D0379660

Texas John Slaughter
DEADLY DAY IN TOMBSTONE

William W. Johnstone
with J. A. Johnstone

PINNACLE BOOKS
Kensington Publishing Corp.
www.kensingtonbooks.com

PINNACLE BOOKS are published by

Kensington Publishing Corp.
119 West 40th Street
New York, NY 10018

PUBLISHER'S NOTE
Following the death of William W. Johnstone, the Johnstone family is working with a carefully selected writer to organize and complete Mr. Johnstone's outlines and many unfinished manuscripts to create additional novels in all of his series like The Last Gunfighter, Mountain Man, and Eagles, among others. This novel was inspired by Mr. Johnstone's superb storytelling.

All Kensington titles, imprints, and distributed lines are available at special quantity discounts for bulk purchases for sales promotions, premiums, fundraising, educational, or institutional use. Special book excerpts or customized printings can also be created to fit specific needs. For details, write or phone the office of the Kensington sales manager: Kensington Publishing Corp., 119 West 40th Street, New York, NY 10018, attn: Sales Department; phone 1-800-221-2647.

ISBN-13: 978-0-7860-4279-1
ISBN-10: 0-7860-4279-6

First printing: July 2014

10 9 8 7 6 5 4 3

Printed in the United States of America

First electronic edition: January 2018

ISBN-13: 978-0-7860-3369-0
ISBN-10: 0-7860-3369-X

Authors' Note

This novel is loosely based on the life and times of legendary Old West lawman, rancher, and gambler John Horton "Texas John" Slaughter. The plot is entirely fictional and is not intended to represent actual historical events. The actions, thoughts, and dialogue of the historical characters featured in this story are fictional as well and not meant to reflect their actual personalities and behavior, although the authors have attempted to maintain a reasonable degree of accuracy.

In other words, none of what you're about to read really happened . . . but it could have.

Chapter 1

Stonewall Jackson Howell tensed as he stood on the boardwalk in front of a hardware store and looked along the mostly darkened length of Allen Street, one of the two main thoroughfares of Tombstone, Arizona Territory. The hour was late enough that most of the businesses were closed for the night, including the one where he had stopped abruptly. The only oasis of light came from the notorious Birdcage Saloon down at the other end of the street.

His hands tightened on the short-barreled shotgun he carried as rapid footsteps thudded on the planks not far away.

When somebody hurried like that at night, it usually meant trouble.

As one of the sheriff's deputies charged with keeping the peace in the famed frontier settlement, trouble was Stonewall's business.

He was a well-built young man, not long out of his teens, with a shock of fair hair under his thumbed-back brown hat. Despite his youth, he had already taken part in several cattle drives and had worked as a cowboy on the vast ranch in the San Bernardino Valley that belonged to his brother-in-law.

He was serving as a deputy under that same brother-in-law, John Horton Slaughter, the sheriff of Cochise County. Texas John Slaughter, a lot of people called him, because he had come to Arizona from the Lone Star State.

Stonewall called him John when they were at the ranch some sixty miles east of Tombstone, since they were related by marriage; in town he called the older man "boss" or "Sheriff."

John Slaughter didn't stand for any disrespect, for him or for the office he held.

The frantic, running footsteps came closer. Stonewall, who had been making the late night rounds and checking that the doors of various businesses were locked as they were supposed to be, leveled the shotgun at the sound. "This is the law!" he called. "Whoever that is, slow down and sing out!"

"Stonewall!" The exclamation from the shadows held both surprise and relief as the footsteps came to an abrupt halt. "Stonewall, is that you, pard?"

With a troubled frown on his face, Stonewall asked, "Dallin Williams?"

"Yeah." The man's dark shape loomed from the shadows on the boardwalk as he moved closer. "You gotta help me, Stonewall. Somebody's after me."

A look of disgust, all but invisible in the darkness, passed over Stonewall's normally open, friendly face. "Somebody's after you?" he repeated.

"Yeah. Albie Hamilton."

"This trouble of yours wouldn't have anything to do with Mrs. Hamilton, would it?"

Despite the fact that Williams was breathing hard from running, he chuckled "Well . . ."

"Good Lord, Dallin!" Stonewall exploded. "When are you gonna learn that it means something when a woman's got a wedding ring on her finger?"

"I tell you what. It didn't seem to mean much to Brenda a little while ago."

Stonewall didn't have to see Williams's face in the shadows to know that the man was grinning. Even when he was up to his neck in trouble, as he usually was, a quick grin and a joke were his first line of defense.

He had cowboyed all over Arizona Territory. He was a good ranch hand, a top all-around hand, in fact, but he couldn't hold down a job. He couldn't be trusted around a man's wife and daughters.

Dallin had the uncanny knack of being able to blind any woman over the age of consent with the bright lights of lust and infatuation. He had cuckolded more husbands and outraged more fathers than anybody could count.

As far as Stonewall could see, it was only sheer luck that had kept Dallin from being tarred and feathered, shot, or marched in front of a preacher at the point of a shotgun.

Just about the only place he had ever failed to land a female he set his hook for was the Slaughter Ranch, when he'd worked there a year or so earlier. He had been mightily impressed with the sultry beauty of Viola Slaughter, Stonewall's sister and the wife of John Slaughter. It was inevitable that he would make a play for her, with every expectation for success on his part. After all, Viola was a lovely, vibrant woman, and she was also considerably younger than her husband.

What Dallin had failed to take into account was that Viola was madly, passionately in love with John Slaughter and always would be. When he made his move on her, she had laughed in his face and then grown serious, warning him to get out before she fetched a rifle.

He had taken his defeat with fairly good grace, Stonewall recalled, and left the ranch before Slaughter ever found out about what had happened.

Stonewall knew about the incident because he was working on the ranch at the time and Dallin was his friend. His sister had convinced him there was no reason to tell Slaughter and had sworn Stonewall to secrecy.

Since then, Slaughter had been elected sheriff of Cochise County, Stonewall had gone to work for him as a deputy, and Dallin Williams had drifted on to several other ranches.

Stonewall didn't really consider him a friend anymore. Stonewall was something of a ladies' man himself, or at least liked to think he was, but Dallin always carried things too far. It seemed to be a game with him. An ugly game, as far as Stonewall was concerned.

Lately, Dallin had been working on the McCabe spread, and Stonewall figured it was only a matter of time before he began trying to seduce Jessie McCabe, the pretty, brown-haired daughter of Little Ed McCabe.

Clearly, though, Dallin had decided to set his sights on Brenda Hamilton instead. Brenda's husband Albie drove a freight wagon and was gone from Tombstone quite a bit. Since they didn't have any children, that meant Brenda was home alone.

She was also blond and shapely, with daring blue eyes and a tantalizing smile like butter wouldn't melt in her mouth. All that put together must have been too tempting a target for Dallin to pass up.

"What did you do now?" Stonewall asked in the same tone of voice he would have used if he had framed that rhetorical question to an egg-sucking dog.

"Well, shoot, you know . . ." Dallin replied in that lazy drawl of his that seemed to have a spellbinding effect on most women. "Brenda and me just sorta spent a little time together gettin' to know one another—"

"Where is he?" a man bellowed from up the street. "Where is he, by God? I'll wring his neck!"

"Albie wasn't supposed to be back from his freight run until tomorrow." Dallin started to edge nervously past Stonewall on the boardwalk. "He got in early, though."

Dallin sighed and shook his head regretfully. "Wish I could say the same. Now, Stonewall, what I need for you to do is, when Albie comes stompin' and blowin' down here in a minute like a crazy ol' bull, you just tell him you ain't seen me and order him to settle down and go on home."

"Why should I do that?"

"Well, he's disturbin' the peace, you know. As an officer of the law, you'd be within your rights to march him right down to the hoosegow and lock him up. Come to think of it, that might not be such a bad idea."

"Forget it," Stonewall said. "I'm not gonna lie to Albie Hamilton, and I'm sure not gonna throw him in jail. I won't help you hide from him, either."

"But Stonewall"—Dallin's voice sounded like his feelings were mortally wounded—"we're pards."

"No, we're not. Maybe we used to be, a long time ago, but not anymore."

Albie Hamilton stood in the middle of the street and stopped to look around. He was a tall, brawny man with heavy shoulders and a bushy brown mustache. He lifted a fist, shook it at the sky, and bellowed, "I'll find you, Williams! I'll find you wherever you are, by God, and teach you not to mess with another man's wife!"

Stonewall couldn't see him all that well and without thinking about what he was doing, he edged back deeper into the shadows in front of the hardware store. Hamilton hadn't spotted them yet, but if he continued in that direction he probably would.

"Listen here, Stonewall," Dallin said softly. "If Albie Hamilton tries to lay his hands on me, I ain't gonna let that happen. He ain't packin' an iron, but I am. This could turn into a right messy situation."

"It won't go that far. Mr. Hamilton will listen to me if I tell him to back off."

"You sure about that? What happens if he don't? I'll tell you what happens. One of us will have to shoot him, that's what. You bein' a lawman and all, you don't want that, do you?"

Stonewall grimaced in the darkness. His teeth ground together in frustration as he thought about his options. After a moment, going against every instinct in his body, he said, "All right, blast it! Get out of here. Go down that alley. Where's your horse?"

"Tied at one of the hitch rails down by the Birdcage."

"Circle around through the alleys and stay out of sight. Get your horse and ride out. I'll try to keep Mr. Hamilton occupied and give you a chance to get out of town."

Dallin clapped a hand on Stonewall's shoulder. "Now that's bein' a good pard like I knowed you was."

"Go on. Get out of here before I change my mind and call him down here myself."

"I'm gone," Dallin said over his shoulder.

Stonewall heard him laughing as he disappeared in the darkness of the alley.

After heaving a disgusted sigh aimed as much at himself as at Dallin, Stonewall started walking toward Albie Hamilton, who was still stomping around in the street.

Hamilton saw him coming and charged toward him with fists clenched.

Stonewall swung the shotgun up. "Hold it right there, Mr. Hamilton," he ordered. "It's me, Deputy Howell. What's all the hollerin' about? It's mighty late at night to be disturbing the peace."

"Deputy!" Hamilton toned his voice down a little, but he still sounded as loud as a bull moose. "Have you seen that no-good young cowpoke Dallin Williams?"

Lying rubbed Stonewall the wrong way, but he said, "No, sir, I haven't."

"Well, if I get my hands on him, you'll never see him again, either! I'm gonna wring his neck!"

"Now wait just a minute there. You can't just go around threatening to kill folks. It ain't like the old days in Tombstone, anymore."

That was true. More than five years had passed since the Earp brothers and Doc Holliday had had their run-in with the Clanton bunch down by the photography studio and the corral. Tombstone had settled down since then . . . sort of.

"It ain't a threat. It's a promise," Hamilton blustered.

"I caught him messin' with my wife. I got a legal right to shoot the both of 'em!"

Suddenly, Stonewall was a little worried about Brenda Hamilton. He knew better than to think that Dallin might have lingered to make sure she was all right. No, Dallin would have lit a shuck out of there fast as he could as soon as he realized they'd been caught in the act.

"Mr. Hamilton, you didn't hurt your wife, did you?" Stonewall hadn't heard any shots, but the man could have beaten her to death. Stonewall had to know for sure.

"What?" Hamilton sounded genuinely surprised by the question. "Naw, I didn't hurt her. Of course I didn't! I got to admit, I was mad enough for a second there that I might've, but I love Brenda—God help me!—and wouldn't do nothin' to her. Anyway, I figure it ain't really her fault. That blasted scoundrel Williams has a way of gettin' women to do any damned thing he wants!"

Stonewall knew that was true. It was sort of like magic. Evil magic.

"Listen, Mr. Hamilton, I know how upset you are. Best thing you can do now is calm down, go home, and talk to your wife. I know Dallin Williams. There ain't a serious bone in his body. The last thing he wants is to steal your wife away from you permanent-like. I'll bet if you have a talk with her, you'll see that whatever happened didn't really mean anything."

Hamilton glowered at him. "You think I'm gonna take advice about my marriage from some wet-behind-the-ears kid?"

Stonewall's voice hardened a little as he replied, "My ears ain't all that wet. I've got a badge, a Colt, and a shotgun, too, so I'd say that makes me a little more than a kid."

A tense moment dragged past, then Hamilton made a disgusted noise in his throat. "All right, all right. I'll go home. But you better hope I don't run into that polecat Williams any time soon. If I do, I ain't gonna be responsible for what happens, you hear me?"

"I hear you," Stonewall said.

Hamilton started to turn away, then paused to add, "I'm surprised somebody hasn't killed that varmint before now."

"To tell you the truth, so am I."

"You're not gonna say anything to Sheriff Slaughter about this, are you?" Hamilton suddenly sounded like he was starting to regret making death threats against Dallin Williams.

"I can't think of any reason to mention it as long as you stop raising a ruckus."

"I'm goin', I'm goin'," Hamilton muttered. He stomped away.

As Hamilton walked off, Stonewall heard a faint, swift rataplan of hoofbeats at the other end of town as somebody rode away from Tombstone. He hoped the distant rider was Dallin. It was all right if his former friend just kept going and didn't ever return to Tombstone.

With a lawman's instincts Stonewall was already starting to develop despite being on the job for only a short time, he had a strong hunch that last part wouldn't turn out to be the case.

Chapter 2

John Horton Slaughter was a precise, methodical man. At the same time, he was one who frequently relied on his instincts and played his hunches.

He had always been that way in his personal life. As a prime example, the first time he had seen the young, darkly beautiful Viola Howell over in New Mexico Territory, he had thought to himself that he was going to marry that girl.

The same held true in his professional life as a cattleman and peace officer. His instincts had told him the San Bernardino Valley was where he ought to establish his ranch, and the spread had proven to be very successful. As for being the sheriff of Cochise County . . . well, right from the first time he had met Morris Upton, the Easterner who ran the Top-Notch Saloon and Gambling Establishment, he'd had to rein in the impulse to pull out a gun and shoot the man.

That would have been the simplest and easiest thing to do, but it wasn't exactly legal. As long as Slaughter wore the sheriff's badge pinned to the lapel of his coat, he had to concern himself about such things.

Upton crossed his mind only because he was thinking about gambling. Slaughter knew being a successful gambler was largely a matter of instinct . . . and following your hunches. That was why he had always been good at it. He was a careful, conservative man in many respects, but he knew when to take a chance.

He laid down his hand—a full house, jacks over eights. "Beat that if you can."

The woman sitting at the end of the bed unbuttoned the man's shirt that was the only thing she was wearing, took it off, and tossed it in a corner of the hotel room. She put her cards on the sheets between them.

Slaughter didn't even look at them.

"Do I win?" Viola Slaughter asked.

"No, I do." Slaughter leaned forward, raked the cards off the bed with a sweep of his hand that sent them flying, and reached out to pull his wife into his arms.

Later, when the early morning sunshine slanting in through the gap in the curtains over the second floor window had grown brighter, Slaughter asked her, "Do you really have to go back to the ranch today?"

"You know I do," Viola answered as she snuggled warmly against his side. "No matter how much we might wish it was otherwise, the place won't run itself, you know."

"It almost does. You know we have the best crew in the whole territory."

"Well, of course we do, but someone still has to keep an eye on things."

"And I say, no one is better at that than you, my dear," Slaughter agreed. "All right. I've enjoyed your visit, but I suppose we both knew it had to end sometime."

Since Slaughter had been elected sheriff, Viola had split her time between the ranch and Tombstone. She wasn't willing to move to town full-time, and he knew better than to demand that his strong-willed wife do anything she didn't want to do.

It wasn't a perfect arrangement for either of them, but spending some time together was better than nothing. He wouldn't be sheriff forever, Slaughter reminded himself whenever he got to missing his wife.

However, Tombstone needed him.

Although things weren't as wild as they had been a few years earlier when the Earps and the wild bunch known as the Cowboys had battled to see who was going to hold sway over Tombstone and the surrounding area, life in Cochise County wasn't exactly what anybody would call tranquil. Rustlers and road agents still operated in those parts and bandits raided from across the border. It hadn't been very long, in fact, since such a raid had taken place in Tombstone and Slaughter had had to pursue the bandits into Mexico.

Most of the Chiricahua and Mescalero Apaches had surrendered in their long campaign against the army and were now on reservations, but from time to time some of them decided to go on the warpath and raise some more hell.

All in all, he kept pretty busy, even though he had the able assistance of several deputies including his brother-in-law Stonewall, a reformed—at least for the moment—bad man named Burt Alvord, and the latest addition to the group of officers, former saloon swamper Mose Tadrack, who had given up booze and become a steady, capable deputy.

Slaughter looked at the angle of the sun again and knew that he ought to be getting to the office. He tightened his arm around Viola for a moment and said, "You want to get some breakfast before you start back to the ranch, don't you?"

"That sounds wonderful," she replied. "It's too far to go on an empty stomach."

"I suppose we should get dressed and head down to the dining room, then."

"I suppose."

Neither of them got in any hurry to do so, however.

Eventually, they walked into the hotel dining room and sat down to breakfast. The place was still fairly busy even though the morning was nearly half over.

Hannah, the buxom blond waitress, came across the room to the couple's table and smiled at them. "Good morning, Sheriff and Mrs. Slaughter. I'll get some coffee right out for you. There are still plenty of flapjacks and bacon in the kitchen. Or would you rather have biscuits and gravy with the bacon?"

"Flapjacks will be fine," Slaughter said.

"With some molasses," Viola added, smiling. She had a sweet tooth on occasion.

"Yeah, of course." Hannah started to turn away, then paused and said, "That man Upton was in here a little while ago looking for you, Sheriff."

Slaughter frowned in surprise. "Morris Upton? I

thought snakes didn't crawl out from under their rocks until later in the day."

"John, that's no way to talk," Viola scolded him. "Mr. Upton is a citizen like everyone else in Tombstone."

"Well, maybe," Slaughter said grudgingly. "But saloon-keepers are usually sound asleep at this time of day."

Hannah said, "I told him you and Mrs. Slaughter hadn't come down yet. He said he guessed he'd stop by your office later."

"Wonderful," Slaughter said, still frowning. "That's something to look forward to."

Viola said, "Why don't you just forget about Morris Upton for now and enjoy your breakfast with me?" The look on her face told him he would if he knew what was good for him.

No mistake about that, Slaughter knew. She was good for him. Very, very good. "I suppose I can do that."

He sometimes thought that if he hadn't been lucky enough to marry Viola, he would have wound up shot or on the wrong end of a hangman's rope. He'd had several of his own brushes with the law, back in his younger, wilder days. He had even been accused of being a rustler, but as he saw it, that matter was open to interpretation.

Of course, he had put all that far behind him. A good part of the credit for that was due to Viola.

The food in the hotel dining room was consistently good, and today was no exception. Slaughter enjoyed the meal, and Viola's company made it that much better.

When they were finished, she headed back upstairs to their room to finish her packing, and Slaughter left the hotel to walk to the livery stable.

Some of the townspeople gave him respectful nods as

he passed them. It wasn't just the badge of office they respected. Texas John Slaughter was known far and wide in Arizona Territory as a bad man to have for an enemy.

He wasn't that impressive physically, although his compactly built body was muscular and packed plenty of strength and stamina. In that respect, he was a little like a stubby-legged cow pony that could work all day. His eyes had a compelling intensity to them as they looked out from under slightly bushy brows. The neatly trimmed, salt-and-pepper goatee testified that he wasn't a young man anymore, but he possessed a vitality that belied his years.

He was always well-dressed. He wore a dark suit with a wide-brimmed, pearl-gray Stetson on his graying dark hair. A pearl-handled Colt Single Action Army revolver was holstered on his right hip, handy if he needed it.

Viola's buggy was parked in front of the livery stable with a pair of fine black horses already hitched to it. She would have been just as happy to put on a pair of trousers, fork a saddle, and ride back to the ranch, but Slaughter had been able to persuade her to use the buggy for her trips to town. A tomboy raised in a ranching family, she had a cowboy's mentality. If something couldn't be done from the back of a horse, most of the time, she didn't consider it really worth doing.

One of the ranch hands, Juan Zavala, waited next to the buggy. Two others, Hal Carter and Lucas Brenner, stood nearby with their saddled horses. The three men had accompanied Viola to Tombstone and would see her safely back to the ranch.

More than once, Viola had argued that she didn't need such an escort, that sending men with her took them away from more important work they could be doing at the ranch.

There were enough outlaws and renegades still raising hell in this corner of the territory that Slaughter insisted upon the precaution, however. When it came to Viola, he picked his battles carefully, but he stood his ground when he had to.

Zavala grinned at him. "The Señora Slaughter, she will be ready to go soon?"

"I expect so," Slaughter replied with a nod. "She's packing right now."

"We've asked around some, boss," Hal Carter said. "No reports of trouble between here and the ranch."

Lucas Brenner smiled and added, "It's plumb peaceful around here."

Slaughter winced. "I wish people would stop saying that. Every time somebody does, all hell breaks loose."

"Aw, you ain't gettin' superstitious, are you, boss?" Brenner asked with a grin.

Zavala looked serious. "You should not make fun of superstition, amigo. There are many things in this world that are beyond our understanding."

Brenner slapped the butt of the Winchester sticking up from the saddle boot strapped to his horse. "Maybe so, but I reckon there's nothing better to clear things up than a few .44-40 slugs."

"Just keep your eyes open until you get back to the ranch," Slaughter advised the three cowboys. "I'm not expecting any trouble, but you never know."

A few minutes later, Viola emerged from the hotel carrying her own bags. Slaughter would have gone to help her, but Zavala and Carter beat him to it. Everybody on the ranch in the San Bernardino Valley, from the youngest children of some of the married hands to the crusty old cook, adored Viola. *

That was as it should be, thought Slaughter. She had never lost the common touch. In the olden days, she would have been a hell of a queen.

She was almost as tall as Slaughter, so she didn't have to stretch up on her toes very far to give him a good-bye kiss. "I didn't see Stonewall this morning," she said after she climbed into the buggy.

"He was on duty last night," Slaughter explained. "Probably still asleep."

"I'm sorry I missed him. You'll tell him good-bye for me when you see him again, won't you?"

"Sure." Slaughter took his wife's hand and gave it a final squeeze. "Be careful now. I'll see you next time." That time couldn't come too soon to suit him, he thought as he watched the buggy roll away.

With Viola gone, he turned his steps toward the courthouse where the sheriff's office was located. He found his chief deputy Burt Alvord sitting at the desk in the front room, riffling through a stack of papers with a look of interest on his face.

"Bunch of new reward dodgers came in this morning's mail, Sheriff," Burt announced.

Given Burt's past, he might be checking to see if *he* was on any of those wanted posters, thought Slaughter.

Burt was a stocky, round-faced young man, almost completely bald despite the fact that he was only twenty years old. For the time being at least, he packed a badge and was on the side of the law.

Slaughter worried Burt was one of those young hellions who might stray back over the line, but hoped it would never happen. He would hate to have to arrest Burt.

He would hate it even more if he had to hang him . . . but he would do whatever the law required.

"See any familiar faces on those wanted posters?" Slaughter asked dryly as he hung up his hat.

"No, sir." Burt didn't seem to catch Slaughter's meaning. "But I'll study 'em in case any happen to ride in."

"You do that," Slaughter said with a nod. He knew his chief deputy kept a pretty close eye on strangers who drifted in and out of Tombstone.

Taking a cigar from his vest pocket, Slaughter clamped it between his teeth as he headed to his private office. He left the cigar unlit and turned to ask Burt through the open door, "Stonewall have anything to report from last night when you relieved him this morning?"

"Nope. He said everything was quiet all night. In fact, it was plumb—"

"Don't say it," Slaughter warned as he shook a finger at Burt. "No point in tempting fate."

Burt grinned and said with a chuckle, "I reckon you're right about that, Sheriff."

Slaughter sat down at his desk and picked up a sheet of paper covered with figures scrawled in pencil. He'd been working on a budget for the county commissioners. His eyebrows drew down in a frown as he studied the numbers on the paper.

When some of the leading citizens of the county had talked him into running for sheriff, they hadn't said anything about how much paperwork would be involved. Slaughter had figured he would be out in the open air most of the time, hunting down outlaws and renegade Apaches. Instead, he spent altogether too many hours sitting in an office behind a blasted desk, trying to make sense of all the papers that flowed across it.

Through the open door, he heard someone come into the outer office. A familiar voice asked, "Is the sheriff here?"

"Just came in." Burt didn't sound friendly. "Hold on there. You can't just barge in—"

"It's all right, Burt," Slaughter called as he came to his feet. He wasn't looking forward to this conversation, whatever it was about, but he supposed there was no point in postponing it. "Let Mr. Upton come on in."

Chapter 3

Morris Upton was a tall, lean man with a narrow face that reminded Slaughter of a wolf. His suit, his hat, and his hair were all iron-gray. When the man smiled, his eyes remained cold and stony, like chips of agate.

He was a predator through and through.

Slaughter forced himself to be polite. "Come on in and have a seat, Upton."

"Thanks, Sheriff," the Easterner said as he took off his hat. He sat down in the leather chair in front of the desk and set the hat on his knee.

Slaughter resumed his seat and cleared his throat. "What can I do for you?"

"I wanted to make sure you were aware of my plans. Have you heard about the big game?"

"What big game?" Slaughter asked with a frown and a slight shake of his head.

"Well, I suppose I should say big games, because there'll be a number of them. The Top-Notch is sponsoring a poker tournament. Players will be coming in from all over the country."

"And you didn't think to talk to me about this first?" Slaughter didn't bother trying to conceal the irritation he felt at the news Upton had just given him.

"Sorry, Sheriff, I didn't know I was supposed to clear all my plans with you," Upton said smoothly. "Gambling is still legal in Tombstone, isn't it?" He knew good and well that it was.

The man was just trying to get under his skin, thought Slaughter. He'd be playing right into Upton's hands if he got mad.

"Of course." Slaughter managed to keep his voice cool and level. "Tell me more about this poker tournament."

It was Upton's turn to look a little annoyed, probably because he hadn't been successful at getting Slaughter's goat. "All the best poker players west of the Mississippi will be here. The buy-in is two thousand dollars, and there won't be any limits on the stakes. By the time we get down to the final two players, I suspect there might be as much as a quarter of a million dollars on the table. Maybe more."

It was all Slaughter could do not to let out an impressed whistle. He was a rich man himself, there was no denying that, but Upton was talking about a lot of money, even to a wheeler-dealer like Texas John Slaughter.

"I'm glad you saw fit to tell me about this before it got started, anyway. That much *dinero* might attract trouble."

"That's why I'm here. I figured you needed to know. I plan to take precautions myself, of course. I'm going to hire armed guards. But I'd like to be able to call on you and your deputies for assistance if necessary. Not only that, but the tournament will draw more people to town than usual. You're liable to have your hands full keeping the peace while it's going on."

The same thought had crossed Slaughter's mind. "We'll keep the peace, don't worry about that. But don't forget, Upton, we work for Cochise County, not for you. If you think you can use my deputies as unpaid bouncers—"

Upton held up a well-manicured hand to stop him. "That's not what I meant, Sheriff. I just wanted you to be aware of the added potential for trouble. My men and I will do our best to see that nothing happens, of course."

"All right," Slaughter said with a grudging nod. "I reckon we understand each other. When does this big tournament of yours start?"

"As soon as everyone who responded to my invitation is here. They should start arriving any time now. I figure we'll be ready to get started in two or three days."

Slaughter nodded again. "What do you get out of this, Upton?"

The saloon owner smiled. "Well, a percentage goes to the house, of course. In addition, I expect to sell a lot more liquor while the games are going on. It's not just the players. People will come from all over just to watch, you know. When they get tired of watching, they'll want a drink and maybe a woman."

"Both of which you'll be glad to provide for a price."

"That's why I like dealing with you, Sheriff. You're a businessman, too. You understand how these things work."

Slaughter didn't care for the subtle comparison Upton had just drawn between the two of them. He wanted the saloonkeeper out of there. "I appreciate you letting me know about it. If there's anything else you need to tell me . . ."

"I'll be sure to do that right away," Upton said as he came to his feet. He put his hat on. "Good morning, Sheriff."

When Upton was gone, Burt Alvord appeared in the doorway and propped a shoulder against the jamb. "Every time I see that fella, he reminds me of a hungry coyote scroungin' for anything he can get."

"Morris Upton is more dangerous than a coyote," Slaughter said. "Did you hear what he was telling me?"

"About that poker tournament? Sure. Sounds like it'll really put Tombstone on the map."

"Tombstone is already on the map," Slaughter pointed out. "The Earps and the Clantons took care of that."

"Yeah, but the place's reputation is startin' to fade a mite these days. This'll make folks sit up and take note again. And if there's any trouble . . ."

"It's our job to see that there's not."

Stonewall hadn't seen Dallin Williams since the night his former friend had almost run afoul of Albie Hamilton. That was just fine. Stonewall didn't want to get dragged into Dallin's affairs. The womanizing cowboy could look out for himself.

Like Sheriff Slaughter's other deputies, Stonewall was kept busy by the sudden influx of people into Tombstone because of the upcoming high stakes poker tournament at the Top-Notch. A lot of money would be changing hands, and the free flow of money meant certain types would show up in an attempt to get their fingers on some of it.

The games in the poker tournament weren't the only gambling going on in Tombstone. Plenty of tinhorn card sharps were there to ply their trade on players not involved with the tournament.

A couple wagons full of soiled doves had rolled into town ahead of the tournament, as well. The women camped in a grove of cottonwood trees on the edge of the settlement and set up tents where they could conduct their business.

Some of the community's respectable ladies, who barely tolerated the Top-Notch, the Birdcage, the Crystal Palace, and the other so-called "dens of iniquity," were outraged by these new arrivals and descended on the sheriff's office to demand that Slaughter run them out of town. He had to walk a fine line between placating the indignant ladies and enforcing the law, because like gambling, prostitution wasn't exactly illegal in Tombstone. He couldn't very well allow the established brothels to continue operating while driving out the newcomers.

Stonewall had enjoyed being a deputy so far, but seeing what his brother-in-law had to deal with convinced him more than ever that he'd never want to be the sheriff himself.

A number of hard-faced strangers also drifted into the settlement during the few days leading up to the tournament. Slaughter ordered his deputies to keep a close eye on anybody they didn't know. Some of those drifters might be thieves and cutthroats, hoping to catch some poker player alone and drag him into an alley where he could be robbed and murdered.

With all that going on, Stonewall sure didn't have time for any of Dallin Williams's foolishness. He was standing on the boardwalk in front of the Top-Notch in the middle of the afternoon with a short-barreled coach gun tucked under his left arm when a buggy rolled along the street and came to a stop in front of the saloon. He had picked up the habit of carrying a scattergun from the sheriff, who often had such a weapon with him when he walked around town.

Potential troublemakers always thought twice when they found themselves staring down the dark tunnels of those twin barrels. The effect of a double load of buckshot on human flesh was a powerful object lesson.

Stonewall was taking life easy at the moment. His shoulder leaned against one of the posts that held up the awning over the boardwalk. He stood up straighter when he saw that it was a woman at the reins of the buggy.

She was the sort of woman who would make almost any man look twice. Raven hair curled around a beautiful face that held a hint of exoticism. Her eyes were a rich, dark brown. A small beauty mark lay near her wide mouth.

She was considerably older than Stonewall, possibly near thirty years old, but when he looked at her the feelings he experienced didn't have the least bit to do with their difference in age.

She smiled at him, an expression that Stonewall felt all the way down to the soles of his boots. "Hello, Sheriff. Is this the Top-Notch Saloon?"

She had to know it was; a big sign was mounted on the front of the building above the awning. She might have genuinely mistaken him for the sheriff, though.

His badge had the word *Deputy* engraved on it, but maybe she couldn't read that. Or maybe she was just playing up to him.

Stonewall didn't know and didn't care. All that mattered to him at the moment was that she was talking to him.

"Uh, yes, ma'am, it sure is." He thought he sounded stupid and tried not to wince. "I'm not the sheriff, though. I'm just a deputy. Deputy Stonewall Jackson Howell, at your service, ma'am."

"It's a pleasure to meet you, Deputy Howell." The accent in her voice confirmed his impression about her foreign nature.

If he wasn't mistaken, she was British, which was pretty doggoned exotic to a fella from Arizona Territory.

"My name is Lady Arabella Winthrop. I know I really shouldn't be asking such a thing of such a stalwart peace officer, but if you could help me with my bags . . ."

"Yes, ma'am!" Stonewall practically jumped off the boardwalk to lend her a hand. He stumbled a little when he landed in the street, but managed not to curse.

Loaded down with three bags, he followed her into the Top-Notch a minute later. The place was already busy. Quite a few of the card players who planned to enter the tournament were already on hand, and so were a lot of people who would be spectators once the games got underway.

The crowd didn't stop Morris Upton from noticing the newcomer. He threaded his way across the room toward her with a welcoming smile on his face and held out his hands to her. "Lady Arabella Winthrop, in the very lovely flesh! It's wonderful to see you again. I was hoping you could make it."

"Boston, wasn't it?" she murmured as she clasped his hands briefly. "Or was it New York where we last saw each other?"

"Neither. It was Philadelphia."

"Of course! You haven't changed, Morris."

"You have," Upton told her.

"Oh?" The elegantly curved dark eyebrows arched upward in response.

"Yes, you're more beautiful than ever."

Lady Arabella's faintly cool smile didn't change at his flattery.

Stonewall had a hunch that anybody who looked like her was probably used to it.

"What made you decide to stage a tournament like this, Morris?" she asked.

"Why, that's the only way I could think of to get you here, Lady Arabella," Upton answered without hesitation. "A frontier backwater such as Tombstone is hardly the sort of place you'd ever visit, otherwise."

Stonewall frowned. He didn't much cotton to a Yankee from back east insulting Tombstone that way.

But before he could speak up, Lady Arabella said, "You might be surprised at the sort of places I turn up. Did you know that I owned a saloon in Tascosa for a short time, several years ago?"

"I've never even heard of Tascosa," Upton said.

"It's over in the Texas Panhandle. And I've spent a considerable amount of time here in Arizona Territory, too. I'm a free spirit, Morris, you know that. I go where the wind takes me."

"Well, I'm glad it brought you here." Upton moved in

and linked his arm with hers. "I have a room upstairs reserved for you. The best room in the house, in fact."

"I suppose it's adjoining with yours?"

"Well . . ."

"I've told you before, I don't mix business with pleasure."

Upton chuckled. "You can't blame a man for trying. Come with me—"

Stonewall cleared his throat.

Lady Arabella turned back to him. "Oh, yes, Deputy Howell was kind enough to bring in my bags, but I can't really expect him to carry them upstairs for me like a bellboy in a hotel. Morris, surely you have someone . . ."

Upton snapped his fingers and gestured sharply, and one of his bouncers stepped forward to take the bags from Stonewall.

Lady Arabella smiled at Stonewall. "Thank you so much for your assistance, Deputy. I hope to see you again while I'm here in Tombstone."

"I'll be around, ma'am, so I reckon you can count on it."

Upton gave him a momentary glare, then was all smiles again as he led Lady Arabella upstairs.

So she was a lady gambler, thought Stonewall as he left the saloon. He had seen a few of those, but none as lovely and impressive as Lady Arabella Winthrop.

He might well have spent some time musing about just how good-looking the English woman was, but just as he resumed his casual pose with a shoulder propped against an awning post, the urgent pounding of fast hoofbeats drifted to his ears.

He straightened and looked down the street to see

where the hoofbeats were coming from. At that moment, a rider rounded a corner a couple blocks away and raced along Allen Street toward him.

Stonewall had just enough time to realize that the man leaning forward in the saddle and urging his mount on at breakneck speed was Dallin Williams. Then several other riders rounded the corner behind him and the guns in their hands spouted powder smoke as they opened fire.

Chapter 4

Stonewall dashed into the street. Some of those bullets flying around wildly were bound to hit some innocent bystander unless he stopped them. Putting an end to the chase struck him as the quickest way of ending the shooting. "Dallin!" he yelled. "Dallin, stop!"

For a second it looked like Dallin was going to ride Stonewall down, but then he hauled hard on the reins and tried to swerve around the deputy.

The speeding horse couldn't handle the turn. Its legs went out from under it and dumped man and animal into the street, where they rolled over and over in a cloud of dust. Stonewall could only hope that the horse hadn't crushed Dallin when it fell.

The other riders still charged along Allen Street, yelling and shooting. Stonewall leaped into their path and leveled the scattergun at them.

Unlike their quarry, they had time to stop. One of the men yelled an order only dimly heard over the thundering hoofbeats, but it was enough to make the others pull back on their reins and saw at the bits. They held their fire as they fought their mounts to a halt only a few yards short of where Stonewall stood.

As dust swirled through the street, Stonewall recognized all four men. The barrel-chested, brown-bearded man who had shouted the order to stop was Little Ed McCabe, whose Bar EM spread was northeast of Tombstone.

Little Ed, despite his name, was anything but little. He was built like a bear, and was about as hairy as one, too, with a thick pelt covering the backs of his hands and sprouting from the open throat of his shirt.

The other three men were hands who rode for McCabe. All of them looked as angry as their boss and still held the revolvers they had been firing at Dallin.

"Pouch those irons!" Stonewall ordered with all the authority he could muster. "And you better hope all that lead flyin' around didn't hurt anybody."

"You're gettin' mighty big for your britches, Deputy," McCabe rumbled. "If you know what's good for you, you'll stand aside and let us have that no-good skunk Williams. He's got a date with a hangrope!"

So it had come down to this after all, Stonewall thought bitterly. Dallin hadn't been able to resist going after Jessie McCabe, and Jessie's pa had caught them.

Lynching Dallin for that offense seemed to be carrying things a mite too far, though, and endangering the citizens of Tombstone had pushed the whole situation over the brink.

Barely able to restrain his anger, Stonewall said,

"Holster your guns right now, or I'll blow you out of your saddles!"

An icy voice added in a tone of unmistakable command, "You'd better do what the lad tells you."

From the corner of Stonewall's eye, he spotted the sheriff standing wide-legged on the boardwalk with a Winchester in his hands. Nobody with any sense wanted to put Texas John Slaughter to the test. Despite the rage that filled Little Ed McCabe, Stonewall saw a flash of reason in the rancher's eyes.

With obvious reluctance, McCabe ordered, "Put your guns away, boys."

Slaughter said, "Stonewall, check on Williams."

Stonewall backed away and then turned to see what had happened to his former friend.

Dallin's horse appeared to be all right; the animal had clambered to its feet and didn't seem to be favoring any of its legs, so maybe the fall hadn't broken any bones. Dallin still lay huddled in the dust of Allen Street. He didn't move as Stonewall approached.

Stonewall figured he was knocked out . . . or worse. But as he dropped to a knee beside Dallin and reached for his shoulder to roll him over, one of Dallin's eyes opened a crack.

He asked quietly, "Are they still here?"

Stonewall leaned closer. "You mean Little Ed and his boys?"

"Yeah. They've gone plumb loco, Stonewall. You can't let 'em get me."

"Are you hurt?" Stonewall was a little annoyed. Dallin

was in trouble again, and once more he expected the law to get him out of it.

"Naw, just shook up a mite. I know how to fall without gettin' busted up."

"I don't doubt it, as many bedroom windows as you've had to jump through."

Dallin chuckled, then grew serious again. "What about McCabe?"

"Sheriff Slaughter's got a gun on him. Get up out of the dirt so we can figure out what this is all about." There wasn't much doubt in Stonewall's mind what that was as he straightened and stepped back from the fallen man.

"Is he all right?" Slaughter called.

"Probably better off than he deserves to be," Stonewall answered.

"Now, there ain't no need to be hurtful," Dallin said as he pushed himself to hands and knees. He climbed to his feet, picked up the hat that had flown off his head, and started beating it against his clothes to remove some of the dust.

"Shoot him, Deputy," McCabe urged. "A shotgun shell costs less'n a good rope."

Slaughter said, "Settle down, McCabe. Nobody's shooting anybody . . . unless I'm the one pulling the trigger."

"But he's got it comin'!" McCabe was red-faced and looked like he was about to explode from anger and frustration.

"I'll listen to what you have to say in a minute." Slaughter turned to Mose Tadrack, who had come up beside him. "Mose, is anybody else hurt?"

Tadrack shook his head. "No, everybody scattered and

ducked for cover when the shooting started. They were lucky. The bullets didn't even hit any horses."

Slaughter nodded curtly and turned back to the rancher. "I'd say you and your men are the really lucky ones, McCabe. If you'd killed or wounded someone while you were blazing away at Williams, I'd be arresting you for murder right now."

"It ain't murder when all you're tryin' to do is bring a rapist to justice," McCabe snapped.

The tense situation in the street instantly became more serious. Dallin Williams looked shocked and yelped, "Rapist! I never forced myself on a woman in my life! Ever' gal I was ever with wanted to be there with me!"

"Shut your filthy mouth!" McCabe roared. "You assaulted my daughter!"

Slaughter began, "That's a mighty serious charge—"

"And it's a lie!" Dallin broke in. "I never laid a finger on Jessie McCabe, Sheriff. I swear it."

"I got proof," McCabe insisted.

"What sort of proof?" Slaughter asked.

McCabe turned in the saddle and pointed up the street. "Here it comes now."

Stonewall looked where the rancher was pointing and saw a wagon rolling toward them. A middle-aged woman was handling the reins, while a younger version of herself huddled on the seat beside her.

Stonewall recognized the two women as Hallie McCabe, Little Ed's wife, and Jessie, their daughter. Hallie was grim-faced while Jessie's cheeks shone with tears.

Stonewall looked over at Dallin. "Are you sure you don't want to change the story you're tellin'?"

Dallin appeared a little pale under the permanent tan of a man who spent his days working outdoors. He swallowed hard. "Whatever they claim I did, Stonewall, it ain't true. Did you ever know me to take advantage of a gal?"

"I've known you to take advantage of a dozen girls . . . but I don't recall you ever forcing yourself on one."

"That's because I wouldn't do it."

Slaughter handed his rifle to Mose Tadrack. "Keep an eye on McCabe's men." He stepped down from the boardwalk into the street and walked to meet the wagon.

Hallie McCabe brought the team of mules to a stop.

Slaughter reached up and touched the brim of his hat. "Ma'am."

"Sheriff," Mrs. McCabe responded coldly. "Are you going to arrest that man who hurt my little girl?" Her mouth twisted as she added, "I shouldn't even call him a man. He's an animal."

Dallin opened his mouth to say something, but Stonewall stopped him with a look and advised, "Best just keep quiet for now."

"I can't arrest anybody until I know what happened." Slaughter glanced around at the crowd gathering in the street. "I don't think this is the place to talk about it, either. Let's all go down to my office at the courthouse."

"And then you'll lock Williams up?" McCabe grumbled.

"I'll listen to the story and do what needs to be done."

McCabe let out a disgusted snort. "That lowdown scum needs to be swinging from a gallows, that's what needs to be done."

"We'll see," Slaughter said. "Come along, the three of

you McCabes. Stonewall, bring Williams. Mose, keep an eye on McCabe's men and the rest of the town."

Stonewall gestured with the shotgun for Dallin to get moving. As they started walking toward the courthouse, he said under his breath, "See what chasin' women all the time gets you?"

Dallin sighed and said solemnly, "I never figured it'd get me a hangrope."

A bad taste filled Slaughter's mouth as he surveyed the people who had crowded into the outer office. Stonewall and Dallin stood to one side. The deputy was grim-faced and held the shotgun pointed in Dallin's general direction.

Dallin looked scared . . . and if he had really done what he was accused of, he had every right to be.

Little Ed McCabe and his wife stood in front of the desk that Burt Alvord normally used. Mrs. McCabe had an arm around her daughter's shoulders. Jessie was pale and kept her head down. She avoided looking at anybody as if she were ashamed.

McCabe opened his mouth to say something, but Slaughter stopped him with a raised hand. "Just hold on a minute. I want to hear from Miss Jessie before anybody says anything else."

"She don't want to talk," Mrs. McCabe told him with a shake of her head. "She's too upset."

"Maybe so, and I'm sorry if this is going to upset her even more, but once your husband and his hands started shooting off guns in the middle of my town, they made this my business. And I intend to get to the bottom of it."

Slaughter leaned forward and rested his hands on the desk. "Jessie, can you hear me?"

"I . . . I hear you, Sheriff," the young woman replied in a tiny voice. She was seventeen or eighteen, a pretty girl with long, straight, dark brown hair.

A lot of girls were married by the time they were her age and maybe had a child or two of their own, but Jessie still lived at home with her parents. She'd had a couple older brothers. One had died of a fever, and the other was killed when a horse kicked him in the head. Jessie was the only child the McCabes had left.

Slaughter couldn't blame them for being more protective of her than they normally would have been.

"Jessie, you're going to have to tell me what happened," he said as gently as he could. "Did Dallin Williams do something to you?"

"I never—" Dallin began, but he fell silent when Stonewall dug an elbow into his side.

"You'll get your chance to talk," Slaughter snapped. "I'm speaking to the young lady now." He turned back to her. "Go ahead, Jessie."

"I . . . I don't like to talk about it, Sheriff."

"I'm sure you don't, but unfortunately that's the way the law works. You have to tell us what's wrong before we can do anything about it."

Jessie swallowed hard. Without lifting her head, she said, "He . . . he forced himself on me. Dallin . . . Mr. Williams, I mean. He made me . . . do things with him . . ."

Slaughter glanced at Dallin. The young cowboy looked like he was about to explode from the urge to deny the charge.

"Did this happen today?" Slaughter asked.

"No, sir," Jessie replied with a slight shake of her head. "It was . . . a while back. A couple months ago."

Slaughter frowned. "If that's true, why didn't you tell anybody until now?"

"I was ashamed. I didn't want to tell. And he said . . . he said he'd get me back if I did."

Despite the warning glares from Slaughter and Stonewall, Dallin couldn't contain himself any longer. He flung his hands in the air in obvious exasperation. "I never did! I never touched the poor gal, and I sure as hell never threatened her!"

McCabe turned toward him, fists clenched, and growled, "Shut your lyin' mouth, you—"

"Quiet down, both of you," Slaughter ordered.

When McCabe subsided except for the murderous glares he continued to shoot toward Williams, Slaughter asked, "Why did you come forward now, Jessie?"

Mrs. McCabe said, "She had to, Sheriff. She . . . she couldn't hide it anymore." Her voice dropped to a whisper. "She's in the family way."

Dallin made a frustrated sound and shook his head as he gazed up at the ceiling in evident disbelief. "So now I'm gonna be a daddy?" he asked when he looked down again. "Well, somebody best call the preacher, 'cause we got us a pure-dee miracle here!"

There was no holding McCabe back this time. He roared and launched himself toward Dallin, swinging a big fist at the cowboy's head.

The punch didn't find its intended target. Stonewall tried to get in between the two men, and McCabe's knobby fist crashed into his jaw, instead.

The powerful blow drove Stonewall back against the

cowboy. As both men staggered from the collision, Dallin reached around Stonewall, grabbed the shotgun, and tore the weapon out of the startled deputy's hands.

The move didn't take Slaughter by surprise. His Colt slid smoothly from its holster as he drew with impressive speed. Before Dallin could raise the shotgun, Slaughter had the revolver's sights lined on the young cowboy's face. The Colt's hammer was eared back, and Slaughter's thumb was all that kept it from falling.

McCabe blanched since the shotgun was pointing toward him and his family. Mrs. McCabe screamed and wrapped her arms around Jessie to shield her daughter with her own body.

"Don't do it, Williams," Slaughter warned. "That shotgun comes up another inch, I'll blow your brains out."

Dallin hesitated. "What does it matter, Sheriff? I'm fixin' to be railroaded into a hangin' anyway."

"What matters is that if that scattergun goes off in here, you'll kill some innocent people for sure," Slaughter said. "Whatever else you've done, I don't think you want that."

"I didn't—" Dallin stopped short and sighed. He lowered the shotgun until it pointed toward the floor. "You're right. I don't want to hurt nobody."

"Stonewall, get that gun," Slaughter ordered.

When Stonewall had the shotgun again, the sheriff went on, "Now take him back to the cell block and lock him up."

"What happened to me gettin' to have my say?" Dallin wanted to know.

"That was before you grabbed that shotgun and nearly got somebody killed. Now get him out of here, Stonewall."

Once Stonewall had escorted the still-complaining Dallin Williams out of the office, Slaughter continued. "I'm sorry to hear about your, ah, situation, Jessie." He wished that Viola was there. She would know what to say to Jessie McCabe. Viola always knew just the right way to handle delicate problems.

He, on the other hand, was just a man, and a rather blunt one, at that. "I'm afraid you're going to have to tell me more about what happened. That's a mighty serious charge you're making against Williams. I mean, are you sure he's the only one who could've . . ."

"What are you sayin', Sheriff?" McCabe demanded. His face looked like he was about to cloud up and rain again.

"I'm not saying anything," Slaughter replied. "I'm just trying to find out the truth."

Mrs. McCabe said, "Jessie, you tell him. You tell the sheriff just what you told me."

Jessie looked like she would have rather been almost anywhere else, but she drew in a deep breath and said, "A couple months ago, not long after Dallin came to work for my pa, I was in the ranch house by myself one day. Pa was out somewhere on the range, and Ma had come into town. Dallin showed up. He said Pa had sent him back to fetch a roll of wire. They were fencin' off a waterhole that had gone bad to keep the cows from getting to it."

"That's the God's honest truth, Sheriff," McCabe said. "I remember that day."

"Hold on," Slaughter told him. "What happened then, Jessie?"

"Well, Dallin came in the house—"

"Why would he do that? The wire he'd been sent to fetch would be in the barn, wouldn't it, not the house?"

"Well, sure," she admitted, "but he told me he wanted to see me. He had been, well, courtin' me, I guess you'd say, ever since he went to work for my pa. I told him that I wasn't interested, but he didn't seem to take no for an answer."

That fit with what he knew of Dallin Williams' reputation, thought Slaughter. The young cowboy was persistent when he went after a woman.

"What did you do when he came in the house?"

"I told him he needed to get on about his business," Jessie replied with the first trace of fire that Slaughter had seen in her. "He said his business was getting to know me better. I told him I already knew him as well as I wanted to. That's when he . . . he got mad and took hold of me and . . . and laid me down there on the rug right in front of the fireplace and had his way with me!"

The words came out of Jessie in a rush, and then she put her hands over her face and started to sob. The sounds were wracking in the silence that gripped the office.

Chapter 5

Just on the other side of the door leading to the cell block, which was open a couple inches, Stonewall stood holding the shotgun.

A few feet behind him and to his right, Dallin was inside one of the cells, pacing back and forth, waving his hands around, and muttering to himself in agitation. He was the only prisoner at the moment. After a few moments, he stopped his pacing and gripped the iron bars so tightly that his knuckles stuck out and turned white.

While Jessie McCabe was answering the sheriff's questions, Stonewall listened through the gap and relayed her statement to Dallin in a whisper that the people in the office couldn't hear through the thick door.

Then, like Slaughter, Stonewall stood there in an uncomfortable silence as Jessie sobbed.

"Stonewall!" Dallin said urgently under his breath. "Stonewall, you got to hear me out!"

Stonewall used his foot to ease the cell block door up until it was closed except for a tiny crack. He turned toward the cell and glared at Dallin. "Why should I listen to you? Any man who'd stoop low enough to do such a thing—"

"But that's just it! I didn't do it!" Dallin insisted. "This is the first time I even heard when I'm supposed to have done it." He pressed his face against the bars like he wanted to crawl between them. His eyes were wide and staring, like those of a trapped animal.

"Listen, I remember that day, all right? It's true that Little Ed sent me back to the ranch headquarters to fetch a roll of wire. That's what I done. I drove the buckboard right up to the barn door, went inside, got the wire, heaved it onto the back of the buckboard, and left. That's all I done. I never even went close to the house, let alone set foot inside it!"

Stonewall frowned in the gloom of the thick-walled cell block. If he didn't know better, he'd say that it sounded like Dallin was telling the truth.

And yet Jessie McCabe had sounded like she was telling the truth. The important question was why would any girl make up such a degrading story if it wasn't true?

Stonewall's brain worked quickly as he thought about the implications of Dallin's claim. After a moment he asked, "Did you take the wire right back out to that waterhole Mr. McCabe wanted to fence off?"

"Why? What does that matter?" Dallin asked with a puzzled frown.

"Well," Stonewall said, "if you went back right away, Mr. McCabe might realize that you didn't have time to, ah, do what his daughter's accusing you of."

"Say, that's right! Lemme think . . . Doggone it, Stonewall, I just don't know. That was a couple months ago. I remember puttin' the wire in the buckboard, but after that . . ." Dallin suddenly looked crestfallen. "No, I don't reckon I did go straight back, now that I think about it. Well, I did, meanin' I didn't go nowhere else, but it took me a while to get there because the harness on the buckboard team snapped and I had to stop and fix it. Little Ed, he's a believer in gettin' ever' penny's worth of use outta his gear. He'll hang on to somethin' until it's plumb wore out, like that harness."

"Did you tell him what happened when you got back with the wire?"

"Sure I did," Dallin replied with an emphatic nod. "I didn't want him thinkin' I'd been lollygaggin' around. He wouldn't have took kindly to that."

Dallin's story made sense and sounded believable enough, thought Stonewall, but if he was really guilty of attacking Jessie McCabe, he might have made up the whole yarn about the broken harness to cover his tracks.

"I'll tell Sheriff Slaughter what you just told me, after the McCabes are gone," Stonewall said. "I'm sure he'll want to talk to you some more about it."

"I appreciate that, Stonewall. I'm bein' railroaded here. You know that."

Stonewall just grunted. He wasn't sure what to believe. Even though he didn't really consider Dallin Williams a friend anymore, he hated to think that Dallin might have done the awful thing he was accused of.

Luckily, if there was anybody who could get to the truth of the matter, it was John Slaughter.

Slaughter suggested Hallie McCabe sit down with Jessie while the young woman pulled herself together.

With an arm around her daughter's shoulders, Mrs. McCabe led her to the old sofa pushed up against one wall.

"Ed, you come with me into my private office," Slaughter said. "We'll talk some more about this."

"I don't see why we need to do any more talkin'," McCabe said as he glared at Slaughter. "You got the son of a buck locked up. All we need now is a gallows."

"Haven't you forgotten something?"

McCabe frowned and shook his head to indicate that he didn't know what Slaughter was talking about.

"A trial," Slaughter reminded him. "There's no need for a gallows until there's been a trial and somebody's been found guilty and sentenced to hang."

"I'd say Williams has already been found guilty. That baby my little girl's carryin' is all the verdict I need."

"The law doesn't work that way," Slaughter said coolly. "Come on." His voice was firm enough that McCabe didn't argue.

The two men went into the office, and Slaughter closed the door behind them.

"Sit down," he said with a nod toward the leather chair in front of the desk.

"Don't feel like sittin'."

"Do it anyway."

Grumbling, McCabe sank into the chair.

Slaughter went behind the desk and sat down, too. "Tell me about what happened this morning."

"What do you mean?"

Slaughter's voice hardened again. "I mean, I want an explanation of how you came to be chasing Dallin Williams down Allen Street and shooting up my town."

With obvious reluctance, McCabe said, "I'm sorry

about that, Sheriff. Reckon the boys and me, we just got carried away. We were so mad when we heard what that skunk did that we couldn't think straight."

"Back up a mite. How'd you hear about it?"

McCabe heaved a deep breath into and out of his barrel chest. "We were out at the corral breakin' some horses. Williams is a pretty good hand at bronc bustin', I'll give him that. He was smoothin' the rough edges off that bay he rode in on when my wife came out and got me." He stopped and frowned as if he had to compose himself for a moment before he could go on. "Seems Jessie finally broke down this mornin' and told her what happened. I guess the gal figured that in her condition she couldn't keep it a secret much longer."

He sighed again and rubbed a big hand over his rugged face. Even a big, bear-like hombre like him fell prey to his emotions from time to time. "I went in and talked to her, and when she told me the same thing she told Hallie, I stormed back out to the corral to have a showdown with Williams."

"Did you figure on forcing Williams into a shotgun wedding?" Slaughter asked.

McCabe grimaced and shook his head. "Hell, no! If the two of 'em had been sweet on each other and that's the way the, uh, problem came about . . . well, maybe. I wouldn'ta been happy about it, that's for dang sure, but if Williams had been willin' to do the right thing by her . . . But that ain't what happened. Jessie don't love him. She don't want him for a husband. He forced her! That's rape, pure and simple, and he oughta be strung up for it!"

Slaughter couldn't really make much of an argument

against that, but it was up to a judge and jury to decide what to do about the offense, not him.

"What did Williams do when you confronted him about it?"

"He lied through his teeth, of course. Said he never did anything to Jessie. I asked him if he was callin' my little girl a liar. He didn't answer that. He was still on the back of that horse he'd been breakin'. He put the spurs to it and jumped it right outta that corral. Damnedest thing I ever saw, the way that horse sailed over that fence."

McCabe sounded like he could almost admire Dallin Williams's horsemanship, if nothing else about him.

"Then Williams lit a shuck," he went on. "Took me and the boys a few minutes to throw saddles on horses and get after him. We didn't catch up until we got to town."

McCabe's powerful shoulders rose and fell in a shrug as he paused again. "Reckon you know the rest of it, Sheriff."

Slaughter leaned back in his chair. "You realize there's no proof things happened the way Jessie said they did." He held up a hand to forestall the inevitable angry protest McCabe was about to make and continued. "You've just got her word for it."

"That's plenty good enough for me," the rancher said.

"And I agree that it's good enough to take to Judge Burroughs and get a proper charge filed against Williams. That's exactly what I intend to do."

"You're not gonna turn him loose, are you?"

Slaughter shook his head. "No, I plan to keep him locked up until I've talked to the judge. If he agrees to hear the case, then Williams will stay behind bars. After that, what happens is up to the court."

"I still wish I'd just shot him when I had the chance."

"If you had, you might be the one in trouble," Slaughter pointed out.

"You think so, Sheriff? You really think so?"

Slaughter frowned. McCabe was right. if he had killed Dallin Williams after hearing the news that Williams had raped his daughter, no jury in Cochise County—probably no jury in the whole territory—would have convicted him. In all likelihood, there wouldn't have even been a trial.

But that wasn't what had happened, and Williams was Slaughter's prisoner. That meant things would have to be done legally from here on out.

Slaughter got to his feet. "Let's go see how your wife and daughter are doing." He and McCabe returned to the outer office.

Jessie had calmed down, but she was still pale and had dried tear streaks on her cheeks. Her mother looked up at Slaughter and demanded, "Well, Sheriff, what are you going to do?"

"Williams is locked up and that's where he'll stay until I've talked to the judge," Slaughter told her. "From the sound of everything I've heard here today, he'll be charged and have to stand trial for what he did."

Jessie said, "Does . . . does that mean I'll have to tell about it all over again?"

"I'm afraid so." Slaughter didn't want to get Jessie started bawling again, but he wasn't going to lie to her about what was going to happen, either.

Regardless of what Slaughter wanted, tears began to well from her eyes. "I can't do that! I told you all about it, Sheriff. Won't that be enough? Can't you tell it at the trial?"

"No, the jury will have to hear the story from you. That's the way the legal system works."

McCabe said, "We know what happens at a trial, damn it! But it ain't right that Jessie has to go through the whole blasted thing and feel miserable about it all over again."

"I'm sorry," Slaughter told them with a shake of his head. "If you want to press charges against him, and if the judge agrees, that's the way it'll have to be."

"It wouldn't have to be that way if somethin' was to happen to that varmint Williams before the trial started," McCabe said as his eyes narrowed. "Say, if he was to wind up danglin' from a cottonwood limb somewhere."

"Ed, don't . . ." his wife began, but fell silent when McCabe glared at her.

Coldly, Slaughter said, "I'm going to pretend I didn't hear you say that, McCabe. There's never been a lynching in Tombstone while I've been wearing this badge."

"That ain't been very long," McCabe pointed out.

"And there won't be one, either," Slaughter went on as if the rancher hadn't said anything. "Anybody who tries such a thing will find themselves in a lot more trouble than they bargained for. You probably ought to think twice before you go around making threats like that."

"I wasn't makin' no threat, just talkin'. And now I'm tired of it. We may not have got what we came for— Williams's hide—but I reckon it'll do for now." McCabe jerked his head toward the door and told his wife and daughter, "Come on."

Mrs. McCabe and Jessie got to their feet. Jessie was still sniffling as her mother herded her toward the door.

McCabe followed them, stiff with anger and offended dignity.

When they were gone, the door into the cell block swung open and Stonewall came into the office. "The prisoner's locked up good and tight, Sheriff," he reported.

"That's what I expected," Slaughter said. "Is he still claiming he didn't attack that girl?"

"Yeah, and he sure sounds like he means it, too."

"But . . . ?" Slaughter sensed that Stonewall wanted to say something else.

"I can't help but think that a fella who's done so much sportin' with the ladies . . . well, he'd have learned to lie and make it sound just like he was tellin' the truth, wouldn't he? That's the only way he could make all those gals believe whatever romantic nonsense he told them."

Despite the seriousness of the situation, Slaughter had to smile faintly. "Stonewall, you can be downright profound sometimes."

"Huh? Does that mean you think I'm right?"

"That's what it means." Slaughter reached for his hat. "Keep an eye on things here. I have to go talk to Judge Burroughs."

Chapter 6

Slaughter didn't have to go very far. Judge Thaddeus Burroughs's office was in the Cochise County courthouse, too.

In the judge's outer office, the bespectacled clerk jerked a thumb over his shoulder at the door behind him. "Go on in, Sheriff. The judge is expecting you."

Slaughter grunted in surprise, but he supposed he shouldn't have been shocked that Burroughs expected him to pay a visit. The judge was known for keeping his ear to the ground. He was returning a thick volume bound in black leather to the shelves when Slaughter went into the judge's office.

With a friendly nod, Burroughs said, "Hello, Sheriff. It's always good to see you."

"I wish I was here on a friendly visit, Your Honor."

Burroughs sighed and nodded. "Ah, yes, the McCabe business." He waved a hand toward the chair in front of the paper-littered desk. "Sit down and tell me about it."

Slaughter lowered himself into the chair. Not for the first time, he reflected that Judge Thaddeus Burroughs didn't really look like the hardnosed frontier jurist he really was. On the contrary, Burroughs looked more like a storekeeper or even a schoolteacher.

He was short and stocky, mostly bald with just a fringe of gray hair around his ears and the back of his head. His eyes were big behind thick-lensed spectacles. His voice tended to drone and gave him more of a pedantic demeanor. But he knew the law and handed it out with an iron fist and little mercy for those who broke it.

"I suppose there are already rumors floating around," Slaughter said.

"It would be difficult for there not to be, considering how Little Ed McCabe was out in the street bellowing at the top of his lungs like a maddened bull. I assume you have young Williams locked up, for his own protection if nothing else?"

"He's behind bars, all right, and protecting him is part of it. McCabe wants to forget about a trial and string him up right now."

"I hope you've explained to him that that's not the way things are done around here?"

"I told him. Whether or not he's going to listen . . ."

Both men sat in grim silence for a moment after Slaughter's voice trailed off. Then Judge Burroughs said, "Tell me what you've found out, Sheriff."

Slaughter laid out the story as he had heard it from Jessie McCabe. As he summarized her testimony, he thought about how bad it sounded for Dallin Williams.

"And what does Mr. Williams say?" Burroughs asked when Slaughter was finished.

"He denies the whole thing, of course. Claims he never laid a hand on her."

Burroughs sighed then pursed his lips "I hate cases where the only real evidence consists of conflicting testimony from the opposing parties."

"Well, there's the baby in Jessie McCabe's belly," Slaughter said. "I suppose you could consider that evidence."

"Yes, but we can't exactly wait . . . what was it? Seven more months? And see whether or not the baby has Dallin Williams's eyes or nose before we render judgment, now can we?"

"That might be the fairest way to do it," Slaughter said, "but I don't reckon Little Ed would be willing to wait that long."

"Neither would the Territory of Arizona. Not to mention the expense of feeding the prisoner for that long." Burroughs leaned back in his chair and clasped his hands together over his rounded belly. "No, the case will have to come to trial as soon as possible. The earliest I can get it on the docket is next week. Can you handle things until then?"

"I don't have any choice in the matter, do I, Your Honor?"

"Not really," Burroughs admitted.

"I'm not as well-versed in the law as you are, Judge . . ."

Burroughs spread his hands as if Slaughter's comment went without saying.

"But I was wondering," the sheriff went on. "If Williams is found guilty of raping Jessie McCabe, will he hang?"

Burroughs shook his head. "No. But I can put him in prison for life."

"I don't know if Little Ed is going to be satisfied with that. He wants Williams dead."

"And if his daughter is telling the truth, you can't blame the man. It's the question of who is telling the truth that's the sticking point. A jury will have to decide."

Slaughter nodded and got to his feet. "Let me know what time the trial is, Your Honor, and I'll have Williams there." He hoped that was a promise he would be able to keep.

Lady Arabella Winthrop closed the wardrobe after putting away the last of the things from her bags and paused to look at herself in the mirror attached to the dressing table. She could see the strain of the trip to Tombstone in the tiny lines visible around her mouth and eyes, but she doubted if anyone else would notice.

That was good. She had spent years perfecting the art of keeping the truth concealed.

Someone knocked quietly on the door. Arabella sighed and thought the visitor was probably Morris Upton again. She'd had enough trouble easing him out of the room without offending him after he'd escorted her up to her room. Just like in their past encounters, Upton had made it all too clear that he wanted her, a feeling that she didn't return at all.

But she couldn't afford to offend him, she supposed. A series of financial reverses had left her in need of money, and the poker tournament would be a good way to get it, not to mention an intriguing challenge. It had been a while since she had really tested her skill at the game.

She turned to the door and opened it as she put a smile on her face. "I didn't expect to see you again so soon, Morris—" The forced smile became genuine when she realized it wasn't Upton standing there in the corridor after all.

The man who grinned at her was much better-looking in a rugged way, with a rawboned, tanned face and prematurely silver hair under his brown hat. His voice held a soft drawl that betrayed his Virginia heritage. "I hope you're not disappointed, Arabella, but it's only me."

"Steve!" she said as her eyes widened in surprise.

Steve Drake stepped into the room and took her in his arms. His mouth came down on hers in a kiss that seemed to melt her inside. He had always had that effect on her, damn him, ever since she'd first met him back in Charleston all those years ago!

She had been little more than a girl then, alone and trying to make her way in a foreign country, ready to do whatever was necessary to survive. He'd been a smuggler and a gambler, and he had taken her under his wing and kept her from having to resort to selling herself.

He had dressed her, tutored her, and come up with the idea of adding *Lady* in front of her name, even though she didn't have a drop of noble blood in her veins. It could be argued that the beautiful and aristocratic Lady Arabella Winthrop was wholly Steve Drake's creation.

And he had never asked anything from her in return except her friendship. When she had finally come to his bed, it was entirely her own idea.

Unless that had been his subtle plan all along, she had thought more than once. But she didn't really believe that was the case. Steve Drake was certainly capable of scheming to get what he wanted, but not with his friends.

He stepped back and rested his hands on her shoulders. "I was hoping you'd show up for this game, Bella. It's been too long."

"Yes. Yes, it has. Five years?"

"Closer to six."

When the time had come for them to go their separate ways, they had parted as friends. Arabella had never figured they would be together for the rest of their lives. Both of them were too restless for that.

"I wasn't sure whether to accept Upton's invitation or not," she said. "Now I'm glad I did."

Steve Drake made a face like he had just bitten into a worm-infested apple. "Morris Upton's a jackass, and I don't trust him any farther than I could throw him. But the stakes in this tournament of his are to my liking. As long as Upton doesn't try to pull any tricks, I'm willing to put up with him."

Arabella turned the palm of her right hand up and used her left hand to pull back the lacy cuff of her sleeve. The move revealed the snout of a wicked little over/under derringer. "If he tries any tricks, he'll be sorry."

That brought a laugh from Steve Drake. "I see you're as ready for trouble as ever. Still have that stiletto strapped to your thigh?"

She smiled. "Why don't you find out?"

"Later on, I just might. Right now, I want to see if you'll have dinner with me."

"Of course I will. Upton's probably counting on me dining with him, but . . ."

"But he'll just have to be disappointed," Steve Drake said with a chuckle.

She wouldn't be disappointed with her visit to Tombstone, Arabella thought, no matter how the poker tournament turned out. Not with Steve Drake there.

Oscar Grayson sat at a corner table in the Top-Notch and nursed a beer. He couldn't afford a real drink because he was saving as much money as he could for the game. It would take almost everything he had for the buy-in. Once he was in the game, he had to win. It was as simple as that.

Of course, he was working on a plan in case he didn't win. He always had a plan to fall back on.

Jed Muller ambled over to the table and sat down without waiting for an invitation. Unlike the dark, slim Grayson, he was big and hearty, with a broad, sunburned face. Despite his cream-colored suit, he looked more like a farmer than a gambler, but he was good at the game, just like Grayson himself.

"Did you see that Drake's here?" Muller asked.

"Yeah, I saw him," Grayson said.

"You reckon he's forgotten about what happened in Wichita?"

"Have you forgotten about it?"

"Hell, no," Muller said with some heat. "He nearly got us both killed. Gettin' up on his high horse like that and spoutin' that stuff about him runnin' an honest game and how he wasn't gonna put up with us cheatin'. He didn't have to let on that the two of us were workin' together."

That had been a close shave, all right, Grayson reflected. He and Muller had raked in several thousand dollars from the other players before Drake caught on to what they were doing and called them on it.

Grayson had come close to drawing on the Virginian that night, but he had stopped himself when he remembered that Drake had a reputation for being quick and deadly with a gun.

He and Muller had gotten out of town just a couple steps ahead of several of their outraged victims. At best, they would have been tarred and feathered; at worst there might have been gunplay or a hangrope.

Muller rubbed his big right fist in his left palm. "I sure would like to catch Drake alone and teach him a lesson."

An ugly laugh came from Grayson's mouth. "If you tried, you'd probably wind up getting hurt. Drake may look a little like a city slicker, but he's plenty tough."

"Yeah, maybe," Muller said with a frown. "I'd still like to settle that score with him."

"Maybe you'll get the chance. For now, you'd be better off worrying about this tournament."

Muller grinned. "I plan to win that big pot at the end. It's liable to be enough dinero that I could drift down to Mexico and lay around for the rest of my life with some pretty little señorita waitin' on me."

"Everybody plans on winning," Grayson said. "You, me, Drake, Lady Arabella, and all the other players."

"The English gal is here?" Muller got a wistful look in his eyes. "She sure is pretty."

"Yeah, and while you're thinking about how pretty she

is, she'll bluff you right out of the game. Listen to me, Jed. I've got an idea how to come out of this as rich men, no matter who wins the final hand. Are you interested?"

"Shoot, yeah, but I don't see how anybody can wind up rich without winnin' the tournament."

"That's because you haven't thought it all through." Grayson drained the last of the beer in his mug, shoved the empty aside, and leaned forward. "Now just listen . . ."

Chapter 7

Morris Upton was at the bar chatting idly with one of the bartenders when Arabella came downstairs with Steve Drake. The saloon owner's forehead creased in an uncertain frown as he spotted the two of them. He abandoned the conversation and hurried across the room to intercept them as they headed for the front door.

Arabella saw him coming and wasn't surprised by his reaction. She had considered suggesting to Steve that they find a rear door, but neither of them was the type to sneak out of a place. That was just too undignified.

"Well, hello again," Upton said as he stopped in front of them. He wasn't exactly blocking their exit, but they would have had to step around him to leave the saloon. "I didn't realize the two of you knew each other. I guess I shouldn't be surprised. We all move in the same circles, don't we?"

"You could say that," Drake replied. His left hand rested lightly on the back of Arabella's right arm. "Lady Arabella and I are old friends. Aren't we, Bella?"

"That's right." She had never been in the same place

at the same time as both men. That was pure coincidence, but it explained Upton's surprise at seeing her and Steve together.

"Are you going somewhere?" Upton asked. "I thought we might have dinner, Lady Arabella . . ."

"I'm afraid I've agreed to catch up on old times with Steve," Arabella said. "Another time, Morris."

"Of course." Upton gave them an obviously forced smile. "The two of you enjoy your evening."

"I'm sure we will," Drake said. "Say, you wouldn't happen to know a decent place to get a steak here in Tombstone, would you?"

"Try the Red Top Café," Upton suggested. "It's up on Fremont Street and two blocks west."

Drake smiled and nodded. "Thanks, we'll do that." He linked arms with Arabella to walk her out of the Top-Notch.

Arabella felt Upton watching them as they left. Quietly, she said, "He's upset. I hope he doesn't do anything to hurt our chances in the tournament."

"What can he do? That's one of the good things about the game, it has rules. And there'll be plenty of people watching Upton to make sure he abides by them."

"I suppose you're right."

She felt him stiffen a little as they passed one of the saloon's front windows. He broke stride, but so briefly that most people probably wouldn't have noticed it.

Arabella did, though. "Steve, is something wrong?"

"Thought I caught a glimpse in there of a couple hombres I know." The flat tone of Drake's voice told Arabella he wasn't fond of the men he thought he had spotted.

"I wouldn't be surprised. A tournament like this draws

players from all over, and like Upton said, most of us move in the same circles. When I came in earlier, I saw three or four other people I know."

"Yes, but these fellas have a particular reason not to like me. If they're in town, I'll have to be sure and keep my eyes open. They're the sort who'd hold a grudge . . . and they wouldn't be shy about trying to settle old scores."

"Would they be here for the tournament?"

"Maybe," Drake mused. "They're not at the same level as a lot of the other players who were invited, but they might be ambitious enough to give it a try. Unfortunately, they don't always play a straight game."

"That could cause a lot of trouble here."

"It sure could. I'll look into it . . . later. Right now I just want to enjoy some good food and better company."

They walked a block north to Fremont Street and found the Red Top Café, a square building made of large blocks of sandstone topped with a red tile roof in the Spanish style.

The place wasn't much to look at outside, but the people who ran it were friendly and the food was excellent. Drake declared the steaks as good as Delmonico's in Kansas City.

When they stepped out of the café after their meal, Arabella noticed right away that a hot wind had sprung up, not unusual in that part of Arizona, of course. The arid breeze stirred the dark wings of her hair since she hadn't worn a hat when she left the Top-Notch.

She pushed several ebony strands back from her face. "I don't much care for that wind. It feels as if a storm might be brewing."

"I'd be more worried about that if the air was still, ma'am," commented a man they were passing on the boardwalk.

Arabella stopped to look at him. He wasn't very tall, about the same height as her, in fact, but something about the way he carried himself made him seem bigger. He gave her and Steve Drake a friendly nod and raised a hand to tug on the brim of his pearl-gray Stetson.

She couldn't help but notice a lawman's badge pinned to his vest just under the edge of his suit coat.

"Sheriff John Slaughter, folks," the man introduced himself.

"I'm Steve Drake," the Virginian said as he put out his hand. "And this is Lady Arabella Winthrop."

"Ah, the English lady," Slaughter said as he shook hands with Steve Drake. "My deputy Stonewall mentioned meeting you when you came into town earlier today, Lady Winthrop." Slaughter chuckled. "I must say, you made quite an impression on the boy."

"He was very polite, Sheriff," Arabella said. "You should be happy to have him as one of your deputies."

"Oh, I am. I'm even happier to have him as my brother-in-law. I married his sister, you see."

"Keeping law enforcement all in the family, eh?" Drake said with a grin.

"Something like that. Am I right in guessing that you folks are in town for the big poker tournament?"

"That's right. We're on our way back to the Top-Notch now."

"The games aren't getting started tonight, are they?" Slaughter asked.

Arabella said, "Not everyone has arrived yet. At least

that's the impression I was under. The tournament will probably start tomorrow or the next day."

"I'll wish you luck, then," Slaughter said with another nod. He started to move on.

"If I was a lawman, I'd be a little worried about the tournament," Drake said. "Lots of high rollers in town and a lot of money, too. Sometimes that brings trouble with it."

"You're right about that, Mr. Drake," Slaughter said. "If things were different, I might be more concerned than I am."

"What do you mean, if things were different? If you don't mind my asking."

"Don't mind at all," Slaughter said. "What I mean is, trouble's already come to Tombstone." He didn't explain that he was talking about the prisoner he had locked up in the jail. That wasn't really any of their business. He bid them good night and continued his evening rounds.

He often took that particular duty on himself, especially when Viola wasn't in town. He liked to see Tombstone settling down for the evening.

He wasn't sure that was going to be the case tonight. The hot wind seemed to have everyone on edge. People he spoke to on the boardwalks and the street were either curt or unusually nervous, even when they had no reason to be.

By the time he reached the Birdcage at the end of Allen Street, Slaughter's instincts told him the air was thick with impending violence.

As he paused in the saloon's doorway, he understood better why that feeling had gripped him. Men were crowded around someone who stood at the bar talking loudly.

"No better than an animal!" the man said. "Hell, he's a mad dog! We all know it. And we all know what you do when an animal turns bad, too. You put it down!"

Slaughter recognized the voice, even though the crowd prevented him from getting a good look at the speaker. The man haranguing the saloon's other customers was Charlie Porter, the foreman on the Bar EM. He had been ramrodding Little Ed McCabe's crew for several years and was one of the riders who had chased Dallin Williams into Tombstone that afternoon with guns blazing, endangering the citizens.

That was enough of a reason right there to make Slaughter dislike the man. The way Porter was trying to stir up more trouble made it worse.

Slaughter pushed the batwings aside and stepped into the Birdcage. The hot wind came in with him and poked some of the sawdust on the floor into lazy swirls.

Porter was still yelling about what Williams had done, or at least was accused of doing, and he had the crowd so worked up that the men weren't even watching the two scantily-clad soiled doves in the cages that gave the place its name. The girls looked bored as they sat on the stools inside the cages that hung from the ceiling and waited for some business.

"You fellas all know what Williams is like," Porter went on. "How many innocent girls has he ruined? How many fine, decent married women has he taken advantage of? A man like that is lower than a snake's belly! I don't know about you, but when I see a snake, I step on it and cut off its head!"

"What do you think we ought to do, Charlie?" one of the men in the crowd asked. His voice was a little slurred and unsteady, proof that he had been drinking.

Slaughter suspected that most of the men in this bunch had put away quite a bit of liquor, probably paid for by Charlie Porter . . . although there was a good chance Porter had been using Little Ed McCabe's money.

"It's not my place to say," Porter replied, which Slaughter thought was a little sanctimonious of him, considering the rabble-rousing he was doing. "Williams has been arrested, and it's up to the law to deal with him now."

"I'll tell you what we oughta do!" a man shouted as he looked around at the others for encouragement. "We oughta get ourselves a rope and string him up! That's what he's got comin' to him, the no-good polecat!"

Cheers went up from most of the men in the crowd. They sounded eager, even bloodthirsty. Several of them angrily pumped fists in the air.

Stirring around in their excitement created a narrow gap through which Slaughter saw Charlie Porter standing at the bar with a satisfied grin on his face.

Porter had done exactly what he'd set out to do, Slaughter thought. He had gotten the men in the Birdcage so drunk and worked up that one of them had made the suggestion Porter had been careful not to make himself. It was a classic manipulation of a crowd into a lynch mob.

And it made John Slaughter mad as hell.

The fact that he could see Porter meant that the Bar EM foreman could see him as well. A look of alarm appeared on Porter's face as Slaughter started across the room toward the bar. Then the crowd shifted again and Slaughter lost sight of him.

The crowd was still making a lot of racket. No one had noticed Slaughter's approach. His route took him past one of the cages. The girl sitting inside was wearing only a nearly transparent wrapper. She smiled at him. "Good evening, Sheriff."

"Ma'am," Slaughter said with a nod. He walked on by and drew his Colt. The Single Action Army slid smoothly from leather. He thumbed back the hammer, pointed the gun at the ceiling, and squeezed the trigger.

The boom of the revolver seemed louder than it really was in the close confines of the low-ceilinged barroom. Slaughter had been careful not to aim at one of the lamps hanging from the ceiling. The last thing he wanted to do was start a fire.

One shot was all it took to make silence come crashing down hard in the saloon.

Some of the men in the crowd jumped at the noise and reached for their guns when they turned to see what was going on. They froze when they saw the grim-faced lawman standing there holding the pearl-handled Colt. Hands eased carefully away from gun butts.

"Porter!" Slaughter thundered, seeming almost as loud as the gunshot. "What the hell do you think you're doing?"

Like Moses and the Red Sea in the Good Book, the crowd parted before Texas John. Nobody wanted to be standing too close to the object of his wrath.

All by himself, Charlie Porter stood at the bar with a mixture of anger and dread on his rough-hewn face. "You got no call to threaten me, Sheriff—"

"I didn't threaten you. I asked you a question. What are you trying to do here?"

"Just havin' a drink and talkin'," Porter said. "That's all."

"Really? Because it sounded to me like you were trying to stir up a lynch mob! Do you think you're going to take Dallin Williams out of my jail and string him up?"

"Now, I never said that," Porter insisted.

"Maybe not, but I saw how pleased you were when somebody else came up with the idea."

Porter's rock-like slab of a jaw jutted forward defiantly. "I got a right to my opinion, Sheriff, and I think a good-for-nothing rapist like Williams deserves to hang."

Several men in the crowd shouted their agreement.

They were in the back of the bunch where they weren't very visible, noted Slaughter.

"I won't abide any lynch mobs in Tombstone." His voice was flat and hard as flint. "The law will take care of Dallin Williams. He'll go to trial and answer for the charges against him."

"Seems to me like a trial is a waste of time and money," Porter said with a sneer. "It's all gonna wind up the same in the end, anyway."

Slaughter's thoughts flashed back to his conversation with Judge Burroughs that afternoon. Clearly Porter and the other men didn't know that Williams would escape the hangrope even if he were found guilty.

Slaughter sure as blazes wasn't going to inform them of that fact, either. That would just inflame them more.

"You need to head back to the McCabe spread, Porter," Slaughter said. "You're done here tonight."

"You're runnin' me out of town?" Porter sounded like he couldn't believe it.

"That's exactly what I'm doing."

Several men jeered and shouted that Slaughter couldn't do that. He wondered if they were some of McCabe's hands, too.

"You can ride out or you can spend the night in jail for inciting a riot and disturbing the peace," Slaughter went on as he stared coldly at Porter. "It's up to you."

For a few seconds Porter looked like he wanted to argue or put up a fight, but then the defiance went out of his eyes. He shrugged. "Reckon I ought to be gettin' back to the ranch anyway."

"Take the rest of McCabe's men with you." Slaughter raised his voice and added, "You hear that? If you ride for the Bar EM, get out of Tombstone. Go home and let the law handle things here in town."

Porter started toward the door. Several members of the crowd followed him, all of them glaring at Slaughter and grumbling as they left the Birdcage.

Slaughter swept a cold gaze over the rest of the men in front of the bar. That was all it took to make them start drifting apart. He heard some angry words muttered, but he chose to ignore them in the interest of keeping the peace.

In a few minutes, the level of conversation in the room was back to normal. Slaughter started for the door. As he passed the cages, he nodded and said, "Ladies."

He had headed off trouble for a little while, he thought as he stepped out into the street, but it would be back soon enough. Maybe not tonight, but it wouldn't take very long for anger to build up again and for people to start talking about how Dallin Williams deserved to dance at the end of a rope.

The week or so before the matter could come to trial was going to be a mighty long one, Slaughter reflected. He'd be surprised if the situation lasted until then without violence breaking out. He was going to need the luck of one of those poker players in Morris Upton's big tournament just to keep the lid on.

And if the hot wind kept blowing, it would only make the pot boil even more.

Chapter 8

Since the terrain around Tombstone was dry and desert-like, the air often cooled off considerably during the hours of darkness. Sometimes it was downright cold before morning. That wasn't the case as the hot wind continued to blow all night, feeling like the searing breath from the mouth of a blast furnace.

The wind didn't die down until just before dawn, and by then it was too late to do any good. As the sun rose, blistering heat settled over the landscape.

Men who were out and about on early errands pulled bandannas from their pockets and mopped already sweating foreheads. Mongrel dogs that normally would have been scrounging in the trash behind the cafés for something to eat sought out any patch of shade they could find, instead.

As a matter of habit, John Slaughter was an early riser. He stepped out of the hotel following his breakfast and paused on the boardwalk. He frowned as he realized just how hot and still the air was.

By the time he reached the courthouse, he had shed his coat and was giving serious consideration to taking off his string tie and unfastening his collar. He liked to dress well, especially when he was carrying out his duties as sheriff. He believed that would make people more inclined to respect him and his office. But there was no point in being miserable all day, he told himself.

Burt Alvord was at the desk in the outer office, pushing some papers around listlessly. Sweat glistened on the chief deputy's mostly bald pate as he looked up at Slaughter. "Gonna be a real scorcher today, ain't it, Sheriff?"

"I'm afraid you're right, Burt," Slaughter replied as he hung up his hat and coat. He pulled his tie off and shoved it into one of the coat pockets. "Everything quiet this morning?"

"Yes, sir. When I took over for Mose a little while ago, he said there weren't any problems overnight."

Slaughter nodded. Mose Tadrack had had the graveyard shift. As a former saloon swamper, he was used to being up at all hours of the night.

"How's the prisoner?"

Burt leaned back in his chair. "Pretty scared, I'd say. I reckon it's starting to soak in on Williams just how much trouble he's really in."

"And he doesn't even know what happened in the Birdcage last night," Slaughter said with a frown.

That put a matching frown on Burt's face. "What happened in the Birdcage?"

"Charlie Porter was buying drinks and doing his best to stir up a lynch mob."

"Little Ed McCabe's foreman?"

"That's right."

"You reckon McCabe put him up to it?"

"I don't know," Slaughter said. "Porter's ridden for the Bar EM for quite a while. It's possible he was doing it just out of loyalty to his boss. I don't think so, but it doesn't really matter why he was trying to cause trouble."

"What did you do, Sheriff?"

"Put a stop to it, of course. I told Porter to get out of town and take the rest of the McCabe hands with him, or I'd jail him for disturbing the peace and inciting a riot." Slaughter paused. "He decided not to put me to the test."

Burt grunted. "Probably a good thing for him. Now I understand some of the talk I overheard in the hash house while I was havin' breakfast before I came to work this morning."

"What sort of talk?" Slaughter asked sharply.

"Just a lot of muttering about how Williams had gotten away with too much already and how folks around here needed to make sure he didn't get away with attacking the McCabe girl."

Slaughter closed his eyes for a second, sighed, and shook his head. "I had hoped that such talk would have died out by this morning."

"Nope, people are still plenty upset about it. You'd think as hot as the weather is, trying to stay cool is all folks would care about right now."

"Hot weather means hot blood."

"I reckon you're right about that, Sheriff. If I hear any more gossip about a necktie party, I'll step in and put a stop to it right away, just like you did last night."

Slaughter nodded in agreement. He went on through

to his private office and sat down to wonder if there was any way he could get Judge Burroughs to speed up Dallin Williams' trial date.

The sooner the law did its job in this case, the better.

Oscar Grayson had stayed up late the night before playing in a low-stakes game that was nothing more than practice for the tournament. A couple times he had been tempted to deal from the bottom of the deck or palm an ace, but in the end he hadn't gone to the trouble. Cheating was just a matter of habit, and the amount of money on the table didn't seem worth it.

He didn't wake up until noon in the squalid hotel on Sixth Street where he was staying. It was one step above a flophouse, but at least he only had to share his bed with fleas and not another guest. He couldn't afford one of the second-floor rooms at the Top-Notch or at a better hotel.

He threw back the grimy sheets and sat up in bed to scrub a hand over his face. His palm rasped against the beard stubble on his jaw. He sighed, then let out a startled exclamation as he realized he wasn't alone after all.

A man sat across the room in the lone, rickety chair and pointed a gun at him.

A .22 caliber Colt Open Top pocket revolver lay on the little table beside the bed. Grayson's eyes darted toward it, but his hand didn't make a move. The gun in the other man's hand was rock-steady, and Grayson knew the unwelcome visitor could drill him before he reached the little pistol.

"That's pretty smart of you, Oscar," Steve Drake said.

"I figured you'd think about making a try for that little toy, but I wasn't worried. That's why I left it there."

Grayson's mouth twisted in a snarl. In a voice hoarse from sleep, he said, "What the hell do you want, Drake?"

"Just thought I'd pay you a visit and renew our old acquaintance."

The air in the room was stifling and Grayson felt sweat springing out under his arms, but Drake looked cool as could be.

"Wichita was where we last saw each other, wasn't it?" he asked.

"You know damned good and well it was."

"Your old pard Muller is here, too. I thought I spotted both of you in the Top-Notch last night, so I asked around and made sure of it. It wasn't hard to find you, Oscar."

"I don't need to hide from the likes of a tinhorn like you," Grayson declared with a sneer and some forced bravado that he didn't really feel.

Drake laughed. "That's pretty rich, you calling someone else a tinhorn. You can't win at poker without cheating. I doubt if you could win at solitaire."

"I don't know what you're talking about. I always play an honest game."

That statement brought another laugh from Drake. Then amusement vanished from his face. "I thought about warning Morris Upton about you and Muller. But Upton can look out for himself. To be honest, I don't have much more use for him than I do for the two of you." He leaned forward, and cold menace glittered like ice in his pale blue eyes. "So I'm here to give you a warning instead, Grayson. This tournament is important to some of us.

You'd be wise not to try anything funny. And if you happen to find yourself sitting at the same table as Lady Winthrop, you'd better be on your best behavior. If there's even a hint that you're trying to cheat her, I'll kill you. Simple as that."

"You're full of big talk," Grayson said.

"I can back it up."

That was the thing, Grayson thought. He probably could. Steve Drake had killed three or four men in shootings over card tables, and that was just the last Grayson had heard. The Virginian's score might be even higher.

"You've got me all wrong, Drake." Grayson struggled to keep a whining note out of his voice. "I don't work with Muller anymore."

"I saw the two of you together last night."

Grayson shrugged. "What can I say? We're old friends. He comes over to have a drink with me, I'm not going to tell him to leave. But we're not partners, and I play the game fair and square now. That's the truth, whether you believe me or not."

Drake cocked his head to the side a little. "You know, I almost do believe you, Oscar. But I know what a talented liar you are. It comes to you almost as naturally as breathing." He stood up, but the gun in his hand didn't waver. "I've said my piece. You're on notice."

"I'm just here in Tombstone to play poker. That's all."

Drake grunted. He backed to the door, reached behind him with his free hand, and opened it. He didn't lower the gun or take his attention off Grayson until he was in the corridor and closed the door behind him.

Grayson looked at his pistol again and wondered if he could grab it, charge out there, and take his old enemy by surprise before Drake reached the stairs.

That was doubtful, he decided. Knowing Steve Drake, he was probably waiting in the hall for him to try something reckless. Grayson wasn't going to play right into his hands.

He got up and pulled on his clothes, then left the hotel to look for Muller.

He had to search through several saloons before he found the big man lounging against the bar in the Oriental nursing a beer.

"What's wrong, Oscar?" Muller asked. "You look like you got a hungry wolf on your trail."

"Almost that bad," Grayson said as he motioned for the bartender to bring him a drink despite the fact that it was barely noon. "Drake spotted us in the Top-Notch last night."

Muller frowned. "So what? We got as much right to be in Tombstone as he does." The frown deepened as something occurred to him. "He don't know anything about what you were talkin' to me about, does he?"

Grayson shook his head. He picked up the drink the bartender set in front of him and tossed it back. The whiskey hit like a rock in his empty stomach. There was a good reason some people called the stuff rotgut.

After a moment, he was able to draw a little strength from the fiery stuff and welcomed it.

"No, I don't see how he could know anything about that," Grayson said in answer to Muller's question. "He just warned me not to try to cheat in the tournament, especially if I'm in the same game as the Winthrop woman."

"Sweet on her, ain't he?"

Grayson slid the empty glass across the hardwood. "They're old friends."

"I wouldn't mind bein' old friends with her, if you know what I mean," Muller said with a leer.

Grayson shook his head. "She'd never give the likes of us the time of day. She acts like she's doing us a big favor just by sitting down at a poker table with us." Anger and resentment stirred in his brain like snakes coiling on a hot rock as he thought about Lady Arabella Winthrop. "One of these days I'd like to teach her not to be so high and mighty. Right now, though, I'm more interested in the money. I've been thinking about it, and I'm not sure we can pull this off by ourselves, Jed."

"You want to bring somebody else in on the plan? Who?"

"Rourke is in town."

Muller's shaggy eyebrows rose. "Max Rourke? He's loco as he can be!"

"I know," Grayson said as he nodded slowly. "And that might be just what we need."

Stonewall took off his hat and fanned himself with it, but it didn't do much good. He was still so hot he felt like his brain was baking inside his head. What he needed, he thought, was a nice cool root cellar where he could catch a nap. There was one on the ranch in the San Bernardino Valley.

Unfortunately he was working, not to mention being a long way from the ranch. He walked along Fremont Street and thought that it was almost hot enough to burn himself on the metal of the rifle he carried.

He paused in front of Schieffelin Hall to wipe his face. The meeting hall was named after Ed Schieffelin, the prospector who had founded Tombstone almost a decade earlier, and had been built by Ed's brother Al. Several old-timers were sitting in rocking chairs in front of the impressive two-story adobe structure, taking advantage of what little shade they could find.

"Howdy, Deputy," one of them greeted Stonewall. "Still got your prisoner over there in jail?"

"Of course we do," Stonewall replied. "Where else would a prisoner be?"

"Well, I don't know," the lanky old man drawled. "From the talk I been hearin' around town, I figured maybe he was decoratin' the limb of some cottonwood tree by now."

The man's elderly cronies slapped their thighs and cackled with laughter over that comment like it was the funniest thing they had ever heard.

Stonewall didn't find it the least bit amusing. "Who did you hear talking about lynching Dallin?" he asked sharply.

"Oh, I don't know," the old-timer replied with a dismissive wave of his hand. "Wouldn't tell you if I did. And don't think I didn't notice the way you referred to that scoundrel by his given name, Deputy. You and him are friends, ain't you?"

"I wouldn't say that."

"But Williams used to ride for John Slaughter."

"Yeah, but he doesn't anymore," Stonewall pointed out. "And it wouldn't matter if he did. Sheriff Slaughter enforces the law fair and square, no matter who somebody is."

"Hmmph," the old man said. "That ain't the way it looks to me. I didn't vote for the man, and I don't blame folks for not trustin' him to see that justice is done."

Stonewall struggled to rein in the anger that welled up inside him, but he couldn't stop himself from saying, "Why, you old coot! I ought to—"

"Ought to what? Arrest me for speakin' the truth? Is that how John Slaughter's deputies do things now? You don't agree with the sheriff and you go to jail?"

Stonewall wasn't sure how this conversation had turned so hostile and become an ugly confrontation instead, but he realized that several people who'd been passing by in the street had stopped to watch and listen.

He didn't want to do anything to embarrass his boss and brother-in-law. With an effort, he was able to keep his voice calm and steady as he said, "Nobody here is getting arrested. You just need to stop accusing the sheriff of things that aren't true. Nobody works harder to see that the law's enforced fairly and impartially than Sheriff Slaughter."

"Well, you'd say that, wouldn't you," the old-timer responded with a sneer, "since he's married to your sister."

Stonewall saw that there was no way he was going to come out ahead in this argument. "You're entitled to your own opinion, mister. I reckon most folks in Tombstone know what they can expect from the sheriff."

"I reckon they do. That's why they're talkin' about takin' the law into their own hands."

Stonewall didn't say anything else. He just walked on down the street with the heat from the brassy sky pounding on his head like a hammer. If things were bad enough that the old codgers in front of Schiffelin Hall were talking about a lynching, there must be a real danger of it, he thought. When he got back to the courthouse and the sheriff's office from the turn around town, he probably ought to tell his brother-in-law about it. John probably already knew, but it wouldn't hurt to apprise him of how the sentiment was running in town.

The heat might make it worse, too. By nightfall, folks would be primed to explode, and it wouldn't take much of a spark to set off the blast.

It had already been a long day, but Stonewall suspected the coming night would be even longer.

Chapter 9

Slaughter looked around the sheriff's office at the men assembled there late that afternoon.

They were a pretty salty bunch, he thought. Stonewall, Burt Alvord, Mose Tadrack, Jeff Milton, G.W. Farrington, Viola's and Stonewall's cousin Tommy Howell, Enoch Shattuck, and a lean, hawk-faced, middle-aged Mexican named Lorenzo Paco who was maybe the best tracker in the whole territory.

All of them had worn deputy badges for Slaughter at different times in the past, and although most of them weren't working full-time for Cochise County anymore, they had all responded without hesitation when he'd called on them for help. It was the sort of loyalty he inspired, and he was proud of that fact.

"Thank you all for being here," Slaughter began. "You know why I asked you all to come in. There's a lot of talk in town about taking a prisoner out of here and hanging him."

"You're talkin' about Dallin Williams, aren't you, John?" Tommy asked.

Slaughter frowned at the informality. It was true that Tommy was a relative by marriage, but law enforcement required a certain decorum. That was one reason he wasn't the jailer anymore; he was more happy-go-lucky and carefree than Stonewall.

When Tommy had worked there full-time, he had not only allowed Mexican prisoners to play their guitars and sing, he had encouraged it and joined in the festivities. He had let their favorite señoritas in to visit, as well, and as a result the place often had been more like a fandango than a jail.

"That's right, Deputy Howell," Slaughter said with a frown. He hoped Tommy would catch the hint that a little more solemnity would be appreciated.

"I ain't sayin' he deserves to be hanged, but he's sure been ridin' high, wide, and handsome through all the womenfolk in the county for a long time."

"That's totally irrelevant," Slaughter said, aware that he sounded more like the judge than the sheriff. "He's charged with a particular crime, and that's our only business. We're going to keep him safe to stand trial on that charge." His cool-eyed gaze went from man to man. "If any of you don't agree with that, you can leave right now and no one will hold it against you."

That wasn't strictly true. He'd hold it against anybody who decided to rabbit, although he wouldn't admit that.

"Shoot, John—I mean, Sheriff—nobody wants to run out on you," Tommy said. "We're here to help, whatever you need. Ain't that right, boys?"

Nods and mutters of agreement came from the assembled deputies.

"All right," Slaughter said. "There are eight of you, so

you're going to split up into four pairs. One pair will always be posted here at the jail, one pair off-duty, and the other two circulating through the town. You'll operate in two-hour shifts. I don't care how you pair up or who does what first, as long as things are set up that way. Is that understood?"

"You can count on us, Sheriff," Burt said.

"If you run into trouble and need help, three shots will be the signal," Slaughter went on. "Someone should always be fairly close by. I'm planning to spend most of the night making the rounds of town myself."

"Shouldn't you have somebody with you, Sheriff?" Stonewall suggested. "I thought the reason you paired us up like this was so that no one man would be out there in the line of fire by himself."

"We don't know that there'll be a line of fire," Slaughter pointed out. "I'm hoping that all the reckless talk is just that—talk. Spouting off in a saloon is a lot easier than facing a gun in the hands of a man who's prepared to use it." He smiled. "Besides, I can take care of myself."

None of the deputies were going to argue with the sheriff about that.

"All right," Slaughter went on after a moment. "Go get yourselves some supper and get ready for a long night. I'll hold down the fort here for the time being."

The deputies filed out of the office and left the courthouse. When they were gone, Slaughter went over to the cell block door, unlocked it, and went inside.

Dallin Williams sat on the bunk in his cell with his hands clasped between his knees. His shoulders were hunched and his head hung down in a posture of despair.

He didn't look up when Slaughter's footsteps echoed from the stone floor.

"Your supper will be brought over in a little while, Williams," Slaughter said.

"It don't matter. I ain't hungry."

"You have to eat. No prisoner in my jail goes hungry."

"I just told you I don't want anything, Sheriff." Williams unclasped his hands and rested them on his knees. They gripped tightly. He began to rock backward and forward a little.

"I don't have no appetite when I'm locked up like this. I can't stand it, Sheriff. I just can't stand it. Havin' all these walls and bars around me, they start to close in on me. It . . . it makes me go a mite loco, I think."

"Everybody feels like that when they're locked up. You'll get used to it."

Williams' head swung slowly from side to side. "I don't think I will," he said quietly without looking at Slaughter. "I just don't think so."

Slaughter suppressed the irritation he felt. He wanted to tell Williams that if he didn't like the idea of being locked up, he shouldn't have attacked Jessie McCabe.

But that charge hadn't been proven yet, Slaughter reminded himself. He didn't see how it could be. There was no real evidence one way or the other.

The jury would just have to decide whether they believed Jessie or Williams.

Slaughter had a pretty good hunch whose story they were more likely to accept. If Williams had a hard time being locked up in the county jail for a week, he really wasn't going to like it when he was sent to prison for twenty or twenty-five years . . . or the rest of his life.

"Your supper will be here," Slaughter said again. "Whether you eat it or not is up to you."

He left the cell block and locked the heavy wooden door behind him. He heard Williams muttering on the other side of the door but couldn't make out the words. He recognized the sound of desperation in the prisoner's voice, though.

Stonewall's cousin Tommy had asked to be his partner, but Stonewall figured the sheriff wouldn't want the two of them working together. For one thing, they were both young, and for another, Tommy needed a steady hand to keep him in line. Stonewall had suggested that Tommy work with Lorenzo Paco. There was nobody steadier than Paco.

After grabbing some supper at the hash house, Stonewall was on his way back toward the jail when he heard someone behind him call his name. He paused on the boardwalk and turned to see a young, dark-haired man in canvas trousers and a work shirt coming toward him. The man also wore a canvas apron over his shirt.

Stonewall recognized Roy Corbett, who worked in one of the general stores.

"Howdy, Roy." During the time Stonewall had been in Tombstone serving as a deputy, he and Corbett had become friends. They were about the same age, and Corbett had been a cowboy at one time, too.

It didn't make sense to Stonewall that somebody

would give up a job like cowboying to work inside in a store all day, but despite his youth he had already learned that it took all kinds of folks to make up the world.

"Stonewall, have you heard all the talk around town?" Corbett asked.

"Talk about what?"

"You know." The light was fading rapidly now that the sun had gone down, but Stonewall could tell Corbett looked uneasy. "About Dallin Williams. I've heard it all day in the store. People are whispering to each other about how Williams deserves to be strung up without waiting for a trial."

Stonewall nodded. "I appreciate the warning, Roy, but the sheriff knows all about it. Charlie Porter started talkin' up a necktie party last night in the Birdcage. Doesn't seem like the talk has let up much during the day, either."

"Do you think they'll actually do it? Do you think a lynch mob will take Williams out of the jail and hang him?"

"They might try. Sheriff Slaughter's not about to let that happen, though."

"Good. I wouldn't want to see Williams lynched."

The fervent declaration made Stonewall curious. "Why do you say that, Roy? You and him aren't friends, are you? I wasn't sure you even knew the fella."

"No, we're not friends, but I don't believe in people taking the law into their own hands. That's a dangerous thing to have happen, especially in a town like Tombstone with its notorious history."

"Yeah, things used to be pretty rugged around here.

But that's all changed now. Tombstone's got law and order, thanks to Sheriff Slaughter."

Corbett looked unconvinced, but he nodded. "We can hope so."

A frown creased Stonewall's forehead. "Hold on a minute. You used to ride for Little Ed McCabe, didn't you, back when you were cowboyin'?"

"For a while," Corbett said with a nod.

"Then you knew Jessie McCabe."

Corbett waved a hand. "Yeah, sure, but she wasn't much more than a knobby-kneed little brat, always underfoot, when I was there. Still, I liked her, I guess. She wasn't a bad kid. I felt sorry for her when her brothers died."

"Seems to me that you wouldn't be worrying about what might happen to Dallin Williams, then, after what he did."

"I don't give a damn about Dallin Williams. I just don't want him strung up without a trial first." Corbett hesitated, then went on. "I haven't told anybody this, but I've sort of got it in my mind to be a lawyer one of these days. That's why I quit cowboying and went to work in the store. It takes money to get the schooling to be a lawyer, and I figured I'd never save up enough as long as I was just a wild young cowhand going on a bender at payday every month."

Stonewall grinned at this revelation and lightly punched his friend on the shoulder. "Why, you ol' dog. Keepin' a secret like that. I always wondered why you gave up a riding job. Figure on being a lawyer, do you?"

"That's what I'd like," Corbett said with a nod. "So

you can understand why I want Williams to be tried properly. If the West is ever going to be truly civilized, there won't be any room for hangrope justice."

"I reckon not." Stonewall leaned closer and added, "To tell you the truth, though, I'm not all that sure about that so-called civilization. Sometimes it seems to me like it's just a different set of rules for the same old warrin' and killin'."

"Maybe someday that won't be the case." The two young men stood there in silence for a moment, then Corbett went on. "I'd better let you get on about your business. I just wanted to warn you about all the talk that's going on, if you hadn't heard about it already."

"Don't worry," Stonewall assured him. "No lynch mob is gonna take a prisoner out of Texas John Slaughter's jail. I can guaran-damn-tee that."

Mose Tadrack had been paired with Stonewall and he was waiting at the jail when Stonewall got there. The newest deputy was a nondescript man in his thirties, the sort of hombre you'd glance at in the street and five seconds later have no recollection of what he looked like.

Stonewall had no idea what Tadrack had done for a living before arriving in Tombstone; the man wasn't talkative, and he wasn't the sort to invite questions.

Until fairly recently, he had been a boozehound, and the only job he'd been able to hold down was that of a swamper. Even at that, he hadn't stayed in one place for too long but had moved from saloon to saloon.

That had all changed when he'd volunteered for the

posse that went after the Mexican bandits who had raided Tombstone and carried off Viola Slaughter as a hostage. That violent ordeal had burned all the liquor cravings out of him, and he hadn't gone back to it.

"We're going to take the first shift here at the jail," Tadrack told Stonewall. "Is that all right with you?"

"Sure. I don't reckon it really matters who does what, as long as everything's covered. Where's the sheriff?"

"He's already out making the rounds in town. It wouldn't surprise me if he stayed awake all night." Tadrack's voice held a note of admiration when he talked about John Slaughter. The sheriff was the only one who'd been willing to take a chance on him, maybe ever.

Stonewall took down a pair of shotguns from the rack and loaded them. He and Tadrack each carried a revolver, but there was nothing better for facing down a mob than a shotgun. Those street-sweepers could cut a wide swath of destruction.

Stonewall didn't want to have to shoot anybody, particularly citizens of the town he was sworn to protect. He was confident that he would do his duty if it came down to that, but at the same time he couldn't be sure how he would react if he found himself looking at somebody he knew over the barrels of that scattergun. What if it was someone he considered a friend, someone he might have shared a hymnal with during church services some Sunday morning? Could he really pull the trigger and blow somebody like that to kingdom come, just to save the miserable life of Dallin Williams?

"You look like you're a thousand miles away, Stonewall," Mose Tadrack commented.

"I sort of wish I was. If I was a thousand miles away, I wouldn't have to be worried about what's gonna happen tonight."

"Maybe nothing will happen," Tadrack told him. "You know how people are. They talk and talk, but when it comes time to actually do something dangerous, most folks find an excuse to be somewhere else."

"Yeah, I hope that's how it turns out—" Stonewall stopped short as he heard something from outside. The windows in the office were open to let in any cooling breeze . . . if there had been such a thing in Tombstone that night, which there wasn't. Darkness hadn't brought much relief from the heat.

The open windows also admitted a low rumble. Stonewall thought at first it sounded like distant drums, but then he realized what he was hearing were voices.

Angry voices.

Tadrack heard it, too, and picked up one of the shotguns from the desk. "We'd better see what that is," he suggested.

"You know what it is," Stonewall replied bleakly as he reached for the other shotgun.

"I know what it sounds like. Let's not get ahead of ourselves, though."

Carrying the shotguns, the two deputies went to the door. They opened it and stepped outside.

The courthouse didn't have a porch or a boardwalk in front of it. The entrance opened directly onto Toughnut Street.

Stonewall peered along the broad, dusty avenue and saw a crowd of men round the corner from Fifth Street.

The area around Fifth and Sixth Streets where they crossed Allen and Fremont was where most of Tombstone's saloons were located. He had no doubt that the men who strode purposefully toward the courthouse were well-lubricated and filled with liquid courage.

Some of them carried torches, and the garish glow from the flames filled the air along with loud, angry words.

"Mose, does that look like a lynch mob to you?" Stonewall asked.

"I'm afraid it does," Tadrack replied.

And it was headed straight for the jail.

Chapter 10

Arabella heard some sort of commotion going on outside, but she didn't really pay much attention to it. She focused instead on listening to Morris Upton as he explained the rules of the tournament to the assembled players.

"There are six of you at each table," Upton said unnecessarily, since they could all count. "You'll play until all but one has either dropped out voluntarily or been cleaned out and can't continue. The four winners will play until the same situation applies. Then the one player still left in the game . . . will play me."

She hadn't known that Upton was going to participate in the tournament until now. Evidently none of the other players had, either. A few mutters came from the tables where the gamblers were seated. Upton had set things up to favor himself, which struck some of them as unfair.

But it was his saloon and his tournament, thought Arabella, and there was no rule that said things had to be fair in life.

No such rule at all.

"Does everyone understand?" Upton asked.

The players—two dozen of the best poker players in the entire country—responded with nods and words of agreement.

"All right," Upton went on with a smile. "I'll wish you good luck, then, gentlemen . . . and ladies."

Two other women besides Arabella were in the game. Copper Farris had gotten her name from the lush mane of red hair that she counted on to provide a distraction for the other players, along with her peaches-and-cream complexion and the ample bosom she always made sure was displayed to its best advantage.

Copper wasn't one of the top players, in Arabella's opinion, but she was good enough to get by in most games.

Not this one. Not against this competition.

The other female in the tournament was Beulah Tillery. Short, dumpy, well into middle age, her looks weren't going to distract anybody the way Copper's would. But she was smart and had good instincts.

And was dangerous on the other side of a poker table as far as Arabella was concerned. She was glad the luck of the draw hadn't put her at the same table as Beulah starting out.

Copper wasn't at her table, either. Arabella wouldn't have minded that. She was immune to the redhead's charms and knew that she outclassed Copper as a player.

She was also glad that the draw had put Steve Drake at one of the other tables. She had confidence in her ability to match up with him, but she didn't want to. Not at this point in the tournament, anyway. If she had to face him once the game was down to one table, then so be it.

She knew the five men who shared this table with her, at least by reputation. She had played with three of them—Jim Snyder, Angelo Castro, and J.D. Burnett. Arabella had never shared a table with the other two, Donald Lockard and Wade Cunningham.

She knew from experience that she was better than Snyder, Castro, and Burnett, and she had never heard anything about Lockard and Cunningham to make her think that she couldn't handle them as well.

A new, sealed deck of cards sat in the middle of each table. Cunningham reached out with a long arm and picked up the deck ."I think we should let the lady have the privilege of opening these cards and dealing first."

Dark, heavyset Jim Snyder grunted. "I figured we'd cut for first deal."

"I have no objection to Lady Winthrop commencing the game," Angelo Castro said. The Italian acted in public like he was a ladies' man, but Arabella happened to know that his tastes in private ran in other directions.

The other men didn't object, either, so Arabella took the deck of cards from Cunningham and used her thumbnail to slit the seal. She made sure all her movements were precise and in plain sight as she opened the deck, spread the cards so everyone could see them, and then began to shuffle.

It was all second nature to her, a matter of habit and instinct and reflex. She didn't really have to pay attention to what she was doing as she manipulated the cards. Instead, she looked at her opponents without seeming to, weighing them, gauging them, speculating on the best approach to take with each one.

Some players could be broken in a hurry. Others took more time and effort.

The saloon was full of sounds. A large crowd was on hand to watch the tournament and to drink and enjoy the regular games of chance in the Top-Notch.

The customers knew there was a lot of money in the place, and that seemed to increase their excitement. The roulette wheel, the faro layout, and the blackjack tables were all busy.

Morris Upton could lose that final game and still make a small fortune on this tournament, Arabella thought.

"The game is five card stud, gentlemen," she said. "Would any of you care to cut the deck?"

Before the other players could respond to the offer, a man pushed the batwings open, leaned into the saloon, and shouted, "There's a lynch mob on its way to the jail! They're gonna get that damn rapist and string him up to the nearest tree!"

Mose Tadrack drew his revolver from its holster and said to Stonewall, "Sheriff Slaughter told us the signal for trouble was three shots, right?"

Stonewall had never been face to face with a lynch mob before. He had to swallow hard before he was able to nod and tell Tadrack, "Yeah, that's right."

The former swamper pointed his gun into the air and fired three times as fast as he could pull back the hammer and squeeze the trigger. The booming reports made the oncoming mob stop for a moment.

Somebody in the crowd yelled, "They're shootin' at us!"

"Uh . . . Mose, that might not've been such a good idea."

"Blast it, Stonewall, get back inside!"

The two deputies turned and dived for the door as several men in the forefront of the mob clawed out revolvers and opened fire.

Bullets thudded into the thick walls of the courthouse as the deputies reached the door. Glass shattered in one of the windows. Stonewall got hold of the door and swung it closed behind them. He felt it shudder under the impact of bullets smacking into it.

He and Tadrack had come close to getting ventilated. A shudder went through Stonewall at the thought.

Brackets were mounted on each side of the door so that it could be barred. Stonewall wasn't sure where the bar was, though.

Neither was Tadrack. The older deputy shouted, "Where's the blasted bar?"

"I don't know. We haven't used it since John's been sheriff." Stonewall glanced through the nearest window and saw the torches bobbing around as the mob charged toward the jail. "Maybe in the cell block."

"See if you can find it," Tadrack told him. "I'll try to hold them off."

Stonewall made a run for the cell block door. He heard Tadrack's shotgun roar behind him.

Part of him hoped that Tadrack had fired over the mob's head in an attempt to scare them off, but after the way those bullets had come so close to him, he wasn't as worried as he had been about innocent citizens getting hurt.

Dallin Williams stood at the door of his cell, tightly

gripping the bars as he stared at Stonewall with wide, frightened eyes. "What's goin' on out there? It's a lynch mob come to get me, ain't it?"

"Just keep your head down," Stonewall replied without really answering the prisoner's question. "We won't let anything happen to you."

"Damn it, Stonewall, they're gonna string me up!"

"Not if we can do anything about it." Stonewall spotted the thick beam used to bar the door leaning in a corner of the storage area at the back of the cell block and hurried to fetch the bar.

Out in the office, Mose Tadrack's shotgun exploded again.

Stonewall grunted as he swung the heavy beam off the floor and into his arms. He turned and dashed back into the office, staggering a little from the awkward weight.

Tadrack crouched beside one of the windows. A slug whipped through just before he slapped the inside shutters into place and latched them closed. It hit the wall at the back of the room separating the outer chamber from the sheriff's private office. More bullets struck the thick shutters, but wouldn't get through.

The courthouse had been built in 1882 when folks still worried with good cause about renegade Apaches and Mexican banditos. It had been constructed with an eye toward defense. Besides the thick shutters, the windows had decorative but functional ironwork over them. Nobody was going to break in that way.

Whoever designed it probably hadn't figured that someday the courthouse would be under attack by the very citizens of Tombstone themselves, thought Stonewall as he hurried to the front door.

Outside, something slammed against it, but the latch held . . . for now. It wouldn't stand up to repeated ramming, but the thick bar would.

He struggled to drop the heavy beam into place. The job was easier when Tadrack sprang across the office and grabbed the other end.

Together, they slid the bar into the brackets. That made Stonewall feel a little better, but not much. Another bullet came through a shot-out window, hit the cast-iron stove, and ricocheted off with a wicked whine.

"We gotta get those other shutters closed." Stonewall bent low to stay out of the line of fire as much as possible and moved in a crouching run toward the nearest unshuttered window.

He reached up, grabbed the shutter on one side, and then jerked his hand back down with a gasped curse.

"You hit?" Tadrack asked.

Stonewall shook his hand and then looked at the back of it, where he saw a faint red line. He knew it had been left there by a slug passing close enough to burn the skin. "Not really. Just damn near."

He tried again and managed to close and latch the shutters. Across the office, Tadrack fastened the shutters on the remaining window.

For now they were safer, but Stonewall's guts still jumped a little every time he heard a bullet thud against the outside wall or the door.

"What about the back door?" he asked Tadrack.

"It was barred to start with," the older man replied. "I checked on that first thing, before you and that mob even showed up."

"Hey, don't make it sound like I'm with them!"

Tadrack shook his head. "That's not what I meant."

Stonewall picked up the shotgun he had set on the desk earlier when he went to fetch the bar. He pressed his back against the wall near the door and tried to calm his rampaging pulse without much success.

On the other side of the door, Tadrack took shells from his pocket and slid them into the barrels of his shotgun.

"When you shot at the mob," Stonewall said, "did you aim over their heads?"

Tadrack hesitated before answering. Finally he said, "Yeah, I did. Both times. I can't guarantee nobody got plinked by the buckshot, but I tried not to kill anybody." He sighed. "When I looked out there, I saw faces I recognized, Stonewall. Fellas who drink in the saloons where I used to work. I know they were trying to kill us, but they're just worked up and liquored up. Most of 'em really aren't bad hombres, when you come right down to it."

"Maybe not, but they're bound and determined to hang Williams, and they'll stampede right over us if they have to."

"I know." Tadrack closed the shotgun's breech. "You think the sheriff's on his way with some help by now?"

"I surely do hope so."

Slaughter stood at the corner of First and Fremont Streets with a shotgun tucked under his left arm and looked at the small adobe house sitting behind a couple cottonwood trees. It was a nice, neat place, nothing fancy, but he thought it might suit him.

He had been staying at the American Hotel, Tombstone's best, since he'd been elected and taken office, but he didn't want to have to bed down in a hotel room for the entire duration of his service as sheriff. Lately, he had given some thought to buying a house. He decided that he would bring Viola to have a look at the house on the corner the next time she was in town.

He would value her opinion on the matter, as he did on just about everything else in life.

A trio of shots followed by a sudden burst of gunfire several blocks away made him jerk his head around. A startled curse came from his lips.

He had been making the rounds of Tombstone all evening, judging the temper of the town, but had allowed himself to be distracted by thoughts of buying a house and making a home there, albeit a temporary one.

Those three shots had been the signal for trouble, and they jolted him back into the present. Holding the shotgun at a slant across his chest, he broke into a run toward the courthouse. The unmistakable boom of a shotgun drifted through the night air.

He had heard plenty of muttering from the towns-people while he was walking around, but they always shut up when he came close enough to make out any words. Those abrupt silences made him sure the gossip in town was about Dallin Williams and the idea of break-ing him out of jail and hanging him.

As shots thundered through the night, Slaughter ran past the school, hoping none of his deputies had been hurt.

A tall, lean figure emerged from the shadows to join him. Slaughter glanced over and recognized the hawk-like visage of Lorenzo Paco.

"Trouble, eh, Sheriff?" the Mexican deputy said.

Another shotgun blast sounded.

"It was bound to happen," Slaughter said, then saved his breath for running.

As they turned the corner from First Street onto Toughnut, Slaughter saw the courthouse two blocks away. He slowed at the sight of muzzle flashes winking from the opposite side of the street. A few torches lay in the street, guttering out where they had been dropped when the men carrying them had scattered.

Slaughter and Paco paused behind a parked wagon. To Slaughter's experienced eye, the scene was as plain as if it had been written in a book.

"A lynch mob showed up and tried to rush the jail," he said quietly. "Whoever is in there signaled for help and then forted up. A couple loads of buckshot scattered the mob, but they took cover and now they're trying to flush out the deputies."

"Sí, that is how I see it, too, Señor Slaughter," Paco said. "Do you know who is inside?"

Slaughter shook his head. "No, I left you fellas to work that out among yourselves, remember?" He frowned at Paco. "Aren't you supposed to have another deputy with you? You were going to patrol the town in pairs."

"I was with Tommy. He felt the call of nature and went behind a shed to answer it. Then the shooting started, and I did not wait for him to return."

Slaughter nodded. He hoped his wife's wild young cousin would have the sense not to rush right into all that flying lead.

He didn't have to worry about that. A few moments later, while trying to figure out his next move, he heard someone behind them calling softly, "Lorenzo! Blast it, where'd you go, Lorenzo?"

Paco stepped out from behind the wagon and waved an arm at the young man who hurried along the street, buttoning up his fly as he trotted through the shadows.

"Over here!" Paco said.

Tommy veered toward the wagon and joined them. His teeth gleamed in the light of the rising moon as he grinned. "Boy, it sounds just like a war, don't it?"

"And our side is outnumbered," Slaughter said as he tried to suppress the irritation he felt. Tommy was too young to take much of anything seriously, but before the night was over he might realize what a grim business this really was.

"Who's in the jail?"

"We don't know."

"Come to think of it," Tommy went on, "I think I heard that fella Tadrack say that him and Stonewall were gonna take the first guard shift, so it's probably them."

Slaughter nodded and tried not to think about the fact that his young brother-in-law might be in there. If the door was barred and the shutters were closed on the windows, Stonewall and Tadrack ought to be relatively safe, he told himself. The mob could shoot at the courthouse all night without doing much real damage.

At the same time, the idea of a bunch of drunken fools trying to take the law into their own hands outraged him. He wasn't going to stand for that. His hands tightened on the shotgun as he straightened from his crouch behind the wagon.

"Sheriff, what are you going to do?" Paco asked with a note of worry in his voice.

"Put a stop to this madness." Slaughter stepped out from behind the wagon.

Before Paco or Tommy could stop him, he strode forward determinedly, heading straight for the torrent of lead slashing at the front of the courthouse.

Chapter 11

The startling announcement that a mob was about to attack the jail caused quite a stir inside the Top-Notch. Some of the people who had come to watch the poker tournament moved toward the batwinged entrance. For them, the lure of potential violence outweighed the attractions of a game of chance.

Gunplay, after all, had higher stakes.

Morris Upton moved quickly to intercept the customers who were about to leave. He put himself in front of the door and raised his hands and his voice. "Hold on there, folks, hold on. You don't want to go out there."

"We sure as hell do," one whiskery old-timer said. "It ain't every day there's a lynch mob here in Tombstone."

Several men shouted their raucous agreement with that sentiment.

"But it could be dangerous," Upton argued.

"We'll take our chances, mister. As long as we stay out of the line of fire, we ought to be all right."

Upton hesitated.

From her place at the table, Arabella could practically

see the wheels of his brain turning. If half the crowd deserted the saloon to watch the showdown at the courthouse, he might sell only half as much liquor tonight.

Of course, once the trouble was over many of the bystanders would drift back to the Top-Notch, but probably not all of them. That would still cut into his profits.

"If you leave now," Upton said, "you'll miss out on the free drinks to celebrate the beginning of the tournament."

"Free drinks?" someone in the crowd called.

"That's right." Upton nodded decisively now that he had made up his mind on his best course of action. He waved a hand toward the bar. "The next round is on me, boys."

That broke the back of the burgeoning stampede. A few men weaved around Upton to push through the batwings and leave, but most of them turned back to the bar to collect that free drink.

Upton must figure he would make more money in the long run that way, thought Arabella. And he might be right about that. One drink usually led to another and another, and he would be charging full price for those next shots of watered-down booze.

As the commotion subsided, Arabella looked around the table at the other five players. "As I was saying before we were so rudely interrupted, gentlemen, the game is five card stud. . . ."

Oscar Grayson didn't like the sound of the words *lynch mob.* They gave him the fantods. Although nobody had ever come after him with the intention of stringing him up, more than once he'd had to flee from groups of angry men who wanted to tar and feather him and maybe ride him out of town on a rail.

He had only a vague idea of who the prisoner in the jail was, but he decided he felt sorry for the poor guy anyway.

He pushed those thoughts out of his mind. He had to concentrate on what he was doing. The cards were being dealt at his table, as well as at all the others.

The game was underway.

Grayson didn't really know any of the other players at the table, although when they'd introduced themselves, some of the names were familiar to him. He supposed they must have reputations as good poker players, or else Upton wouldn't have invited them to the tournament.

Grayson wasn't really worried about the competition. He had confidence in his skills.

He also had the knowledge that it didn't matter if he won or not. He wanted to be able to stay in the game for a while, but that was no longer his ultimate goal. The payoff from his other plan would be even better.

He checked his hole card. Seven of clubs.

They had cut the deck for the first deal, and the man who had won passed out the cards deftly as the betting went around the table, giving Grayson the jack of diamonds, two of hearts, seven of hearts, and ten of clubs.

The pair of sevens wasn't good enough, Grayson judged. He dropped out of the hand.

His instincts were correct. One of the other players took the hand with the other three jacks. Grayson was starting the game down a little, but not too bad.

Somewhere in town—down around the courthouse and jail, he supposed—more shots began to ring out. He ignored them. If the guns weren't aimed at him, he didn't care. It was none of his business.

Half an hour later he had won only a single hand, but that pot was a good one, big enough so that he was almost even again as he raked it in.

Play paused briefly as a couple men rolled cigarettes. Another lit up a cigar. One signaled for a drink to be brought over to him.

During that break, Grayson glanced over at the table where Jed Muller sat. The game continued there. That ugly she-devil Beulah Tillery was one of the players at that table, and Grayson could tell by the pile of money in front of her that she had been fairly successful so far.

But it would be a long game. Things still had quite a ways to go, and fortune could change at any time.

His gaze drifted over to the fourth table. His guts tightened with anger as he saw Steve Drake sitting at that one and remembered the high-handed way the silver-haired gambler had invaded his hotel room that morning. Grayson hoped the high-and-mighty blackguard lost everything.

Seated to Drake's right was Copper Farris. Grayson's eyes lingered on her. Any man would have trouble taking his eyes off of her, he thought. She was spectacular . . . but in a gaudy, flashy way. He wasn't sure Copper was actually any more lovely than Arabella Winthrop. The English woman's beauty was just more subtle, that was all.

Still, most men would have trouble concentrating on their cards with the creamy expanse of Copper's bosom staring at them from a low-cut gown across the table. He had no doubt that she counted on that.

At the moment, Grayson was actually more interested in the man who sat two chairs to Steve Drake's left. Max Rourke was also a redhead, although his hair was a much more subdued shade than Copper's flaming mane. He was lean, with a face that reminded Grayson of a fox. Rourke's cheeks were faintly pitted from a childhood illness. His green eyes were flat and hard, like a stone. Like an emerald.

Rourke had killed even more men in gunfights than Steve Drake had, at least six. That didn't count the Indians and whores he was rumored to have done for. His temper was said to be uncontrollable.

But he was supposed to be relatively trustworthy if you were working with him. At least Grayson thought so, and he hoped the hunch was right. Before the tournament was over, he might have a lot riding on Max Rourke.

Everything, in fact.

Burt Alvord and Jeff Milton ran up behind the wagon where Lorenzo Paco and Tommy Howell were crouched. Burt asked, "What in blazes is the sheriff doing?"

"He said he was gonna put a stop to the shootin'," Tommy replied. "I don't see how, though."

If Slaughter had heard that, he might have admitted that he didn't really know, either. Anger had prompted him to step out into the open.

Sheer stubborn determination kept him going.

He reached the intersection of Second Street and Toughnut. The courthouse was on the south side of Toughnut at the far end of the block.

The businesses on the north side of the street were all

dark at that hour. The members of the mob had taken cover in alleys, behind rain barrels and water troughs, and anywhere else they could find that offered a little protection. Muzzle flame continued to spurt from their guns as Slaughter approached.

Someone must have spotted him coming along the street. A man yelled hoarsely between shots, "It's the sheriff!" The gunfire slowed but didn't stop.

Several more men shouted. "There's Texas John!"

"Hold your fire, boys! That's the sheriff!"

A grim smile tugged at Slaughter's mouth for a second. He was glad that at least some of the men weren't so drunk or caught up with blood lust that they didn't realize who he was.

Most of Tombstone's citizens were law-abiding, at least deep down, and he had hoped that the sight of the town's top peace officer would make some of them pause.

He stopped and held the shotgun one-handed, propping the butt against his hip. At the top of his lungs, he bellowed, "Hold your fire! Hold your fire, I say!"

The shots dwindled even more, but a few stubborn members of the mob continued shooting at the courthouse for several seconds before their companions forced them to stop.

As the echoes of the onslaught rolled away in the hot, still, night air, Slaughter resumed his approach. He stalked forward until he was planted smack-dab in the most dangerous place of all, right between the mob and the courthouse.

If they opened fire again, he would be shot to pieces in a matter of seconds. But it was the iron will of Texas

John Slaughter that ruled over the scene and maintained order.

A tense silence reigned over Toughnut Street.

Slaughter called out, "Who's the leader of this group?" He didn't really expect an answer, and he didn't get one.

No one spoke up.

After a long moment, he continued in scathing tones, "That's just what I'd expect from a bunch cowardly enough to form a lynch mob."

"This ain't a lynch mob," a man called from the mouth of an alley. "We come to bring justice."

"That's the law's job," Slaughter shot back instantly. "It's not the responsibility of a motley horde of drunkards, bar flies, and layabouts."

Back along the street, behind the wagon, Tommy Howell said, "Dang, John, are you tryin' to get 'em to shoot you?"

"John Slaughter believes in speakin' his mind," Jeff Milton said with a note of admiration in his voice.

Another member of the mob called from behind a rain barrel, "Dallin Williams deserves to hang for what he done to that poor McCabe girl, Sheriff. You know that just as well as we do."

"It's up to a judge and jury to decide what the prisoner deserves," Slaughter said stubbornly. "It's not up to you or me. My job is just to hold Williams until he comes to trial, and that's exactly what I intend to do."

"You'd risk your own life for no-account trash like that?"

"I'm risking my life for the law, not for Dallin Williams," Slaughter said.

Silence hung over the street again, broken by agitated muttering among the men.

Slaughter figured his words were having an effect on some of them. Whether enough of them would decide to be reasonable and the mob would break up was still very much in question, however.

From the corner of his eye, he spotted Enoch Shattuck and G.W. Farrington taking up positions farther to the east along Toughnut Street. Along with the other deputies to the west, they could lay down a deadly crossfire if the mob tried an all-out frontal assault on the courthouse. Slaughter was confident that his men could drive them back. The members of the mob would lose their courage in a hurry once some of them started dying.

But he didn't want things to come to that. He wanted to head it off without anybody losing his life.

"Is Charlie Porter here?" Slaughter called. "Charlie, are you out there? Or any other McCabe men?"

"We don't need Little Ed McCabe or any of his hands to lead us," one of the men responded. "We know what's right."

"What's right is for all of you to go home and forget this foolishness. I ought to arrest each and every one of you for disturbing the peace and malicious destruction of county property. There are broken windows and bullet holes in the county courthouse, by God, and I don't appreciate that." Slaughter drew in a deep breath and glared in the direction of the men he couldn't see in the shadows.

"But I won't do that. I'll let you all leave . . . but only if you do it now. Any man who's still on this street in five minutes is going to jail. You hear me? Five minutes."

He heard one of the men say quietly, "The sheriff's got

plenty of sand, facin' us all down and givin' orders like that. You got to give him credit."

Another man said, "Yeah, you're right. I think I'm goin' home while I've got the chance." He stood up from behind the water trough where he had knelt. He had a rifle in his left hand, but he held it out well away from his body to show that he wasn't going to use it. "Deal me out, boys."

Several men followed his example, stepping into the open with their hands either empty or held so that it was obvious they didn't intend to use their guns.

"What the hell are you doing?" another member of the mob demanded. "You're gonna let Williams get away with what he did? What if it was your wife or daughter he attacked?"

"Then I'd blow a hole in him if I got the chance," a man said. "Otherwise I reckon I'd have to let the law handle it."

"But he's liable to get away with it!"

Slaughter said, "What makes you think that? You men all know Judge Burroughs. He's a fair man and he'll conduct a fair trial. The jury will be made up of men from Cochise County. Maybe even some of you. Williams will answer for the charge against him, and he'll get what's coming to him, whatever the trial determines that to be. That's the way the law works."

More men moved into the open, ready to abandon the idea of taking Williams out of the jail and hanging him. Like a shift in the wind, Slaughter felt the change that came over the rest of the mob. The danger was slipping away.

Then he spotted a flash of flame to his right and

wheeled in that direction to see a man running into the street with a can of coal oil in his hand. The man had stuffed a rag into the can's spout and set it on fire to make a crude bomb. As he dashed toward the courthouse, he yelled, "Come on, boys! We'll burn them out!"

The outside of the stone and adobe courthouse wouldn't burn, but the interior might if he succeeded in setting the shutters on fire. As the man drew back his arm to hurl the bomb toward the windows, Slaughter palmed his Colt from its holster, aimed, and fired. The whole process barely took the blink of an eye.

Slaughter's gun roared, and an instant later the slug ripped through the man's thigh and spun him off his feet. He howled in pain as he fell. The can of coal oil slipped from his fingers and thudded to the ground beside him, rolling a few feet away as the makeshift fuse continued to burn.

The man stared at the bomb and then screamed as he tried to scramble to his feet and get away from it before it exploded. But his wounded leg wouldn't support his weight, so all he could do was crawl. That wasn't going to get him far enough away.

Then Slaughter was beside him, reaching down, gripping his arm, and hauling him to his feet. Slaughter ran, dragging the wounded man with him.

On the north side of the street, the straggling members of the mob yelled in alarm and scurried for cover.

Slaughter dived over the top of a water trough. The wounded man flopped into the water itself, causing it to splash high into the air.

At that instant, the can of coal oil exploded in a ball of flame that sent jagged pieces of metal flying. As

Slaughter rolled in the dirt, he heard some of the debris striking the buildings behind him.

He hoped everyone had reached safety and no one had been hurt except the man he had shot. He came up on one knee and looked into the water trough, where the bomber was sputtering and flailing, apparently unharmed except for the bullet hole in his leg.

Slaughter had dropped his shotgun in the street when he went to rescue the would-be bomber, but he still held the revolver. He reached into the trough, grabbed the man's shirt front, and hauled him out of the water.

Putting the Colt's muzzle in the hollow of the man's throat, Slaughter said, "You don't know how badly I want to blow your head off right now, mister."

"P-please, don't shoot, Sheriff!" the man sobbed. "I . . . I'm hurt. You already shot me!"

"You're just lucky I didn't do a better job of it," Slaughter told him.

Rapid footsteps nearby made him glance around. Several of his deputies were on hand, having run down the street from where they had taken up positions earlier.

Slaughter dragged the wounded man the rest of the way out of the water trough and let him sprawl in the dirt. "Lock him up, and then fetch a doctor to tend to his leg."

Burt and Jeff got hold of the man's arms and lifted him between them. As they marched the man toward the jail, Paco asked Slaughter, "You are all right, señor?"

"Yeah, just mad as a hornet." Slaughter looked around. Quite a few of the men in the mob were emerging from hiding. As they felt the power of the sheriff's cold stare, they left the vicinity in a hurry.

"Damned fools," he muttered.

Since the bomb had gone off in the middle of the street, it hadn't done any real damage except to blast a hole in the ground that could be filled in and repaired easily enough. Small flames still licked up from some of the burning coal oil that had splattered around in the explosion.

By that garish light, Slaughter brushed some of the dust off his clothes, took his shotgun when Tommy Howell handed it to him, and told the others, "Let's go make sure Stonewall and Mose are all right in the jail."

Chapter 12

The time he and Tadrack spent in the jail while guns went off and bullets thudded into the wall, door, and shutters were some of the most nerve-wracking moments in Stonewall's life.

Tadrack, who was risking his life by peeking through the narrow crack between two shutters, exclaimed, "Sheriff Slaughter's out there!"

The news came as a great relief. Stonewall knew if anybody could put an end to the trouble, it was his brother-in-law.

Sure enough, the shooting stopped a few moments later. Stonewall took a chance and pressed his eye to the gap between the shutters on one of the other windows. He watched as the sheriff confronted the lynch mob and talked them out of their deadly plans. His admiration for Texas John Slaughter grew even more as those tense few minutes unfolded.

Just as he thought it was over, a man rushed into the street with a makeshift bomb, and Stonewall figured that hell was going to pop after all. A bomb like that wouldn't blow a hole in the wall, but it might set the courthouse on fire.

Like a lot of Westerners, he had a mortal fear of fire. More than one frontier town had burned to the ground from what had started as one small blaze.

Glued to the window, Stonewall watched Sheriff Slaughter deal with the threat in his usual blunt, efficient manner then stride toward the courthouse behind Burt Alvord and Jeff Milton with their prisoner.

"Let's get that bar off the door," Tadrack said.

Stonewall hurried to help him, and together they lifted the heavy beam from the brackets and set it aside.

Tadrack opened the door so Burt and Jeff could bring in the wounded prisoner. The man moaned as the blood-stain from the bullet hole continued to spread down his trouser leg.

"We're supposed to put him in a cell and fetch the doctor," Burt said.

Stonewall grabbed a ring of keys from a nail on the wall behind the desk and used one of them to unlock the cell block door. He swung it back and stood aside while his fellow deputies half-carried, half-dragged the wounded man past him.

"Harley Court!" Stonewall exclaimed as he recognized the man. Until that moment he would have said that Harley, who worked at the blacksmith shop, was a friend of his.

Court looked at him. "I'm shot, Stonewall. The sheriff shot me."

Stonewall followed them into the cell block. "Well, considerin' that you were trying to blow us up at the time,

I can't say as I blame him. In fact, I'm pretty doggoned glad that he did!"

Burt and Jeff took the prisoner into the cell across the aisle from Dallin Williams's cell and lowered him onto the bunk.

Court groaned and looked up at Stonewall "I didn't even think about that at the time. Hell, I didn't want to blow you up, Stonewall."

"It sure looked like it from where I was standin'."

Court shook his head. "I just got so worked up, like the rest of the fellas. It seemed like the most important thing in the world was gettin' our hands on that rapist so we could teach him a lesson."

Across the aisle, Dallin came to the barred door and said hotly, "I didn't rape nobody. I keep tellin' people that. Why won't anybody believe me?"

Jeff Milton gave him a cold stare. "Because everybody in Tombstone knows what you're like, Williams. You're used to getting whatever you want from women. For most folks, it's no stretch to believe that when the McCabe girl turned you down, you just took it anyway."

With a despairing look on his face, Dallin shook his head and muttered, "I didn't do it. I didn't."

Burt clanged the door shut on the other cell. "We'll be back with a sawbones for you, Court. Try not to bleed to death in the meantime."

Court just moaned.

Stonewall, Burt, and Jeff went back into the office where Sheriff Slaughter was getting Tadrack's version of the evening's events.

Tadrack glanced at his fellow deputies then back to

Slaughter. "Do you think there'll be any more trouble tonight, Sheriff?"

"That's a good question," Slaughter replied with a frown. "When that mob broke up, the men looked pretty cowed. That explosion may have knocked the lynch fever out of them for the time being. But we'll continue to stay on our guard all night, anyway."

"I'll fetch the doc." Jeff left the office as the other deputies were coming in.

"Did everyone go home?" Slaughter asked them.

"They took off like scalded dogs," Tommy said. "Reckon nobody wanted to take a chance of gettin' any part of the blame for what that hombre did."

"Everything is quiet now," Paco added. "Do you still want us patrolling the streets tonight, señor?"

"Indeed I do," Slaughter said. "That lynch mob could try to form again, and that's not the only potential trouble we have in town right now. There's still that big poker tournament going on at the Top-Notch."

With everything else that had been happening, Stonewall had forgotten about that. He recalled that pretty English lady whose bags he had carried into the saloon and couldn't help but wonder how she was doing.

Arabella placed her cards facedown on the table, slid them over to the discard pile, and murmured, "I fold."

She'd had to do that all too often tonight, she thought. She couldn't win if she didn't play, and yet sticking with a hand when it was obvious she just didn't have the cards was the same as throwing away money. Arabella was too smart to do that.

A few minutes later, Angelo Castro let out a satisfied chuckle and raked in the pot. He was doing well tonight, probably better than any of the other players.

But the game was a long way from over. None of the others at the table were anywhere close to being cleaned out. A game like this was a distance race, not a sprint.

And as for the tournament itself . . . well, that was a bloody marathon.

Since Castro had won the hand, he had the deal again. He called seven card stud as the game as he began to shuffle.

That was fine with Arabella. She didn't really care which particular game they played. She was equally adroit at all the variations of poker.

Again the right cards didn't come her way, or at least not ones that she felt confident enough about to risk much. She dropped out of the hand early when it became evident to her that she wasn't going to win.

Tall, lanky Wade Cunningham took the pot instead and changed the game to five card draw.

A couple tables over, the players took a break. From the corner of her eye, Arabella saw Steve Drake stand up, stretch, and then light a cigar he took from his vest pocket.

She would have enjoyed spending a few minutes with her old friend. Instead, she had to settle for the quick grin of encouragement that he sent her way. She turned her attention back to her cards.

Holding a pair of treys, a pair of sevens, and a jack, Arabella threw away the jack. Instead of the three or seven she needed for the full house, Cunningham dealt her an eight. That left her with two pair, the best hand she'd had in a while, so she decided to stick with it, at least for the moment.

As the betting went on, the pot got big enough to force out Snyder, Lockard, and Burnett, leaving Arabella to go against Cunningham and Castro.

In the end, her two pair beat Cunningham's pair of queens. Castro had nothing but a busted flush.

"You were bluffing," she said to the Italian with a smile.

He gave an eloquent shrug. "Something that must be done from time to time. To keep the other players in the game honest, you know."

"Part of the game's price, you mean."

"Exactly, *signorina*."

She knew all about paying the game's price. She could have been married, had a family, children. Instead, she had spent half her life in smoky saloons like this one, sleeping by day and truly existing at night, when the only pleasures were transitory ones. She really didn't know how to do anything else.

Arabella gathered the cards to shuffle. "Let's keep the game five card draw for now, gentlemen."

Across the room, Oscar Grayson had forced himself to keep his mind on the game even while some of the spectators were rushing out to see what was going on. It was a little hard to concentrate with guns going off, followed by a muffled explosion.

He heard the talk as people drifted back into the Top-Notch. Something about a lynch mob trying to break into the jail and string up a prisoner. It was nothing to do with him or the game, so he didn't pay much attention to it as things settled back down in the saloon.

The players at each table took a break whenever they all agreed. When the game broke up momentarily at the table where Steve Drake and Max Rourke were, a hand had just concluded at Grayson's table as well.

Grayson looked at the others. "I could use a few minutes, fellas."

"So could I," one of the other men said. He grinned. "Too much coffee, but a man's got to keep his brain alert somehow and running to the privy will do it."

Grayson watched Rourke stroll outside. He followed as unobtrusively as possible. Pushing through the batwings, he stepped onto the boardwalk and saw Rourke standing to his left. The red-haired gambler lifted a small silver flask to his lips and took a sip.

Not wanting to startle him, Grayson cleared his throat and made some noise as he approached. Rourke glanced around at him, put the cap back on the flask, and slipped it into his pocket.

Grayson was close enough to catch a faint whiff of what was in the flask. He'd figured it was whiskey, but he recognized the smell as something else.

Laudanum.

He didn't see how anybody could take nips of a powerful drug like that and still be able to concentrate on his cards, but if that was how Rourke played the game, then more power to him. Grayson nodded. "Hello, Max."

"Grayson," the man said, his voice curt but not unfriendly. They had met several times over the years, in various places, and gotten along all right, although they certainly weren't close.

"How's luck treating you so far?"

Rourke made a disparaging noise. "Luck has very little to do with it. They call poker a game of chance, but it's really a test of skill. But to answer your question . . . I'm down a little. But my luck will change."

He said it in all seriousness, not even realizing the self-contradiction, thought Grayson.

Rourke went on. "I expect to come out on top in the end."

"A fella who didn't feel like that wouldn't have any business sitting down at the table for a game like this one," Grayson said. "You've got to plan big to win big."

Rourke made another sound that might have been a laugh. "What's your plan, Grayson?"

"I'll tell you . . . but not here and not now."

That seemed to catch Rourke's interest for the first time. He turned his head to look at Grayson and asked with a slight frown, "What are you up to?"

"I've got an idea how to come out the big winner, no matter what the cards do, but I can't do it by myself, Max. I'm going to need help. If you'd like to know more about it, be part of it, we can talk tomorrow, when the tournament breaks up for a few hours so folks can get some sleep."

Rourke regarded him solemnly for a few seconds. "This sounds like a double cross of some sort."

"Just a different kind of game," Grayson said.

Rourke's hand strayed to the pocket where he had put the flask. It rested there for a second, then moved away.

He wanted another nip of the laudanum, thought Grayson, but he wasn't going to take it with somebody else standing right there watching him.

"I'll think about it," Rourke said. "Where can I find you?"

Grayson didn't want to admit that he was staying in such a squalid dive. "Which hotel are you in?"

"The American."

"So am I," Grayson lied. "I'll find you there tomorrow afternoon, around three o'clock?"

"That's fine," Rourke said with a nod. Grayson started to turn away, but the red-headed gambler stopped him by adding, "You'd better not be thinking about playing some sort of trick on me, Oscar."

"I wouldn't do that." Grayson didn't have any problem sounding sincere because he meant it.

Double-crossing a lunatic with a hair-trigger temper like Max Rourke possessed was the best way Grayson could think of to wind up dead.

Unless he was able to do it very, very carefully.

Chapter 13

The violent confrontation on Toughnut Street might not have completely put an end to lynch talk for the night, but the memory of what had happened kept anyone from taking it seriously enough to do anything more about it.

At least, that's what Stonewall supposed, since no more trouble had broken out overnight. He and Mose Tadrack had stayed at the jail until midnight, when Shattuck and Farrington had relieved them.

Stonewall had gone to the boarding house where he had a room. He tried to get a couple hours sleep before going back on duty, but he hadn't been able to do more than doze fitfully.

Tired, he was up before dawn. He and Tadrack joined the patrols walking around the streets of Tombstone. The big saloons were the only things that were open.

As they passed by the Top-Notch, Stonewall looked through the windows and saw the poker games going on, although many of the spectators had drifted away. More than likely the tournament would continue until dawn, he thought, and then break up for a while so the players could get some rest.

He caught a glimpse of the English lady through the glass, but couldn't tell how much money she had in front of her. Of course, that wasn't his problem, he reminded himself. Keeping the prisoner safe was.

As the sky lightened in the east, they turned toward the courthouse. Stonewall wanted to make certain nothing had happened there during the night.

"I'm going to stop by my shack." Tadrack still lived in the same run-down jacal that had been his home when he was a saloon swamper. "It won't take me but a few minutes."

"That's all right," Stonewall said. "Everybody's asleep except us. I'll go on to the courthouse."

"I'm sure if there had been any more trouble, we would have heard."

"Yeah, I reckon," Stonewall said, but he knew he would feel better about everything once he had seen Dallin Williams safely behind bars with his own eyes.

When he reached the courthouse, he saw that the shutters were still closed over the windows inside. It had to be hot as blazes in there with no air moving around, but opening the shutters risked some hungover sorehead taking a potshot at the deputies on duty.

The door was barred, too. Stonewall knocked on it and called, "Hey, it's me. Open up." He heard the bar being lifted from its brackets.

The door swung open, and his cousin Tommy stood there. "Anything goin' on out there?"

"Nary a thing," Stonewall replied.

Lorenzo Paco leaned the beam against the wall near

the door and picked up his rifle. "I will go to the café and bring back breakfast for the prisoners. Where is Mose?"

"Stopped at his place. He'll be along directly."

Paco nodded. "You and Tommy can stay here until I get back unless Mose shows up first. Then you can go home, Tommy. It's been a long night."

Stonewall couldn't argue with that, but he didn't much like the way Paco was giving orders. The Mexican wasn't even a regular, full-time deputy. Stonewall was.

But Paco had been around those parts for a lot longer, and John Slaughter had a lot of confidence in him. Stonewall decided it wasn't worth worrying about. He lifted a hand in farewell as Paco left the courthouse.

Stonewall glanced at the beam and wondered if he and Tommy should slip it back into the brackets. That seemed like too much trouble. It was already getting light outside. Nobody would try anything. Folks would be too sleepy to even think about lynching anybody.

"I'm gonna go check on the prisoners," Tommy said. "They've been mighty quiet."

"Sleeping, more than likely." Stonewall thought about how filled with despair Dallin Williams had been and added, "Probably a good idea, though."

More than one man had given up hope while locked behind bars and done away with himself—usually by tearing strips off his bedding, making a rope out of it, and hanging himself.

Stonewall really didn't see Dallin doing such a thing . . . but it never hurt to be sure.

Tommy unlocked the cell block door and went inside, carrying the ring of keys with him. Stonewall saw that but didn't take any real notice of it. He went over to the gun rack to put up the Winchester he'd carried while he and Tadrack were on patrol.

A frown creased his forehead as a thought occurred to him. It wasn't a good idea to go into the cell block alone with the keys. You didn't need them unless you were going to unlock one of the cells, and you wouldn't do that unless you had another deputy standing by with a gun, just in case the prisoner tried anything . . .

He drew in a sharp breath and turned toward the cell block. At that moment, he heard a commotion—the quick shuffle of feet, a sharp outcry cut short, a dull thud.

Stonewall bit back a curse and lunged toward the open door, grabbing at the butt of his revolver. The Colt hadn't cleared leather when he reached the doorway. He stopped short at the sight of a cell door swinging open. As it clanged back against the bars of the adjoining cell, Dallin Williams stepped out into the aisle and pointed the gun in his hand at Stonewall.

In the cell across the aisle, the wounded Harley Court cowered on his bunk with a bandage wrapped around his ventilated leg. From the frightened look on his face, he didn't want anything to do with what was going on.

"I'd sure take it kindly if you was to let go of that gun, Stonewall," Dallin said quietly. "I didn't wake up this mornin' feelin' like killin' anybody."

Stonewall hesitated with his hand still on the revolver. It wouldn't take much time for him to finish his draw and bring the weapon level.

But in that time, Dallin could press the trigger of the gun he had taken from Tommy. Stonewall knew he couldn't beat the shot.

His startled gaze dropped to Tommy, who lay sprawled

on the stone floor just outside the cell. Blood trickled from a wound on the young man's head.

"Did you—"

"Kill him? Shoot, no." Dallin seemed offended by the idea. "I just walloped him hard enough to knock him out for a few minutes. He'll be fine except for a little headache when he wakes up."

Stonewall suspected that Tommy's head would hurt more than just a little, but at least his cousin wasn't dead.

"You're still holdin' on to that gun and makin' me nervous," Dallin went on.

With a sigh, Stonewall released the Colt and let it slide back down into its holster. Dallin nodded in satisfaction and moved a step closer to him.

"Let me guess," Stonewall said. "Tommy got too close to the bars, and you grabbed him and took his gun and knocked him out. Then you got hold of the keys and let yourself out."

"That's just about the size of it," Dallin admitted. "Ol' Tommy, he wasn't really payin' close enough attention to what he was doin'."

"He didn't expect you to jump him like that."

Dallin's voice sharpened. "Well, hell, I didn't really have any choice, now did I? I got to do somethin' to get out of here while I got the chance, otherwise I'm gonna wind up swingin' from a tree branch. You think I didn't hear all that ruckus last night?"

"We didn't let that mob get you, did we?"

"Not that time. What happens next time?"

"We'll stop them again," Stonewall said with an emphatic nod.

"Maybe. Maybe not. What if Little Ed grabs you or

one of the other deputies and uses you as a hostage? He could threaten to kill you unless the sheriff turned me over to him."

Stonewall shook his head. He hadn't considered that possibility, "John would never do that."

But Dallin had had more time to sit and think, locked up the way he was. "You really think so? You figure he'd let his wife's little brother die just to protect the likes of me? I'd be plumb surprised if he did. So surprised I don't want to risk my life on it."

Dallin might have a point, thought Stonewall, but he said, "It'll never happen. McCabe knows what would happen if he tried something like that. He'd have Texas John Slaughter on his trail for the rest of his life."

"Maybe so, but it's my life I'm talkin' about." Dallin motioned with the gun. "Back up now, slow and easy."

Slow was fine with Stonewall. The longer he could delay Dallin's attempted escape, the better the chance Tadrack or Paco would show up at the courthouse. That would put a stop to Dallin's loco idea.

Dallin followed him out of the cell block, then jerked the gun barrel again. "Turn around."

"Why? So you can shoot me in the back?"

"Dadgum it! I told you I ain't gonna hurt you unless I have to, Stonewall. Why would I do that? We're friends. I got nothin' against you. You've just been doin' what the sheriff tells you to do."

"You know you're not going to get away. John's one of the best trackers in the territory, and Lorenzo Paco is even better. They'll find you, wherever you go."

"Maybe. But maybe by then things'll be different, and it won't matter if they find me."

"What in blazes do you mean by that?" Stonewall asked with a confused frown.

"Never you mind. Just turn around like I told you so I can get your gun. Then you can drag ol' Tommy boy into that cell and I'll close the door behind you. I ought to be able to find a horse and get out of town before anybody comes to help you."

"I'll yell," Stonewall said.

"Won't do you much good. This early all the courthouse offices are still closed, and with these thick walls all the yellin' in the world won't go very far."

Dallin was right about that, Stonewall thought bitterly. And he didn't doubt that while Dallin was telling the truth about not wanting to shoot, he would if he was forced into it.

Try as he might, Stonewall didn't see how he was going to stop the prisoner from getting away.

"Turn around and put your hands up," Dallin said. "I ain't gonna tell you again."

Still moving slowly to stall for time, Stonewall turned around and lifted his arms. He heard the scrape of Dallin's boot leather on the floor close behind him.

At that instant, Tommy groaned in the cell block.

Stonewall was so keyed up he couldn't stop himself from jerking his head around to look over his shoulder. He saw that Dallin had reacted the same way and was looking back into the cell block, not at him.

Without a second's hesitation, Stonewall threw himself backward and crashed into the prisoner. The collision sent both men reeling toward the cell block.

Stonewall didn't try to draw his gun again. He didn't

want anybody to die, either. He wrestled with Dallin in an attempt to take the gun away. "Tommy!" he shouted. "Tommy, wake up and help me!"

He didn't hear any response from Tommy, but Dallin grunted with effort. "Damn it, Stonewall—"

Stonewall lowered his head and butted Dallin in the face.

Dallin yelped in pain and jerked back as blood welled from his nose. Stonewall had both hands on the wrist of Dallin's gun hand as he forced the barrel away from him and tried to wrench the weapon loose.

Dallin's left fist came up and around in a hooking blow that landed solidly on Stonewall's jaw and drove his head to the side. His grip started to slip, so he redoubled his efforts to hang on tighter.

Given Dallin's history as a ladies' man, it was no surprise that he had been in plenty of fights. He had been caught more than once by angry husbands and outraged suitors. He'd had to battle his way free, so he was skilled and experienced at bare knuckles brawling.

Stonewall had been in his share of fights, too, but none as desperate as this one. The blow Dallin had landed had muddled his brain a little. He tried to shake off the dizziness and blurriness. He surged forward and lifted his knee, aiming it at Dallin's groin.

Normally, he never would have attempted such a despicable blow, but he had to protect himself and Tommy and stop Dallin from escaping.

Unfortunately, Dallin twisted aside and caught Stonewall's knee on his thigh. He used his free hand to grab the front of Stonewall's shirt and heaved, swinging the young deputy around so that Stonewall slammed into the doorjamb.

That jolted Stonewall's hands off Dallin's wrist. The gun darted up, fell swiftly. The barrel smashed against the side of Stonewall's head with stunning force.

He felt his knees start to fold up and fought to stay on his feet, but his muscles had stopped responding to him.

"I'm sorry, Stonewall," Dallin said.

Another blow exploded through Stonewall's brain, and that was the last thing he knew before spiraling down into darkness.

from its muzzle. Arabella gasped as a slug whined through the air an inch or two in front of their faces.

If they hadn't stopped when they did, one or possibly both of them would have been hit.

Drake reacted instantly. In the blink of an eye, he produced a gun from somewhere under his coat, pushed Arabella behind him, and returned the shot.

Between the still dim light and the shock of being ambushed, she couldn't see very well, but she thought she spotted a shadowy figure at the far end of the alley.

Another muzzle flash ripped through the gloom, and Drake fired a second time from his crouch.

The would-be killer darted out of sight.

Drake grated a curse. "Get back in the saloon where you'll be safe, Arabella."

She clutched at his arm. "Where are you going?"

"I'm going after that varmint."

"Steve, no!" She held on tighter to him. "He'll kill you."

"Nobody takes a shot at you and gets away with it, Bella."

"But he's gone now. I'm safe."

"We don't know that. He could still be lurking."

"Let's find the sheriff or one of his deputies. This is a job for them, not us."

Drake looked like he wanted to pull away from her, but with a grimace, he nodded and put his pistol away, sliding the weapon back into a holster under his left arm. "People are coming now to see what the shooting was about. I doubt if the bushwhacker will make another try for us with witnesses around."

"Steve . . . was he shooting at you . . . or me?"

Drake frowned in thought and shook his head. "Now that's a question I just can't answer, Bella."

Slaughter was about to go into the dining room of the American Hotel for his breakfast when he heard the shots coming from somewhere else in town. Four of them, and they came relatively fast and close together.

But from two different guns, he judged, and that meant a fight.

He sighed and turned away from the dining room entrance. Moving quickly through the hotel lobby, he went out onto the boardwalk.

People were already out and about despite the early hour. Slaughter saw several of them running along the street and figured they were headed for the source of the shooting. The guns had fallen silent after that flurry of reports. He hoped that didn't mean he would find dead men lying in the street.

He didn't see any bodies as he approached a knot of people near the mouth of an alley. He raised his voice as he came up behind them. "I say, what's going on here?" he demanded.

The crowd parted in response to his commanding tone. They had been gathered around a man and a woman, both of whom looked familiar to him.

"Sheriff Slaughter," the man said. "It's good to see you again, although not so much under the circumstances."

"What circumstances are those, Mr. Drake?" Slaughter had searched his memory quickly for the man's name and had recalled his brief conversation with these two a couple days earlier.

"Someone took some shots at Lady Arabella and myself," Drake said.

"Are either of you hurt?"

"No, thank goodness, but it wasn't for lack of trying on the part of the man hiding in that alley."

"I reckon you returned his fire." Slaughter was certain he had heard two different guns.

"It seemed like the thing to do at the time," Drake said coolly.

"Did you hit him?"

"I don't think so. He was moving pretty fast, the last I saw of him. I started to go after him, but . . ." Drake glanced at Lady Arabella.

"I asked him not to. We were both all right, and I was afraid Steve might be hurt if he gave chase."

Slaughter glanced at Drake and thought that the decision not to pursue the bushwhacker probably hadn't set very well with him. The gambler looked like the sort of man who wouldn't take it kindly if anybody shot at him and his ladyfriend.

And in this case, that description of the brunette was even more apt.

"He was hiding in the alley, you say?" Slaughter asked.

"That's right," Drake said.

"Let's take a look."

It was light enough to see in the alley and avoid the trash that littered it. After telling Lady Arabella to wait on the boardwalk, Drake joined Slaughter.

"Whereabouts did you see him?" the sheriff asked.

Drake pointed. "Along in there, behind those crates. I caught another glimpse of him at the end of the alley as he fled."

Slaughter fished out a match and lit it to dispel any lingering shadows behind the crates where the would-be killer had waited for his quarry to come along. He saw some footprints in the dirt, but they didn't tell him much.

The tracks weren't left by the sort of high-heeled boot favored by cowboys, but rather had been made by either low-heeled work boots or shoes. There were hundreds of pairs of such footgear in Tombstone.

A cigar butt also lay there behind the crates, but it didn't mean anything, either, as far as Slaughter could tell. Plenty of men smoked cigars.

A quick search of the rest of the alley proved equally futile. As they stood at the far end of it, Slaughter asked Drake, "Did you hear a horse gallop off right after the shooting?"

"No, not at all. If I had to venture a guess, Sheriff, I'd say that the bushwhacker fled on foot and is still here in Tombstone."

Slaughter grunted. "That's the way it appears to me, too. Do you have any idea if the gunman was aiming at you or the lady?"

"The bullet could have easily struck either of us, so it's impossible to say."

"Then it wasn't a warning shot. He was out to kill you."

"It definitely wasn't a warning shot."

"How did he know the two of you would be coming along the street right here?"

"That's something that immediately puzzled me as well, Sheriff. You see, Lady Arabella and I had just left the Top-Notch and were on our way to get some break-fast. I suppose the bushwhacker could have followed us from there and circled around to get ahead of us and set this trap."

"Is the poker tournament over already?" Slaughter figured that was too much to hope for.

Drake confirmed that hunch. "No, the players are just taking a break to get some food and rest. We'll be back at it later today."

Slaughter nodded. "Well, I don't see what else I can do here, except maybe advise you to keep an eye on your back."

"I'd be doing that anyway," Drake said with a nod of his own.

Before either of them could say anything else, someone hurried along the alley toward them and called, "Sheriff! Sheriff Slaughter!"

"That's one of my deputies. What is it, Mose?"

"You'd better get over to the courthouse, Sheriff," Tadrack said. "Looks like Dallin Williams has busted out of jail."

Stonewall was sitting in a chair gingerly rubbing the blood-smeared lump on the side of his head when Slaughter hurried into the office.

"What in blazes—" Slaughter burst out then stopped and looked relieved for a second before a stern, angry expression took over his face again. He snapped, "What happened here?"

Burt Alvord was at the stove pouring a cup of coffee from the pot brewed the night before. "Mose came in and found Stonewall and Tommy knocked out and Williams gone. He was on his way to find you when he ran into me. I came on here to see how bad they were hurt."

"Where's Tommy?"

"Jeff took him home. He was still pretty woozy and not making much sense. I figured you could talk to him later." Burt handed the cup of coffee to Stonewall, who took it and sipped gratefully. "Stonewall can tell you what happened."

"I'm waiting," Slaughter said with his slightly bushy eyebrows drawn down in a frown.

"Well, Sheriff, it was like this." Stonewall could hardly stand to look at his brother-in-law as he explained how the prisoner had gotten the drop on him and then knocked him out. He knew Slaughter would be really disappointed in him.

Slaughter looked angry, all right, but his voice held a touch of concern as he asked, "How badly are you hurt?"

"Ah, hell, John—I mean, Sheriff—you know how hard this head of mine is. It'd take more than a gun barrel to dent my skull. I'll be fine." Stonewall nodded to reinforce his answer, but stopped with a wince as fresh jolts of pain jabbed into his brain.

"You'd better be," Slaughter snapped. "I'd hate to have to explain to your sister how you got your head busted open." He turned to Burt Alvord. "Any idea which way Williams went when he lit a shuck out of here?"

Burt shook his head. "I haven't had a chance to look into it yet, Sheriff. It could be that he's still here in town, hiding out somewhere."

"I doubt it," Slaughter said. "He'll want to put some distance behind him, now that he's on the run. He probably stole a horse off the street and the owner doesn't know yet that it's gone because he's still asleep in some alley or whore's crib."

Stonewall swallowed some more of the bitter coffee. "I'll find him. It's my responsibility, Sheriff. I'm the one who let him get away."

"We'll talk about that, but not now," Slaughter said as he put a hand on Stonewall's shoulder. "Wherever he is, Williams had better hope that the law finds him."

"Why's that?"

"Because when Little Ed McCabe finds out about this, he'll see it as his chance to go after Williams again himself," Slaughter replied grimly. "And if McCabe and his punchers get their hands on him first, there sure won't be any trial."

Chapter 15

Dallin Williams clamped his hand over the horse's nose and held his own breath as the riders passed by about fifty feet from the arroyo where he had taken cover when he spotted them coming. He didn't think they had seen him before he went to ground, but he couldn't be sure. He had to keep his horse quiet and hope for the best.

If they came for him, he would put up a fight. He had five rounds in the Colt he had taken away from Tommy Howell. He wished he had thought to look through the desk in the sheriff's office and see if he could find a box of .45 cartridges before he fled from the jail, but it hadn't occurred to him at the time.

All he'd been able to think of was getting out of there before somebody came along to lock him up again.

He couldn't stand being locked up. It had gnawed at his brain like a hungry coyote with a jackrabbit carcass.

He heard the hands talking, even though he couldn't understand all the words. From what he could tell, it was the typical sort of desultory range chatter that cowboys exchanged while they were riding on some errand or other, casual and mostly meaningless.

He would have given a lot to live that seemingly boring life again. The old saying was sure enough true— a fella just didn't appreciate what he had until it was gone.

Back in Tombstone, Dallin had pulled his hat brim down low over his face and acted casual as he'd walked out of the jail, not wanting to draw attention to himself. He knew he didn't have much time to get away.

The hour was early and not many people had been up and about, but the streets weren't completely deserted. He'd worried somebody might spot him and raise the alarm.

The hitch rails in front of the courthouse stood empty. He'd headed along Toughnut Street toward the closest rail where horses were tied. It was a long hundred yards away, maybe the longest of his life.

There hadn't been any hue and cry by the time he'd reached the three saddle mounts tied there. He chose the best-looking animal of the bunch and untied its reins, well aware that what he was doing made him a horse thief.

He regretted that, he truly did, but they could only hang him once, he'd thought.

He had swung up into the saddle, his movements still easy and unhurried. Clucking to the horse, he'd turned it away from the hitch rail and heeled it into a walk. He'd kept his head down and rocked along, just a cowboy headed back to the home ranch after a night in town.

His pulse had hammered like thunder. He'd expected that at any second he would hear an angry shout or the roar of a gun. His muscles were tensed for the strike of a bullet.

Nothing had happened. He'd ridden out of Tombstone without the least bit of commotion or calamity.

Once clear of the settlement, Dallin had turned his stolen mount toward the northeast.

Toward the Bar EM.

He knew it was a foolish thing. Mexico wasn't that far to the south of Tombstone. He could be across the border in a day, maybe a day and a half. All he had to do was dodge any pursuit for that long and he'd be safe.

Only he wouldn't be. He would never be able to return to Arizona Territory without worrying about the law, and there was a good chance Little Ed McCabe would chase him into Mexico, anyway. If the rancher didn't come after him himself, he could hire gunmen to do it; he had the money.

Dallin had spent a lot of time thinking about it while he was cooped up in that cell. He hadn't had much of anything else to do. And he had come to an inescapable conclusion. The only thing that would free him from having to spend the rest of his life looking over his shoulder was the truth.

And the only person who could tell the truth was Jessie McCabe.

The cowboys were finally out of earshot. Dallin couldn't hear them or their horses anymore. Despite that, he waited another five minutes, baking in the heat that flowed along the arroyo like thick mud, before he risked a look.

The two riders were gone.

He heaved a sigh of relief, took off his hat for a

moment, and sleeved sweat from his face. He thought again about what a loco thing he was doing then mounted up and rode up a caved-in section of bank out of the arroyo.

He had been working for Little Ed McCabe for several months, so he knew the Bar EM range quite well. He knew how McCabe split up his crew and where he was likely to have them working. He could take advantage of that. With any luck, he could make it to the ranch house without being spotted.

He would take all the luck he could get. He would use whatever he had to, do whatever was necessary, to prove his innocence.

In all honesty, he had been a little surprised that it bothered him so much to be accused of attacking Jessie. He had done plenty of things in his life that he wasn't proud of. Not that he was going to apologize for them, that wasn't the way he was made, but he was smart enough to know that he was a pretty sorry excuse for a human being sometimes.

But he wasn't in the habit of hurting folks, especially women. Especially young gals like Jessie, who had a sweet innocence about her that he found likable.

Except it seemed like she wasn't quite as innocent as he had thought, he reflected as he rode toward the ranch house. If she really did have a bun in the oven, he hadn't put it there. That was one thing he was damned sure of.

Which left him with the question of who had.

That was none of his business, he told himself, other than how it related to his current predicament. Jessie was going to have to bite the bullet and tell her pa and the sheriff and anybody else who would listen who really had attacked her . . . or who she had been messing around with of her own free will.

It was one of the first things that had occurred to Dallin. If a gal had been sneaking off to see a boy and got herself caught in a bad situation . . . and if her pa was loco wild as Little Ed could be when he was mad . . . and if she really cared about the fella who'd got her in trouble . . . well, the easiest thing in the world would be to holler that she'd been attacked and point her finger at somebody who was notorious for his tomcattin' around. Her folks had believed her, and so had everybody in Tombstone.

Shoot, even Stonewall had believed her, and that bothered Dallin about as much as anything. He had thought that he and Stonewall were pards.

No time to worry about that, he realized as he topped a little rise and spotted the ranch house a quarter mile ahead of him. The place looked sleepy in the heat and the morning sun.

He reached down to his waist and touched the hard lump of the Colt he had tucked behind his belt and under his shirt. He hoped he wouldn't have to hurt anybody.

But he wasn't going back to jail.

Not ever.

"Jessie, you go out there to the hen house and gather those eggs," Hallie McCabe told her daughter in a stern voice.

"Yes, Mama." Jessie picked up a wicker basket from the kitchen counter. She'd been using it to gather eggs for a long time. That was one of her jobs, along with milking.

Everybody worked on a ranch, her pa was fond of

saying. He drove everybody hard . . . although none harder than himself, especially since Jessie's brothers had died.

The Bar EM was as self-sufficient as the family could make it. A hen house full of chickens provided eggs. There were two milk cows in the barn. Little Ed raised hogs, too, and slaughtered them every year so the family would have something to eat besides beef. Jessie and her mother tended to a vegetable garden, although that was a real struggle in the arid land. Most years the garden didn't make much, but Hallie McCabe didn't give up on it.

As Jessie started to leave the house with the basket, her mother said, "Land's sake, girl, put a bonnet on before you go out there. That sun'll fry your brain in heat like this if you don't cover it up. You've got to learn to take care of yourself." She sniffed. "Especially now."

"Yes, Mama," Jessie said again. It was easier than arguing. She tied on a sunbonnet and went out the back door of the ranch house, pausing just outside to run her hand over her belly.

It was still flat, but it wouldn't be for much longer.

Not wanting her mother to catch her lollygagging, Jessie walked on toward the hen house. She didn't hurry; only a fool hurried in such weather. But she didn't waste any time, either.

A moment later, she stepped onto the hard-packed dirt floor of the hen house. The roof provided shade, although it stunk to high heaven in here. She took only a couple steps toward the nearest setting hen when a shape moved fast out of the shadows inside the gloomy structure and a hand clamped over her mouth to silence her. Another arm wrapped around her waist and held her still.

"Don't you go to fightin' me now, darlin'," a man's voice whispered in her ear.

Jessie stiffened. She recognized that drawling voice. She had heard it often enough, laughing and telling whoppers to the other members of the ranch crew, even though Dallin Williams had never talked much to her.

"I knew your mama would be sendin' you out here about this time to gather the eggs. That's why I waited here for you." Dallin paused. "You know why I'm here, don't you?"

Jessie didn't say anything. She was too terrified to move, let alone speak. Anyway, Dallin still had his hand over her mouth.

"You heard what I said, didn't you?" he prodded.

She ventured a tiny nod in response.

"You give me your word you're not gonna holler?"

Again she nodded, barely.

"Don't think you can trick me. I can get my hand back over your mouth before you get out a peep if I need to. Now you just stay calm. I'm gonna move my hand."

The tight grip left her face, but his hand hovered just in front of her mouth. Jessie's mouth and throat were so dry she had to swallow a couple times before she could say, "Don't hurt me again. Please."

"Again?" Dallin repeated. "Dadgum it, girl, I never hurt you the first time, and you know it. That's why I'm here. We're gonna march in that house, and you're gonna tell your mama the truth. You're gonna tell her I never laid a finger on you, and I sure as hell didn't do what you told the sheriff I done."

"I-I can't," she whimpered.

"Sure you can. Are you really in the family way?"

"Yes." Her voice was just a whisper.

"Well, then, you don't want the fella who really attacked you gettin' away with it, do you?" Again Dallin paused. "Unless the hombre didn't attack you at all."

Jessie didn't say anything. She couldn't.

He took his hand away from her face, evidently convinced that she wasn't going to scream or shout. "I knew it. I knew I'd figured it out. You been sneakin' off to meet some boy, and when you told him what happened, he begged you not to say anything about it bein' him. Ain't that right, Jessie?"

She looked down at the dirt floor, still unable to speak.

"So you decided you'd blame me."

She heard the angry, bitter tone in his words.

"You knew ever'body would believe you if you pointed the finger at that ol' hound dog Dallin Williams, and sure enough, that's what happened."

Finally she was able to get some more words of her own out. "I-I never meant for you to get hurt, Dallin."

He still had his arm around her waist, but he let go of her entirely and stepped away from her to fling his arms out in exasperation.

"Didn't want me to get hurt? Good Lord, gal, don't you know what your pa's like? What'd you think he'd do when you told him I attacked his little girl, the only young'un he's got left?"

"I didn't think about it," she practically moaned. "I was just so scared."

Dallin's angry attitude softened slightly. "Well, I reckon I can't blame you for that. But you got to know it ain't right to get me in so much trouble for somethin' I never done. You got to tell everybody the truth, Jessie, and let things work out however they're gonna."

"I can't. I promised—"

"Maybe so, but do you know what happened in Tombstone last night? A lynch mob stirred up by your pa's foreman Charlie Porter attacked the jail. They were gonna take me outta there and string me up to a cottonwood limb. They were gonna hang me, Jessie. Is that what you want?"

"No!" she cried, horrified by what she had just heard. "Good Lord, of course not, Dallin. I never dreamed you'd get in that much trouble."

"They string a fella up for attackin' a gal. At the very least, they send him away to prison for years and years and years. If that's what you want 'em to do to me—"

"No," she said again as she shook her head miserably. "No, no, no—"

"Williams!" The roar filled the hen house, making Jessie and Dallin spin around.

Little Ed McCabe loomed in the doorway. "Get away from my daughter!" He charged forward like a furious grizzly bear.

Chapter 16

Without thinking, Dallin thrust Jessie behind him as if trying to protect her from her own father. He knew he couldn't stand up to the rancher's maddened charge, so he went low, diving at McCabe's legs.

McCabe slammed into Dallin. His own momentum betrayed him, pitching him headlong, out of control. He crashed to the dirt floor of the hen house.

Dallin rolled over and came up on his knees. Instead of surging to his feet and kicking McCabe while the bigger man was down, he leaped up and grabbed Jessie's hand. "Come on! We're gettin' out of here until your pa comes to his senses and stops tryin' to kill me."

"No!" she cried. "You can't—"

Dallin ignored her protests and jerked her into motion. He hauled her with him as he dashed for the opening at the far end of the hen house.

Behind them, Little Ed McCabe struggled to his feet and yelled, "Damn you, Williams! Come back here!"

Dallin didn't slow down. He didn't dare.

Jessie tried to hang back and pull free from his grip, but she was no match for his strength born of desperation. He knew if he got caught there, in all likelihood he would never leave the Bar EM alive. He had known that when he went there.

But he had been willing to run that risk because his life wasn't worth anything without his freedom, and Jessie was the only person who could give that back to him. He had to convince her to tell the truth.

Now that he'd been discovered, he had no choice except to take her with him. She was his only chance.

They pounded out of the hen house with McCabe lumbering after them. Dallin glanced over his shoulder and saw the rancher draw the revolver holstered on his hip.

McCabe thrust the gun right back in the holster, though, obviously realizing that he couldn't risk shooting at Williams as long as Jessie was so close to the fleeing cowboy. Instead, McCabe started bellowing for help.

Dallin ran for the little clump of brush and rocks where he had hidden the horse he'd stolen in Tombstone. Unwillingly, Jessie went with him, staggering and gasping and begging him to let go of her.

Dallin wished he could, but that was no longer an option. If anything, his daring visit to the McCabe ranch had made the situation worse, but he still clung to Jessie's hand . . . and to a shred of hope.

Thankfully, the horse was still where he had left it. As they lunged toward it, Jessie said, "Please, Dallin, don't do this, please—"

The roar of a gunshot interrupted her and made her squeal in fright and maybe pain. Dallin slowed and looked back at her, hoping she wasn't hurt and hardly believing that McCabe had taken a shot at them.

He hadn't, as it turned out. It had been a warning shot. McCabe's gun was pointed almost straight up in the air. But as the young people kept going, McCabe roared a curse and lowered the weapon to point it in their direction. It looked like his rage was about to get the better of him and make him risk a shot despite the danger to his daughter.

His wife charged up behind him, reached around, and grabbed his arm to force it up just as McCabe pulled the trigger. His second shot went into the air, too, just like the first one, although not at such a steep angle. The bullet went well over the heads of Dallin and Jessie.

They reached the horse, and Dallin pulled Jessie closer to him. He got his hands under her arms, and lifted her onto the horse, setting her down in front of the saddle.

Moving fast, he jerked the reins loose from the bush where he had tied them and vaulted into the saddle. It was a testament to his skills as a top hand and a talented horseman.

He looped one arm around her to hold her on the horse's back and dug his heels into the animal's flanks, sending it leaping ahead. Another glance over his shoulder revealed Little Ed McCabe struggling with his wife as she tried to prevent him from firing another shot at them.

After that, Dallin concentrated on his riding. He headed northwest. McCabe would come after them, no doubt about that, and Dallin knew the terrain was more rugged in that direction. More places where he could give his pursuers the slip, he thought.

He became aware that Jessie was trying to say something over the noise of the hoofbeats. He raised his voice and asked, "What'd you say?"

She turned her pale, frightened face toward him. "Are you going to kill me?"

"Kill you? What the hell! Why would I do that?"

"Because . . . because of what I told my folks and the sheriff about you."

"Shoot, you're my only chance of gettin' out of this with a whole hide. I never wanted to hurt you. I just want you to tell the truth."

"I can't. I promised."

"Promised who?"

She didn't answer.

Dallin didn't think she would. She was still too scared and upset. But maybe once they got away from the ranch and he had a chance to talk to her some more, he might be able to make her see that his life depended on her. All he needed was some time, and a little peace and quiet. He had always been able to make gals believe they were doing the right thing by giving him what he wanted. In this case, it would even be true, so he didn't see why he couldn't convince her.

With that thought in his head, they galloped on, putting more distance between themselves and the Bar EM headquarters.

Stonewall was insistent that he was going to be part of any posse that went after Dallin Williams. Slaughter understood why his young brother-in-law felt that way. He blamed himself for Williams's escape, although as far as Slaughter could tell, Tommy Howell was really more at fault. Tommy was the one who had gotten close enough to the bars of the cell that Williams had been able to grab him.

Blaming Tommy for being careless was like blaming a puppy for being clumsy and enthusiastic, though. There was just no point in it.

Stonewall didn't seem to be suffering any lingering effects from that wallop on the head, but despite that, Slaughter leaned toward ordering him to stay in Tombstone while somebody else went after Williams. Too much personal interest in a pursuit could cause problems.

Of course, he had led the posse after the outlaws who'd kidnapped Viola, he reminded himself. Nobody could have had a more personal interest than that.

He had sent Stonewall back to the boarding house to get a little rest and was pondering his next move when one of the citizens stuck his head in the door of the office. "There's some trouble down the street, Sheriff."

"What sort of trouble?" Slaughter asked.

"Dead man in an alley."

Slaughter frowned. He immediately thought of the shooting involving Steve Drake and Lady Arabella Winthrop and wondered if the would-be killer had struck again and succeeded.

"Who is it, do you know?" he asked the townsman as they left the office.

"No, I don't. Looked like a stranger to me."

The man led him to an alley that ran between Allen and Toughnut Streets although he didn't really need directions. Several people were gathered around the mouth of the alley.

Death always drew a crowd.

"Step back, I say," he ordered.

The knot of people parted to let him through.

A man lay sprawled in the litter of trash about halfway down the alley. He was on his side, but Slaughter could see his face. It was only vaguely familiar, but after a moment of thought, Slaughter recalled where he had seen the man last. In the Top-Notch Saloon.

Burt Alvord came along the alley from Allen Street. "Heard there was trouble back here, Sheriff." He looked down at the corpse and grunted. "Sure enough is."

Slaughter hunkered on his heels to examine the dead man. "Do you know him, Burt?"

"Can't say as I do. What killed him?"

Slaughter pointed to the bloodstain on the man's vest. "Looks like somebody stabbed him. He wasn't shot, I'm sure of that. That's not a bullet hole in his coat."

"Didn't think I'd heard a gun go off in town since Williams busted out of jail. Speakin' of which, what are we gonna do about that, Sheriff?"

"I'll send a posse after him," Slaughter replied with a touch of impatience. "But right now I've got a killing to deal with, not just an escaped prisoner. Go to the Top-Notch, Burt, and bring Morris Upton back here."

"Upton? You reckon he had something to do with this?"

Slaughter wouldn't have put much of anything past Morris Upton, but he was just looking for information.

"I saw this man in the Top-Notch, and Upton might know who he is."

"Oh. Well, that makes sense. I'll be back with him quick as I can."

Burt hurried off toward Allen Street while Slaughter remained beside the corpse. He pulled the bloody vest and shirt aside, revealing the wound on the left side of the man's chest. As he had suspected, the size and shape of the injury confirmed that the dead man had been stabbed with a rather narrow-bladed knife.

Slaughter also checked the man's pockets and found them empty. No wallet, no watch, no other valuables.

He heard the murmur of conversation at both ends of the alley as the townspeople speculated among themselves about who the dead man was and who had killed him. Slaughter wanted to know those things himself. Unlike the past, murder was uncommon in Tombstone and it caused quite a stir.

Burt came back with a sleepy-looking, somewhat disheveled Morris Upton. The saloon owner looked like he'd been rousted out of bed, which was probably what had happened.

"What's going on here, Sheriff?" Upton demanded. "The deputy wouldn't tell—My God! That's Angelo Castro."

Slaughter straightened from his crouch next to the body. "So you know him?"

"Of course I know him. He's a gambler. He's one of the players in my tournament." Upton frowned. "Or he was playing in my tournament, I suppose I have to say now. He is dead, isn't he?"

"Dead as he can be," Slaughter said. "If I had to hazard a guess, I'd say he was killed sometime in the past couple hours."

"Why? Who would do such a thing?"

"I was hoping you could help me figure that out."

Upton shook his head. "I don't know anything about it, Sheriff. Castro was fine when the games broke up for a while earlier this morning. He left the saloon, so I assumed he was going to get some sleep or find something to eat. That's the last time I saw him."

"Do you have any idea who might want him dead? Did he have any particular trouble with anybody in the game?"

Again Upton shook his head. "I don't know of any trouble. He was doing well in the game, though. Probably had quite a bit of money on him. Have you checked his pockets?"

"They're empty," Slaughter said.

"Well, there you go. Somebody robbed and killed him." Upton's voice took on a faint sneering tone as he added, "I thought you had cleaned all the cutthroats out of Tombstone, Sheriff Slaughter."

Suppressing the urge to knock the smirk off the saloon-keeper's face, Slaughter said, "If you hear anything about this, Upton, I expect you to let me know."

"Why do you think I'd hear anything about it?"

"People talk in saloons, especially when they've had too much watered-down liquor. Just keep your ear to the ground, all right?"

"Of course, Sheriff." Upton was still smirking.

Slaughter turned to his chief deputy. "See about getting this body carted down to the undertaker's, Burt."

"Sure thing, Sheriff. What are you gonna do?"

"I need to put together that posse to go after Dallin Williams."

Still standing there, Upton's smirk grew larger and more self-satisfied. "Yes, you have an escaped prisoner to worry about, don't you, Sheriff?"

Slaughter ignored him and strode away.

The wheels of his brain turned rapidly as he walked back toward the courthouse and thought about everything that had happened. He wanted Dallin Williams caught and brought back, of course. Nobody was going to knock two of his deputies unconscious and break out of his jail, Slaughter vowed to himself.

But at the same time, the murder of Angelo Castro was particularly troubling because of the circumstances. Castro was in town only because of that damned poker tournament, and from the looks of things, the tournament had contributed to his death. Somebody in the saloon must have taken note of Castro's success and followed him out to relieve him of his winnings.

It was just the sort of thing Slaughter had worried would happen as soon as he heard about Upton's blasted tournament. Despite his anger at what Williams had done, the sheriff was reluctant to leave Tombstone at the moment. He felt like he needed to stay to keep a lid on things.

Williams didn't have any history of violence until his attack on Stonewall and Tommy. Slaughter figured Jeff Milton and Lorenzo Paco could handle him. Paco was the best tracker, anyway.

His mind made up, Slaughter decided to send those

two after Williams, and he would stay in Tombstone to find Angelo Castro's murderer.

Before anybody else wound up getting killed.

Stonewall's head was starting to throb pretty good by the time he got back to the boarding house. The sun beating down on it didn't help matters. The heat wave that had settled on the town had been in full force only for a couple days, but he felt like it had been burning up for weeks.

Even worse than the pain in his head was the anger that churned his guts.

He had told his brother-in-law he wanted to go along with the posse, but Stonewall had a hunch Slaughter would order him to remain in Tombstone . . . out of concern for his injury and because he had doubts about Stonewall's competence.

Stonewall couldn't blame the sheriff for feeling like that. He had allowed Dallin to escape, hadn't he? He opened the door and went inside.

The elderly widow lady who ran the boarding house greeted him with a worried smile. "Are you all right, Stonewall? I heard rumors that one of the prisoners attacked you."

"I'm fine, Mrs. Mumford," he assured her. "I just came by to pick up a few things and see if you could rustle up some sandwiches for me. You know, for the trail. I'm fixin' to set out after that varmint."

He wasn't sure where the words had come from, but as soon as he spoke them, he knew it was the right thing to do. He wasn't going to wait around and let the sheriff order him to stay in town.

He could track and read sign, couldn't he? Maybe not as well as Lorenzo Paco, but good enough to trail Dallin Williams. He had been in such a hurry to get out of Tombstone that he probably hadn't been very careful about hiding his tracks.

Something else odd was nagging at Stonewall's aching brain, too. Williams had said something about how maybe it wouldn't matter if a posse caught up to him. What in the world had he meant by that?

A vague possibility shifted around in Stonewall's mind. Dallin had sworn up and down, ever since Jessie McCabe had leveled the accusation of rape at him, that he wasn't guilty. Maybe he intended to prove that. Since the only evidence against him was Jessie's word, he would have to get her to change her story.

Stonewall's heart slugged a little harder in his chest as the idea became clearer. Although it seemed unbelievable that Dallin would do something so crazy as to head for the McCabe ranch, it was the only way to clear his name.

The more Stonewall thought about it, the more he was convinced that it would be worth his time to take a ride out to the Bar EM. If he could find Dallin Williams and bring him back, it would go a long way toward clearing his own conscience, too.

"Stonewall, are you sure you're all right?" his landlady asked.

"Maybe not, ma'am"—Stonewall gave a shake of his head—"but I'm gonna be."

Chapter 17

Stonewall kept his horse in a corral behind the boarding house, so he didn't have to go very far to saddle up. He tied the bag of sandwiches Mrs. Mumford had made to the saddle and swung up.

As he started to ride along the back alley, he realized it might be a good idea to buy more cartridges for his Winchester. He didn't expect to have a big fight on his hands when he caught up to Dallin Williams, but it was impossible to predict what would happen.

A desperate man was capable of almost anything.

He left his horse ground-hitched beside the general store instead of tied up at the hitch rack out front and kept his head down with his hat shielding his face as he went inside. He wasn't sure Sheriff Slaughter would forbid him from going after the escaped prisoner, but he didn't want to take a chance on that.

The store wasn't busy. Roy Corbett stood behind the counter at the rear. "What can I do for you, Stonewall?"

"Box of .45s, Roy."

"Going hunting?" Corbett asked as he got the box of cartridges off a shelf and set it on the counter.

"You could say that," Stonewall replied without offering any further explanation. He paid for the cartridges and walked back to the front of the store.

As he went out, he thought he felt Corbett's eyes on him, watching him. He supposed the clerk was curious. As a deputy, the county usually paid for Stonewall's cartridges, but the cost had come out of his own pocket.

He stowed them away in one of his saddlebags and mounted up again. He stuck to the alleys as he made his way out of Tombstone and maintained a slow, careful pace until he put the town behind him.

It was impossible to know which direction Dallin had gone when he left Tombstone, so Stonewall played his hunch and headed for the McCabe ranch. He heeled his horse into a ground-eating lope toward the northeast. If he discovered that the fugitive hadn't been there, he would have wasted time and would have to start over, but he didn't see any other way to proceed.

As he rode, Stonewall kept an eye on his back trail out of habit, and after he had gone a couple miles he thought he spotted something moving behind him. Reining in, he waited to see if he could get a better look.

A moment later, a rider came into view, cresting a rise about half a mile behind him. Stonewall's keen young eyes had been right. Somebody was trailing him.

The rider went out of sight again as he followed the rolling, semi-arid terrain. Stonewall figured that Sheriff Slaughter had somehow found out what he was doing and had sent somebody after him. Slaughter might have even come himself, intending to rein in his impulsive brother-in-law.

Stonewall didn't intend to let that happen. He wasn't going to be swayed from his goal. He decided he might as well wait and have the confrontation, rather than postponing it.

He looked around, saw some good-sized rocks alongside the trail up ahead, and decided he would conceal himself there until his follower caught up to him. He heeled his horse into motion again and rode behind the boulders.

His nerves grew tense as he waited. What would he do if the man on his trail was the sheriff? Could he disobey a direct order to return to Tombstone? If he did, Slaughter might fire him, brother-in-law or no brother-in-law.

If it was another deputy following him, Stonewall might get away with ignoring any such orders, but only for the time being. Sooner or later, he would have to face Slaughter's wrath.

He heard hoofbeats approaching the boulders and knew that he wouldn't have to wait much longer to find out which one it was going to be.

Another thought occurred to him. Maybe the rider had nothing to do with him. That was always possible. He hung on to that hope until the man on horseback had almost reached the rocks then he urged his mount out into the open to block the trail.

The other man let out a startled exclamation and hauled back on the reins to bring his horse to a stop before the two animals could collide.

"Roy! What in blazes are you doin' following me?"

Roy Corbett struggled to bring his mount under control.

The clerk and would-be lawyer had traded his apron for a leather vest and donned a dark-brown, flat-crowned hat. He wore a holstered six-gun and had a rifle in a saddle boot.

"Son of a gun, Stonewall, you scared me. What's the idea of ambushing me like this?"

"I wouldn't call this an ambush. Where are you headed, Roy? How come you're not working in the store back in town?"

Corbett didn't answer. The questions made him uncomfortable.

"Dadgum it, you're followin' me, aren't you?" Stonewall demanded.

"I got to thinking after you left the store. You wouldn't be stocking up on cartridges if you didn't think there might be trouble of some sort. When I saw you ride out, I thought you might be going after Dallin Williams. But the sheriff didn't send you, did he, Stonewall?"

Stonewall frowned. "How do you figure that?"

"You wouldn't be sneaking around like you were if you were just following Sheriff Slaughter's orders." Excitement crept into Corbett's voice as he went on. "You figured out where Williams went, didn't you?"

"I don't know what you're talking about," Stonewall insisted. "This is just loco. I'm . . . I'm . . ." He couldn't think of a plausible excuse for being out there, headed in the direction he was headed.

It didn't really matter. Whatever he might have said, Corbett probably wouldn't have believed it.

"You're riding out to the McCabe ranch, aren't you? You think Williams has gone out there." A look of worry appeared on Corbett's face. "You think he'd hurt the

McCabe girl? Without her to testify in court, there's no real case against him."

"Oh, there's a case against him," Stonewall said. "He busted out of jail, and I've got a lump on my head to prove it. So does my cousin Tommy. Whether he did what Jessie McCabe accused him of or not, breaking out of jail and assaulting a couple deputies is a crime. That's a danged good case as far as I'm concerned."

"Well, sure, but maybe he figures he'd get off easier for that than he would for raping Jessie."

"Actually, I'm thinkin' that he might have some crazy idea about talking Jessie into changing her story. If she said he was really innocent, a jury might not be too hard on him for breaking out of jail to prove it."

"That makes sense," Corbett agreed. "I think it's worth us riding out there to find out."

"Us?"

"I'm going to go with you and give you a hand."

Stonewall shook his head. "You can't do that, Roy. I'm a duly authorized peace officer. You're not."

"Sheriff Slaughter lets civilians go along on posses. He chased those bandits all the way down into Mexico with a posse of townspeople."

Stonewall had to admit that was true, but there had been special circumstances involved in that case. "Why do you want to come along, anyway?"

"I told you, I'm going to be an attorney someday. The more experience I have with the law, the better."

That seemed like pretty shaky reasoning to Stonewall, but he didn't know anything about lawyering or how somebody went about preparing to be one. And he was wasting time sitting there arguing.

"If you want to come along, I reckon I can't stop you. There's no law against you or anybody else ridin' out to the McCabe ranch." Stonewall paused and then added sternly, "But don't interfere with me carryin' out my official duties or I'll have to arrest you."

"I just want to help if I can, not get in the way," Corbett said.

Stonewall lifted his reins and jerked his head toward the trail. "Come on, then."

They had ridden side by side for about half a mile when Stonewall spotted a column of dust rising ahead of them.

Corbett saw it, too "Looks like somebody's coming this way in a hurry."

"Yeah, and that ain't good," Stonewall muttered. "Nobody hurries in heat like this unless there's real trouble."

It didn't take long for the gap between them to close. Stonewall and Corbett reined in as the rider galloped toward them. When the man was close enough that he couldn't miss seeing them, Stonewall held up his left hand in a signal to stop.

At first he thought the rider was going to gallop right past them, but the man slowed his mount and gradually brought the horse to a halt. He looked at Stonewall. "Thank the Lord it's you, Deputy. I was on my way to town to fetch the law."

Stonewall recognized the man as one of Little Ed McCabe's cowboys. "What's wrong, Tom? Trouble at the ranch?"

"Damned right there's trouble! Dallin Williams showed up there."

Stonewall couldn't help but feel a little satisfaction because his hunch had turned out to be right.

But that feeling vanished the next moment when the Bar EM puncher continued. "He kidnapped Miss Jessie!"

"What!" Corbett cried.

If the cowboy was curious what a store clerk was doing with Stonewall, he didn't show it. "Yeah, Williams got in a fight with Little Ed, threw Miss Jessie on his horse, and rode off with her."

"Was anybody hurt?" Stonewall asked.

The cowboy shook his head. "I don't reckon so."

That was a little surprising, considering that the man had said Dallin got in a fight with McCabe. Stonewall would have figured that Little Ed would bust Dallin in half. "You said Little Ed sent you to town?"

Tom nodded. "Yeah, he told me to let the sheriff know what happened."

"And what's he doing?"

"What do you think? Him and some of the boys lit a shuck after that varmint. They're gonna catch Williams, get Miss Jessie away from him, and string him up!"

That was exactly the answer Stonewall expected, although it wasn't what he wanted to hear. He wanted Dallin behind bars again, where he could answer to the law, not to hangrope justice.

Tom went on. "Now that I've told you, Deputy, I reckon I don't have to go all the way on into Tombstone—"

"Yeah, you do," Stonewall broke in. "I'm out here on a job of my own. I can't turn around and go back to report this. You go ahead and find Sheriff Slaughter and tell him what happened."

"Dadgummit! I hoped I could catch up to Little Ed and

the rest of the boys. I don't want to miss what's gonna happen when they get their hands on Williams."

"Which way did he go when he rode off with Jessie McCabe?" Stonewall asked.

"Northwest toward the Santa Catalinas."

Stonewall nodded. The terrain in that direction was pretty rugged. There were a lot of places where a man could hole up or maybe give his pursuers the slip. Stonewall had hunted some up there and knew the country.

Dallin Williams knew it, too, quite possibly better than he did.

One thing was certain. Williams wouldn't live very long if Little Ed and the rest of the Bar EM bunch caught him. Guilty or innocent, he would hang.

Stonewall was bound and determined to prevent that. Every moment he sat there jawing increased the odds against success. "You go on to Tombstone like I told you," he said to the McCabe puncher, then pulled his horse's head around.

No point in riding to the ranch. Dallin had already been there and gone. Stonewall headed northwest toward the distant gray humps of the Santa Catalina Mountains.

Roy Corbett fell in beside him, pushing his horse to keep up.

"Still plan to come with me, do you?" Stonewall asked.

"I've made up my mind. I'm in this to the end."

Stonewall didn't say anything. He just hoped it didn't end with Dallin Williams dangling at the end of a rope.

Chapter 18

After they had eaten breakfast, Drake escorted Arabella back to the Top-Notch. She was tired and wanted to get some sleep, so she said her goodbyes downstairs and went up to her room.

She hadn't seen Morris Upton when they came in, and when she reached her room she heard snores coming through the wall from the adjoining room. Obviously, Upton had turned in, too.

She checked the door between the rooms to make sure it was locked. She didn't want to take a chance on Upton deciding to pay her a visit if he woke up in an amorous mood.

With that precaution taken care of, Arabella pulled the curtains securely to keep out as much of the light as possible, took off her dress, stretched out on the bed in her underclothes, and dropped off to sleep almost immediately.

She had never been one to dream much, and today was no exception. She slept soundly for several hours and woke up feeling rested.

When she pulled back the curtain and looked through the window, the intensity of the light outside told her it was probably early afternoon.

She didn't hear the snoring coming from next door anymore, so she supposed Upton was awake, too.

After freshening up and getting dressed, she went downstairs. Upton stood at the bar nursing a drink, while a number of the players from the tournament sat around a big table in the back, talking animatedly.

He beckoned to her, but Arabella pretended not to see the gesture and went over to the table where the other players were. As she approached, she could tell that some of them were upset about something.

"There you are, Lady Winthrop," Wade Cunningham said. "We were a bit worried about you."

Arabella smiled. "Why would you be worried about me?"

"You haven't heard, have you?" Donald Lockard asked.

"Heard what?"

With a solemn look on his narrow face, Cunningham told her, "Angelo Castro was murdered early this morning, sometime soon after the games broke up."

Arabella's eyes widened in shock at the news. Her breath seemed to freeze in her throat for a second. She hadn't considered the Italian to be a friend of hers, and they certainly hadn't known each other well, but she had always gotten along with him and felt no animosity toward him.

"What happened?" she asked as she took one of the empty chairs at the table.

"Someone stabbed him in an alley and stole his

stake, along with what he won last night," Cunningham explained.

"The killer got away?"

"That's right," Lockard said. "The sheriff questioned some of us, but I don't think he has any idea who killed Castro."

"Do any of you?" Arabella asked.

The men around the table murmured negatives or shook their heads.

Cunningham said, "We've been doing a head count of the players in the tournament, trying to see who's already back here ready for the games to start up again."

"Because you think the murderer might be . . . one of us?"

"That . . . and we were sort of worried that there might be some other bodies out there that haven't been found yet."

Arabella leaned back in her chair as Cunningham's words soaked in. The lanky gambler was right. The murderer who had stalked and killed Angelo Castro might have targeted some of the other players from the tournament as well.

Worry for her old friend's safety sprang up inside her. "Has anyone seen Steve Drake?"

The men around the table shook their heads again.

Lockard said, "Drake's staying down at the American Hotel. Maybe somebody should go check on him."

"I'll do that." Arabella scraped her chair back. She stood up and headed for the saloon's entrance.

Morris Upton wasn't going to be ignored any longer. He got in her way and said, "I need to talk to you, Arabella."

"I'm in a bit of a hurry—"

"I just want to make sure you're all right. I'm sure you've heard by now about Castro—"

"I have, and that's why I'm in a hurry. I want to go find Steve."

Upton made a face. "That's right. The two of you are old friends, aren't you?"

"That's right. I'm sorry, Morris. I'll be back before the tournament starts again." She paused despite her anxiety over Drake. "You are going to continue with the tournament?"

"What? Of course. The tournament will go on as planned. We can't end it because of the unfortunate death of one of the players."

"We don't know yet that Angelo was the killer's only victim. There may be others who haven't been found yet."

Upton frowned and looked like he hadn't considered that possibility.

While he was distracted by that new worry, Arabella made it past him and out the door onto the boardwalk. She knew where the American Hotel was. She hurried toward it, trying not to think about the possibility that something had happened to Steve.

There was no reason to believe that it had, she told herself. After leaving her at the Top-Notch, he had probably gone back to the hotel to get some sleep himself.

The oppressive heat still lay over Tombstone. By the time she reached the hotel, her face glowed with a fine sheen of perspiration. She went inside and crossed the lobby to the desk. "Steve Drake's room."

The clerk hesitated and glanced at the board where room keys hung before he said, "I'm pretty sure Mr.

Drake is here, ma'am, but I don't know if he wants to be disturbed."

"He won't mind," Arabella assured him. "Just tell me his room number."

The clerk couldn't hold out in the face of her forceful insistence. "Mr. Drake is in Room 27, ma'am."

"Thank you." Even in a state of anxiety, Arabella was gracious. She turned toward the stairs.

The clerk called after her, "I'd be glad to send someone up to summon Mr. Drake."

Arabella ignored him and kept going.

Room 27 was on the second floor. She had no trouble finding it. She paused in front of the door in the carpet-runnered hallway with its potted plants and sand-filled ashtrays and took a deep breath before she knocked on the panel.

"Steve?" she called. "Steve, are you there?"

At first there was no response. Then Arabella heard a footstep on the other side of the door. "Arabella? Is that you?"

A tide of relief went through her at the sound of his voice. She sighed. "Thank God. I was worried that something had happened to you."

"I'm fine, Bella."

"Then open the door and let me in. Something has happened, and we need to talk."

She frowned slightly as seconds ticked past and there was no response from him.

Finally he suggested, "Why don't you meet me downstairs in the dining room in a few minutes? I'll get dressed—"

"Steve, what's wrong? There's no need for false modesty between us."

The doorknob rattled and the door swung open, but only a few inches. Drake looked out at her through the gap with his usual grin. He appeared to be dressed only in the bottom half of a pair of long underwear. "It's just that the room's rather messy and I don't see any need to offend your sensibilities, Bella—"

"You don't want to offend her, but you don't seem to be worried about me!" a new voice broke in.

Arabella's carefully curved eyebrows shot up. She recognized that voice. "Copper?" she said in a disbelieving tone. "Copper Farris?"

Drake's grin disappeared as he winced. "Arabella, I didn't mean to upset you. That's why I suggested that we meet downstairs."

"It's all right, Steve," she forced herself to say. "We have no claim on each other."

Someone jerked the door out of Drake's hand and threw it open the rest of the way. Arabella found herself facing Copper Farris, who was undeniably spectacular in a short, thin shift that hugged the contours of her heavy breasts. Her mass of red hair was tousled from sleep . . . and other activities that had gone on in the sheet-tangled bed visible behind her.

"If you don't have any claim on him, what are you doing here?" she demanded in an angry, challenging voice.

Arabella struggled to hang on to control of her temper. "Steve and I are friends, and I just heard some news I thought he ought to know."

"Well, here's some news for you," Copper said. "You can just stay away from him from now on."

Drake looked like he would have rather been almost anywhere else. "There's no need to argue, ladies."

"I'll say there's not," Copper said as she slid her arm through his and pressed herself against him. In their state of undress, it was a blatantly intimate gesture. "How could anybody argue that they'd rather be with this dried-up foreigner rather than me?" She smirked at Arabella.

Drake swallowed hard and began, "There's no need—"

"There's certainly not," Arabella broke in. "You've always been free to do whatever you wanted, Steve." She turned away but added over her shoulder, "I just thought you had better taste than to take up with such a common tramp as this." She walked along the corridor toward the stairs with her chin held up in what she hoped was a reasonably successful attempt to retain a little dignity.

She heard Copper's outraged gasp behind her

"Why, that" Copper started spewing obscenities.

"Copper, don't!" exclaimed Steve Drake.

The rapid rush of footsteps as she reached the landing was all the warning Arabella got. She turned just as Copper crashed into her, still spitting curses and clawing at her eyes. Arabella let out a startled cry as she felt herself going over backward.

"Bella!" Steve Drake cried.

She grabbed at Copper in an attempt to catch her balance and steady herself, but all that succeeded in doing was pulling the redhead down with her.

Both women landed hard on the steps and began to tumble down out of control. The impacts jolted Arabella to her core and drove the breath out of her body. When she finally reached the bottom of the staircase and spilled onto the floor of the hotel lobby, she was gasping for air.

Copper sprawled alongside her, seemingly stunned.

Arabella started moving her arms and legs in an attempt to discover if she had broken any bones in the fall. Everything seemed to be working, she realized. She ached and she might be covered with bruises by the next day, but she decided that she wasn't seriously hurt.

She looked over at Copper. The redhead's shift had hiked up so it was definitely immodest. Her bosom threatened to escape completely from the thin fabric, and the fact that she was breathing hard because the fall had knocked the air out of her, too, didn't help matters.

Arabella reached toward her. "Copper."

With a snarl, the redhead slapped her hand aside and then lunged for her throat. She got both hands on Arabella's neck, rolled on top of her, and started to squeeze.

Arabella hadn't gotten her breath back fully and was still desperate for air. The hotel lobby seemed to spin crazily around her. Her blood rushed in her head like a great river. Over that roar, she barely heard men shouting.

She looked up at Copper looming over her. The redhead's face was twisted with anger and didn't look so beautiful anymore. Her hair hung down around her head in crazy tangles.

With a black haze starting to close in around her, Arabella clenched her right hand into a fist and shot it upward into Copper's face. Copper might have expected scratching or hair pulling, but the short, hard punch seemed to take her by surprise.

The blow landed solidly on her jaw and drove her head to the side. Her grip on Arabella's throat slipped. Arabella bucked up from the floor and wedged her left forearm under Copper's chin. She pushed Copper's head back and heaved to the side, forcing the woman to let go and roll off of her.

Scrambling to survive in Liverpool all those years ago had taught Arabella some hard lessons. She didn't trust that the redhead wouldn't come after her again, so she took the initiative despite the fact that her head was pounding and she was still gasping for air. She lunged after Copper and plunged her hands into that mass of red hair.

With that grip, Arabella was able to lift Copper's head and slam it down against the floor. She did that once and then again before someone grabbed her from behind and pulled her away from the redhead.

"Stop it!" Drake yelled. "Damn it, Bella, you're going to kill her."

"That redheaded slut . . . tried to . . . kill me," Arabella panted. "Let go of me!" She writhed in Drake's grip, but couldn't break free.

A few feet away, the hotel clerk danced nervously around Copper's senseless form. Several men and women, more than likely guests in the hotel, watched the scandalous scene from the other side of the lobby.

Chapter 19

It had occurred to Slaughter that he ought to talk to Stonewall again and make sure the deputy hadn't heard Dallin Williams say anything that might offer a clue to where the fugitive was going. He went to Clara Mumford's boarding house, stood on the porch, and knocked on the door.

The widow lady answered the summons almost immediately. As she swung the door open, she beamed at him. "Why, Sheriff Slaughter! It's so good to see you again. Please, come in. Come in and have a seat."

Slaughter took his hat off and held it in front of him. "I won't take up much of your time, Mrs. Mumford. I'm just looking for Deputy Howell—"

"Goodness gracious. Time is the thing I have the most of, Sheriff. Please come in."

"If you could just tell Deputy Howell I'm here."

She wouldn't be denied. "I just made a pitcher of nice, cool lemonade to go with lunch, but I think I can spare a glass of it for the sheriff of Cochise County."

The walk in the blazing sun seemed to have baked every drop of moisture out of Slaughter, so the idea of a glass of lemonade sounded very appealing. Too appealing to turn down. "All right. Thank you, Mrs. Mumford."

She led him into a parlor with a woven rug on the floor and lace doilies on the backs of the furniture. There was a mantel on one wall, but no fireplace to go with it. Above the mantel hung a portrait of George Washington, a Currier & Ives print, and a framed needlework picture of praying hands. An enormous pedestal clock sat in one corner and its rhythmic ticking somehow had an ominous sound.

"Now you have a seat, Sheriff," the elderly, white-haired woman said, "and I'll be right back with that lemonade."

"Thank you," Slaughter said again. He sat on a divan that had elaborate scrollwork on its arms and listened to the clock tick. After a minute or two it began to sound to him like the pounding of a drum. There wasn't a breath of air in the room.

Luckily, it didn't take Mrs. Mumford long to fetch the lemonade. She brought the glass to him and sat down opposite him in an armchair.

Slaughter sipped the cool, tangy liquid and immediately felt better. He was tempted to gulp it all down, but he controlled that impulse. "I can just go up to Deputy Howell's room when I finish this."

"Oh, Deputy Howell's not here," Mrs. Mumford said.

Slaughter was taking another drink of the lemonade and almost choked on it as he drew in a sharp breath. "Not here?" he repeated. "I told him to go home and get some rest after that wallop on the head he got."

Mrs. Mumford shook her head. "I'm afraid I don't know anything about that, Sheriff. Stonewall left more than an hour ago."

"Did he take his horse?"

"Yes, he did. He took along some sandwiches he asked me to make for him, too. I'm under the impression that he thought he might be gone for a while."

Slaughter kept a tight rein on his temper. The old woman could have told him that when he first got there, instead of luring him into the house with the promise of lemonade. "Did he happen to say where he was going?"

"No, not at all, and I didn't ask." Mrs. Mumford tightened her lips primly. "I don't make a habit of prying into the personal affairs of my boarders, Sheriff."

"Of course not." It didn't really matter. He had a pretty good idea where Stonewall had gone, or at least what the deputy was doing.

He leaned to set the half-full glass of lemonade on a spindly-legged table in front of him, then changed his mind and downed the rest of it in one long swallow. He might as well get something out of this visit, he told himself.

He set the glass down and stood up. "I have to be going."

"Is there anything you want me to tell Deputy Howell when he gets back?"

Slaughter could think of several things, but the elderly widow would be too shocked and scandalized to repeat them, so he just shook his head. "No, thanks, ma'am. And thank you for the lemonade."

"You're very welcome, Sheriff. Come back any time."

But she was talking to Slaughter's back as he left the house.

There was no doubt in Slaughter's mind that Stonewall had gone after Dallin Williams. The boy was young enough to take it personally that Williams had knocked him out and escaped from jail while Stonewall was supposed to be responsible for him.

They weren't sure which direction Williams had gone, though. Mose Tadrack and Jeff Milton had spread out through Tombstone, questioning merchants and others who had been out and about early and might have seen Williams flee the jail. Lorenzo Paco was making a wide circle around the town, searching for likely tracks.

If Stonewall had been gone for more than an hour, as his landlady had said, that meant he must have had an idea where Williams might go and was checking out his theory.

What it amounted to for Slaughter was that he had a second person to find, which meant his work had doubled.

He was just about to the jail when a man coming from the opposite direction hailed him. "Sheriff, I was just lookin' for you." Judging by his clothes, he was a cowboy, and his voice held a Texas drawl.

"I'm afraid I'm a little busy right now," Slaughter said.

"But my horse has done been stole," the man insisted. "I'm set a-foot. Can't get back to the spread I ride for."

Slaughter started to brush past the man. "You can file a report with one of my deputies—" He stopped short and looked at the man again. "You say your horse was stolen?" He remembered the theory he had mentioned earlier, that Williams had stolen a horse but the horse's owner didn't know about it yet.

"That's right, Sheriff. Pretty little chestnut mare. Best cow pony you'll ever find."

"When did this happen?"

The man took off his battered old hat and raked his fingers through straw-like hair as he frowned. "Well, I don't rightly know. You see, I, uh, had a mite to drink last night, and I just woke up a little while ago in one o' them cribs up by the Birdcage. Went to get my horse, and it was gone."

"Where did you leave it tied up?"

The cowboy pointed along Toughnut Street. "Down yonder at one o' them hitch racks, the one in front of the gunsmith's shop. Had to have him do a little work on this ol' hogleg o' mine, and when he was finished I just left the hoss there and walked around to the saloon. Didn't really plan on spendin' the night in town or I would've put her in a stable." He frowned. "I sure hope she's all right."

Slaughter understood the man's concern about his horse, although the cowboy shouldn't have allowed himself to get so distracted by whiskey and whores that he had forgotten all about the animal. At the moment, however, Slaughter was more concerned with the timing of the theft. The horse that Dallin Williams had ridden into town—with Little Ed McCabe and the Bar EM punchers in hot pursuit—was still at the livery stable; that was one of the first things Slaughter had checked on when he found out about the prisoner's escape.

Williams had stolen a horse to get out of Tombstone,

and nobody else had reported a missing horse this morning. The fact that this one had disappeared from a hitch rack not far from the courthouse and jail was just more of an indication that Williams had taken it.

"You said it's a chestnut mare?"

"That's right. Answers to Milly."

"Anything unusual about its hoofprints?"

The Texan frowned in thought for a moment. "Well . . . the shoe on the right front hoof has a little moon-shaped nick in it. You know, like on an outhouse door."

That was a stroke of luck, thought Slaughter. To an experienced tracker like Lorenzo Paco, such a mark was almost as good as a painted sign.

"Anything else distinctive about her tracks?"

The cowboy shook his head. "Naw, not that I can think of. You're gonna find her, aren't you, Sheriff?"

"We're certainly going to try," Slaughter said, and he meant it.

There was a good chance that if they found the stolen horse, Dallin Williams would be riding it, and Stonewall wouldn't be far behind.

He went back to the courthouse and sent Jeff Milton to find Lorenzo Paco. While he waited for the men to return, he unlocked the cell where Harley Court had spent the night and let the man go.

"You're not gonna charge me with anything, Sheriff?" Court sounded like he couldn't believe his good fortune.

"I've got too much on my plate right now to worry about you, too," Slaughter snapped. "But the next time you're tempted to join a lynch mob, just remember how you wound up with a bullet hole in your leg."

Court winced in pain and declared, "Not gonna be a next time, Sheriff, I can promise you that."

When Court was gone, Slaughter tried to do some paperwork, but he couldn't concentrate. The air in his office was too hot, and too much was going on. It didn't help matters when Morris Upton showed up looking for him.

"Sheriff, I want to know if you've made any progress finding Angelo Castro's killer," Upton said without preamble.

"It's only been a couple hours since the body was found," Slaughter said.

"I know, but the players in my tournament are worried. Some of them are afraid that they've been targeted for death, too."

Slaughter almost snorted at the melodramatic way the saloonkeeper phrased that. "You had to know that if you invited a bunch of gamblers into town with a lot of extra money, there was a chance of trouble."

"It's your job to handle that trouble."

Unfortunately, Slaughter couldn't argue with that statement. The people of Cochise County had elected him to deal with whatever came up . . . and he had been damned fool enough to accept the job!

"I know you have an escaped prisoner to go after," Upton went on, "but the murder of my friend is important, too."

"Nobody said it wasn't. We'll do everything we can to find out who killed Castro. In the meantime, why don't you let us go on about our jobs, Mr. Upton?" Slaughter sounded a lot more polite than he felt, or at least he hoped he did.

After a moment Upton nodded curtly and left the courthouse.

Slaughter had a strong hunch that he would be seeing more of the saloonkeeper than he wanted to until the mess was cleaned up.

Jeff Milton and Lorenzo Paco came in a few minutes later, along with Burt Alvord. Slaughter explained what he had learned from the Texan.

"It must've been Williams who stole that horse," Burt said. "If anybody else had lost a saddle mount, chances are we would've heard about it by now."

"I think so, too," Slaughter said. "Lorenzo, did you notice any tracks like that while you were searching?"

"No, but now I know what to look for. I will go back out right away, Sheriff."

"You can cool off a little first if you want to."

Paco shook his head. "The heat doesn't bother me. I have lived with it all my life . . . and that life has been a long one." The leathery Mexican left.

Once Paco was gone, Burt said, "There's a lot of talk around town, Sheriff. Folks aren't happy that nobody has gone after Williams yet."

"Where would they have us go? We're trying to find out which direction he went when he left Tombstone."

"All of us know that, but after the way you stopped that lynch mob last night, they think you're draggin' your feet on purpose so Williams will have a better chance to get away. They think you're takin' his side in this deal."

"Then they don't know John Slaughter very well, do they?" He felt anger burning inside him to go along with the heat outside. He didn't like being accused of not trying to do his job the best he could.

Mose Tadrack came in with a worried look on his face. "Sheriff—"

"What is it now? Some new trouble?"

"Well, I don't know. A fella told me there was some sort of ruckus going on at the American Hotel."

That was unusual. The hotel's owner, Nellie Cashman, ran an orderly establishment. Reports of trouble there were rare. Nellie was a forceful personality, and usually if there was a problem, she handled it herself.

Slaughter sighed and heaved himself to his feet. "I'll go see about it. Jeff, gather some of the men and get ready to ride. You'll lead the posse that goes after Williams as soon as Paco finds the tracks."

"You're not going along, Sheriff?"

"I have the business of that dead gambler to deal with, and as long as Upton's damned poker tournament is going on, there's liable to be more trouble. You'll be able to handle Williams when you catch up to him."

Slaughter hadn't said anything about Stonewall's disappearance and his theory that his young brother-in-law had gone after Williams on his own. He thought that would all be cleared up when they found the escaped prisoner.

He hoped fervently that Stonewall wouldn't go and get himself killed. Viola might not ever forgive him, although she knew the risks that went with a deputy's job.

Slaughter left the courthouse and walked with as much speed as he could muster toward the American Hotel. The hotel's front doors were open to let in air, and they also let out the sound of angry voices shouting at each other. There was some sort of ruckus going on, all right.

Slaughter didn't expect to see two women—one of them nearly naked!—standing toe to toe and yelling at each other while a couple men tried to hold them back. The sheer ludicrousness of the scene irritated him. He raised his voice and shouted, "What the hell is going on here?"

Chapter 20

Slaughter recognized one of the battling women as Lady Arabella Winthrop, although the English woman's hair and clothing were a lot more disheveled than they had been the last time he'd seen her. She had a bruise forming on her jaw, too. Obviously, she and the skimpily clad redhead had been fighting.

The man holding Lady Arabella back was Steve Drake, another of the gamblers who had come to Tombstone for Upton's poker tournament.

The one trying to keep the redhead under control appeared to be a drummer of some sort, judging by his flashy, checkered suit and derby hat.

Slaughter strode forward and put himself between the two women. Holding out his hands like the referee in a prizefighting match, he swiveled his glare from one to the other. "We don't allow brawling in hotel lobbies in Tombstone. And ladies don't have any business brawling in the first place!"

"You see, there's your mistake, Sheriff," Lady Arabella said coolly. "This slut is no lady."

"You're a fine one to talk," the redhead shot back. "At least I'm not a tease like you."

"That's enough." To the redhead, Slaughter said, "Ma'am, you'd better go upstairs and get some clothes on. Can I trust the two of you not to start fighting again if these hombres let go of you?"

"I never wanted to fight in the first place," Lady Arabella said. "Miss Farris attacked me without warning as I was leaving. I just defended myself."

"You thought you could call me names and then walk off," the redhead said. "I don't let anybody get away with treating me like that."

Slaughter started to tell Drake to take Lady Arabella out of the hotel, but then he noticed that the gambler was partially undressed himself, wearing only the bottom half of a pair of long underwear.

The sheriff stepped over to Lady Arabella and took hold of her arm. "Come with me, ma'am."

"Are you arresting me?" she demanded.

"No, ma'am. Not unless you give me more reason to. I'm just getting you out of here so things can settle down."

"There's no need to force me. I'll go with you." Her angry gaze shuttled back and forth between the redhead and Drake. "There's nothing else I want here."

When Slaughter let go of her arm, she took a moment to straighten her clothes, then walked toward the door with her chin held high.

Slaughter stayed beside her to make sure the redhead didn't get loose and try to tackle her from behind. He recalled that Lady Arabella and Drake had seemed quite friendly when he had seen them together before.

He didn't think it was a coincidence that the gambler

and the redhead were both in their underwear. If they had been together like that and Lady Arabella had walked in on them . . .

Well, that was a sure-fire recipe for a ruckus, all right.

Once they were outside, the English woman sighed wearily. "I'm very sorry about this disturbance, Sheriff. I assure you, it wasn't my idea."

"No, ma'am, I suppose it wasn't."

She looked at him. "You've figured out what happened, haven't you?"

"I can make a pretty good guess."

A faint, sad smile curved her lips. "Then you're more perceptive than I was. Never in a million years would I have believed that Steve would take up with such a—"

Slaughter held up a hand to stop her. "You don't want to get yourself all worked up into a state again," he cautioned. "Sometimes, for your own peace of mind, you have to just let these things go."

She sighed again. "I suppose you're right. Besides, there are more important things to worry about. Have you made any progress in finding out who killed poor Angelo Castro?"

"Not yet," Slaughter answered honestly, suppressing the irritation he felt at the question. He couldn't really blame her for asking it. Castro had been a friend of hers, or at least an acquaintance. "There's not much to go on other than the fact that he was killed with a narrow-bladed knife."

"Like a dagger or a stiletto?"

"That's right," Slaughter said.

"I wouldn't think there would be many of those in

Tombstone. Don't most of the men around here carry Bowie knives or other big hunting knives?"

"That's true, but I can't very well go around Tombstone asking everybody what kind of knife they carry and demanding to take a look at it."

"Yes, I can see that that would be a daunting task," Lady Arabella said. "Not to mention the killer would probably just lie to you. I've heard talk that you have an escaped prisoner to go after, or something like that."

"Something exactly like that," Slaughter agreed. "One thing's for sure. There's plenty of trouble on my plate right now."

Lady Arabella smiled. "Well, I wish you luck with that full plate, Sheriff Slaughter. I shall do my best not to add any more heaping helpings of trouble."

Oscar Grayson and Jed Muller strolled into the lobby of the American Hotel a couple minutes before three o'clock that afternoon and asked at the desk for Max Rourke.

The clerk pointed to the entrance to the dining room. "I believe Mr. Rourke is in there . . . gentlemen."

That slight hesitation in the man's voice annoyed Grayson. He knew the clerk thought they weren't dressed well enough to be in there. That they weren't high-class enough.

Grayson had heard all about the trouble earlier, when Lady Arabella and Copper Farris had gotten into a knock-down, drag-out fight. The gossip going around town said that Copper was dressed only in her scanties at the time.

That would have been a sight to see, Grayson reflected. But he had something more important on his mind than the abundantly endowed Miss Farris. He nodded curt thanks to the clerk. "Come on, Jed."

Muller had an unlit cigar clamped between his teeth. He rolled it from one side of his mouth to the other as he followed Grayson across the lobby to the dining room. It wasn't busy in the middle of the afternoon. Most of the tables were empty.

Max Rourke sat at one of them with a cup of coffee in front of him. He glanced up as Grayson and Muller approached, but didn't seem too interested.

"Hello, Max." Grayson was a little nervous about coming up to Rourke. The man had a reputation as a powderkeg that could go off for no reason. "You haven't forgotten about what we talked about last night, have you?"

"We didn't talk about anything except that we'd get together here today." Rourke looked at Muller with cold green eyes. "You're part of this . . . whatever it is . . . too?"

"I reckon I am." With his characteristic bluntness, Muller asked, "Can we sit down?"

Rourke's shoulders rose and fell maybe an inch as he said, "Help yourself."

Grayson and Muller scraped chairs back and took seats at the table.

As an apron-clad waitress came toward them, Grayson said, "Bring us some coffee."

"Yes, sir," the girl said with a smile. "Anything else you need, Mr. Rourke?"

"No."

Grayson passed the time with small talk while waiting

for the waitress to bring two more cups of coffee to the table. Rourke seemed to ignore it all.

When the girl had come and gone, Grayson lowered his voice. "We need some place private to talk, Max."

"This is private enough. Look around."

Grayson saw what he meant. The few other hotel guests had left. They were the only occupants of the dining room. The waitress had gone through a swinging door and was no longer in sight, either.

"Somebody out in the lobby might hear . . ." Grayson said.

"Nobody's going to hear. Nobody gives a damn what you've got to say, Grayson, including me." Rourke took a sip of his coffee. "You've got two minutes to change my opinion."

"Well, what about me?" Muller asked.

"You're just a beast of burden, Muller. I'm here to listen to Grayson."

Muller's face turned brick-red, and he started to stand up.

Grayson put a hand on his arm and said sharply, "Take it easy, Jed."

"I don't cotton to people talkin' to me like that," Muller said.

"Really?" Rourke said. "I would have thought you'd be used to it by now."

"Just sit back and get hold of yourself, Jed," Grayson told the big man. "All three of us can wind up rich men here . . . if we work together."

Muller settled back in his chair and glared at Rourke.

"All right. But there's a limit to how much I'm gonna take."

For a second, Grayson thought Rourke was going to say something else just to put a burr under Muller's saddle. But Rourke looked at him instead. "Tell me what you've got in mind."

"You know there's going to be an awful lot of money on the table during that last game between Upton and whoever comes out of the tournament," Grayson said. "There's a good chance that won't be one of us."

"Speak for yourself," Muller said. "I'm a damn good card player."

"Not good enough. Sorry, Jed, but that's the truth and we might as well admit it. None of us are good enough to come out on top of all the opposition we've got here."

Rourke said, "So you're planning to steal that last giant pot."

Grayson blinked in surprise. "How did you know that?"

"What else could you be talking about that would make us all rich? If one of us could win on his own, he wouldn't need the other two." Rourke drank some more of his coffee. "You know Upton will have guards all over the place."

"That's why we need a distraction. We're going to have bundles of dynamite set to go off all over town, right at the same time. When everybody runs out to see what's going on, you kill the guards and anybody else who gets in the way, I grab the money, and we go out the back to where Jed's got horses waiting for all of us."

Silence hung over the table for a long moment before

Rourke spoke. Grayson was afraid the man would declare the plan to be stupid and unworkable.

Instead, he asked, "Who's going to handle the dynamite? Muller?"

"I used to be a mining engineer," Muller said. "I know how to use the stuff, what length to make the fuses, how to keep from blowing myself up, everything like that."

Rourke reached up and rubbed his rather pointed chin as he frowned in thought. "You'd be running less of a risk than we are, Grayson. Muller has to handle explosives, and I have to shoot it out with Upton's men."

"It was my idea," Grayson said, trying not to sound too defensive. "And I'll probably have to kill Upton when I make a move for the money."

Rourke smiled thinly. "That's true." He inclined his head slightly to acknowledge the point Grayson had made. "I wouldn't expect him to go along with it peacefully."

Grayson leaned forward, "So, what do you think, Max? Does it sound to you like it could be done?"

Instead of answering the question directly, Rourke looked at Muller. "Where do you plan on setting off the dynamite?"

Grayson and Muller glanced at each other. Muller shook his head, and Grayson said, "Well, we hadn't really gotten that far with our planning . . ."

"You want a distraction, don't you? You need to have the blasts in places where they'll attract a lot of attention. If you blow up an empty barn, not enough people will care."

"What do you suggest?"

"Blow up all the other saloons in town."

Grayson's eyes widened. "There'll be people in those places, folks who don't care about the poker tournament and just want something to drink or a whore to dally with."

"That's exactly right. Destruction makes a good distraction. Death and destruction make an even better one."

"That might kill a couple hundred people," Muller said. "Maybe more."

"And there may be a quarter million dollars on the table during that last hand," Rourke said. "Maybe more. Look at it like that and a couple hundred people doesn't seem like such a high price to pay, does it?"

Several seconds ticked by without Grayson or Muller saying anything. Finally, Grayson asked, "Does that mean you're in on it with us, Max?"

"I'm in," Rourke said softly, "but I call the shots. You may have come up with the idea, Grayson, but it's my job now."

Muller said, "As long as the split stays even, I don't care about anything else."

"Neither do I," Grayson said, although it required an effort for him to go along with the idea of Rourke taking over. The money was all that mattered, he told himself, not his pride.

Besides, he might have a surprise or two for Rourke before it was all over.

"All right," Rourke said. "We'll get together again after the tournament has gone on longer and we have a better idea when the showdown will be. Until then, it would probably be a good idea if we're not seen together a lot."

"That's fine with me." Muller's meaning was clear.

He didn't want to be around Rourke any more than he had to.

"Me, too," Grayson said as he got to his feet. "Let's go, Jed." He smiled. "The games will be starting again soon, anyway."

Once the two of them were gone, Rourke finished his coffee. His face was hard and unreadable as he reached under his coat. He slid a knife from a soft leather sheath hidden under his arm, a thin-bladed dagger that he used to trim a rough spot on one of his fingernails.

A tiny rusty spot on the cold steel showed where a drop of blood had dried. Rourke frowned at it for a second, then picked up a napkin from the table and wiped it off. There, that was better, he thought as he slipped the dagger back in its sheath.

Chapter 21

Stonewall and Roy Corbett rode all day toward the Santa Catalina Mountains.

By late afternoon, it seemed that the peaks weren't any closer than they were when the two men started, but Stonewall knew they really were. "We ought to get there by around the middle of the day tomorrow," he said as they paused to rest their horses. The heat was taking a toll on men and animals alike.

"We could make it sooner if we just camped for a couple hours and then rode on through the night," Corbett suggested.

Stonewall frowned. "I don't know. I'd hate for us to get lost. That'd just cost us time."

"How are we going to get lost? The mountains are over there. We can steer by the stars well enough to keep going in the right direction. It's not like we're actually following a trail, so we don't have be able to see hoofprints or anything like that."

Corbett had a point, thought Stonewall. He hoped they were headed in the same direction as Dallin Williams and

Jessie McCabe, but there was no way to be sure of that. The plan was to pick up the trail of the escaped prisoner and his hostage somewhere along the way.

"All right, here's what we'll do," Stonewall said as he'd reached a decision. "We'll push on for a while longer, then find a good place to stop for a few hours. These horses have to rest and cool off, and so do we. Then we'll keep going."

"Sounds like a good plan to me," Corbett said.

As they rode on, Stonewall said, "I sort of expected you to turn back before now, Roy. Chasing down fugitives ain't your job, you know."

"No, I'm in this to the end," Corbett declared. "That's how much the law means to me, Stonewall. I'm going to do everything in my power to see that the system works."

"Maybe you should be a star packer instead of a lawyer, if you feel that strongly about it."

Corbett laughed. "No, I don't mind helping out with something like this, but I'm not cut out to wear a badge permanently. A lawman can't really see a case through to the end. Once you've arrested an outlaw and put him in jail, what happens to him after that is really out of your hands. It's up to a judge and jury to decide his ultimate fate, and that's what I want to be part of."

"Reckon you'd ever want to be a judge someday?"

"Well . . . I don't know. Maybe. But I need to be a lawyer first and get plenty of experience."

"Sort of like I'm bein' a deputy."

Corbett grinned. "You think you might be sheriff someday, Stonewall?"

"You can't ever tell." Stonewall laughed. "I reckon stranger things have happened in this world." He paused, then added, "After seeing how much paperwork Sheriff Slaughter has to do, though, I'm not sure I'd really want the job."

They stopped at the base of a large, rocky upthrust and let it shade them from the last of the sun's burning rays as they unsaddled the horses.

The presence of some grass and a pair of scrubby bushes prompted Stonewall to dig down into the sandy soil. After a couple feet he hit a trickle of muddy water. "If we let this fill in and settle for a while, we'll have some clear water on top we can use to fill our canteens."

"That's why I'm glad I'm traveling with somebody who knows his way around the wilderness."

"Shoot, that's just common sense. You would've figured it out yourself."

"Don't be so sure about that," Corbett said. "I'm not much of a frontiersman."

"Well, everybody has their own strengths, I reckon."

As Stonewall had predicted, a little pool formed in the hole in the ground while they slept a couple hours. They filled their canteens, then ate the last of the sandwiches Mrs. Mumford had packed. Stonewall had intended for the food to last longer than that, but he couldn't expect Corbett to go hungry.

Once they reached the mountains, there would be game to hunt. They wouldn't starve.

The sky turned ebony overhead and the stars came out, but Stonewall waited until the moon rose before he said, "All right, I reckon we can saddle up and head out again."

The mountains were a looming black mass shot through with veins of silver, or so they appeared in the wash of light from the rising moon. The air was still hot, but without the harsh sun glaring down it was more bearable.

After several hours of riding, Stonewall and Corbett reached the foothills. They wound through a vast field of boulders and began to climb into the Santa Catalinas.

Stonewall looked back at the eastern sky and saw a faint gray tinge. "It'll be dawn in a couple hours. We ought to stop and rest a little more, and we can move out again when it's light. We don't know how far Dallin and Jessie made it. We don't want to ride right past them in the dark without seeing them."

"That's a good idea," Corbett agreed. "I could use another hour of sleep."

They stopped at the base of a looming bluff where some grass grew. There was no water, but they still had plenty in their canteens so they could wait until morning to search for a spring or a little creek. They unsaddled their mounts and spread their bedrolls.

"You get some rest first," Stonewall told Corbett. "I'll wake you after an hour or so and you can spell me."

"You think it's necessary for one of us to stand watch?"

"It never hurts to be careful." Stonewall sat down with his back against a slab of rock and his rifle across his knees. With his hat tipped back, weariness made his face gaunt in the moonlight.

Corbett stretched out on his blankets, and a few minutes later he began to snore softly.

Stonewall listened to the night. At first, everything was absolutely still and quiet except for Corbett's snoring, the sound of the horses cropping at the grass, and the shuffle of their hooves on the ground as they moved around a little.

As time passed, though, Stonewall began to hear other things, and he knew the small animals, the desert rats and the lizards that populated the mountains, were starting to come out of their burrows. The creatures had hunkered down, motionless and silent, at the arrival of the men, but they began to feel like it was safe to resume their nocturnal activities.

Had to give the critters credit for being smart enough to know how perilous it was when human beings started stomping around, thought Stonewall. He had hunted mountain lions and bears, but figured there were no greater predators in the world than his fellow men.

His eyelids grew heavy. He fought off the drowsiness. He wasn't going to let Corbett sleep all the way to dawn. His turn was coming, he told himself.

But exhaustion continued to steal over him, and while he wasn't asleep, after a while he wasn't fully awake, either. He hovered in the netherworld in between.

His senses weren't completely deadened. After an unknowable amount of time, something made his head snap up. He blinked rapidly, looked around, and listened intently as he searched for any sign of trouble. He didn't see or hear anything, but he came to his feet anyway, still holding the rifle.

Suddenly, a weight crashed into his back and knocked him forward. Stonewall tried to keep his balance and stay upright, but the impact drove him to his knees.

A bare arm looped around his neck, hooked under his chin, and cruelly yanked his head up and back to expose the taut line of his throat.

He knew what was going to happen next—cold steel slashing into his flesh, the hot spurt of blood, and death.

* * *

Dallin felt sorry for Jessie, but knowing that Little Ed McCabe and most, if not all, of the crew from Bar Em would be on their trail, he pushed the stolen horse at a hard pace all day.

He sympathized with the horse, too. Since the animal had been tied up at a hitch rack in Tombstone, quite possibly since the previous night, there was no telling when it had last been grained and watered. Dallin had no way of knowing how fresh the horse was.

The mount responded well and gave him everything it had. From time to time, he stopped, swung down from the saddle, and walked while leading the horse, just to lighten the burden for a little while.

The third time he did that, Jessie got down, too.

Dallin tensed, ready to go after her if she tried to run away, but she just gave him a scornful look. "Don't worry. I'm not going to take off for the tall and uncut. I know you'd catch me if I tried. But you're killing this poor horse and I don't want to be any more a part of that than I have to."

"It ain't my intention to kill the poor critter," Dallin said, "but I don't cotton to the idea of your daddy and his hands stringin' me up, either."

"My father wouldn't do that," she insisted.

"Oh, no? Then how come Charlie Porter did his best to get a lynch mob to take me outta the jail?"

"Charlie's known me since I was a little girl," Jessie said, flushing. Dallin couldn't tell if the rise in her color was due to embarrassment or the heat. "He was just so upset he got carried away."

"Uh-huh. I almost got carried away, too . . . carried right to the nearest cottonwood with a high enough branch."

She didn't have anything to say to that.

After a while they mounted up again and rode on.

Water was a considerable worry. It was dry country, for the most part, and Dallin hadn't been able to bring any with him from Tombstone.

He had cowboyed all over the region, though, and knew the location of several springs. He headed for the nearest one, and was glad to see that it hadn't dried up yet, as it might later in the summer.

He let the horse drink but was careful not to allow the animal to founder. Then he and Jessie drank as well.

She said, "You don't have anything to eat, do you?"

"Not unless there's something stashed in these saddle-bags," Dallin said.

"You don't know because that's not your horse. You're a horse thief, too."

"I'm a horse thief," Dallin admitted. "I hope they don't hang me for it later on. But we both know I ain't guilty of anything else I been accused of."

She looked away.

He would keep working on her conscience, he thought, and sooner or later she would tell the truth.

He checked in the saddlebags and didn't find anything other than some piggin' strings, a deck of cards, a pouch of chewing tobacco . . . and a six-gun.

Dallin's heart jumped a little when he saw the revolver. He checked the cylinder, saw that five of the chambers were loaded with the hammer resting on the empty sixth chamber. There weren't any extra cartridges in the saddlebags, but if he was cornered, at least he could put a little fight.

Problem was, despite everything that had happened, he didn't want to shoot Little Ed McCabe or even Charlie Porter.

Jessie's eyes widened at the sight of the gun. "Are you going to shoot me?"

"What? Good Lord, gal, you ought to know better than that! Why would I want to shoot you?"

"Because I . . . Because you wouldn't be in so much trouble if it wasn't for the things I said about you."

Dallin shrugged. "I ain't gonna deny I wish you'd told the truth, but I figure you got your reasons for what you done. I'm sure they seem like good reasons to you." He looked at her. "I reckon you must be scared. I don't claim to know you all that well, but you don't seem like a mean gal to me. You wouldn't so somethin' like this outta spite or sheer cussedness. Somethin' must'a spooked you pretty bad to make you come up with that lie and stick to it so stubborn-like."

That thought had just occurred to him, but as he put it into words, he thought about it more and was convinced that he might be on the right track. Instead of wanting to protect the fella who had gotten her in the family way, Jessie was scared of him.

She looked like she wanted to say something else, but gave a little shake of her head and turned away.

"Maybe we can find something to eat later on," she said. "I have to keep my strength up. On account of my condition, you know."

Dallin felt like slapping his forehead in exasperation. He kept forgetting that he hadn't just kidnapped a young woman. He had kidnapped a pregnant woman. That complicated the situation a whole heap more.

"When we get into the mountains we might find a rabbit or two," he said. "I can shoot one of the varmints, build a fire, and roast him right up. It'll be good eatin'."

"Won't a shot and a fire tell anybody who's following us where we are?"

"Well, yeah, I suppose so. I didn't think about that. But I ain't gonna let you and your . . . I mean, I ain't gonna let you go hungry."

She glanced around at him, and for a second he thought she was going to smile. "Thank you." She didn't smile, not quite, but he was convinced that she thought about it.

They rode on, and he carried the gun tucked behind his belt where he could get at it in a hurry if he needed to.

By late afternoon, they reached the mountains and began climbing through the valleys between slopes covered with pines and manzanita.

As they were riding, Jessie asked, "What is it you plan to do, anyway? Where are you going?"

"I don't rightly know," Dallin answered honestly. "I just wanted to get some place where I can hole up and stay away from everybody who's after me until I convince you to tell the truth about what happened."

"You mean if I agree to tell everyone that you didn't . . . well, you know what I mean. If I say that I'll tell everyone, you'll turn around and take me back?"

"Sure. That's the only reason I went out to the ranch and got you in the first place."

She turned her head to look back at him. "But I could lie. I could tell you that I'd do what you want, and then when we got back I could say anything I wanted to." She paused. "I could even tell everybody that you raped me again after you kidnapped me."

He stiffened and drew in a sharp breath. "You wouldn't do that. Not if you'd given me your word."

She looked at him for a long moment, then sighed, shook her head, and faced forward again.

He wasn't sure what she meant by that, but he didn't say anything else. Best just to let her stew in her own guilty conscience, he thought.

Night fell, and eventually it got too dark to go on. They made a cold camp in the trees next to a dry streambed. They hadn't found any game so far, and anyway, Jessie had been right about him not wanting to risk a shot.

Dallin's belly was empty, and he was sure hers was, too. Sooner or later, they would have to eat, even if it meant giving up and turning himself in. He had meant what he said. He wasn't going to let her and her baby starve.

He gathered up a good pile of pine needles, spread the saddle blanket on them, and stomped them out to level them down some. "It ain't much of a bed, but I reckon it'll have to do tonight."

"Why don't you let me go? Leave me here, and you ride on all night. That would put some distance between you and anybody who's coming after you."

"I couldn't do that. That'd mean leavin' you out here in the middle of nowhere by yourself."

"I'm sure somebody would find me."

"Maybe, maybe not. And you might not like what found you if it was a mountain lion or some such."

"There are mountain lions up here?"

"And worse things," he said, thinking about the Apaches. There hadn't been any Indian trouble for a while, but there was no telling when some of the young warriors would decide to leave the reservation and go back to their wild ways.

He didn't say anything about that to Jessie. No need to worry her any more than necessary, he decided.

She bedded down, and even though she swore she wouldn't be able to get to sleep in such primitive conditions, within a few minutes her breathing was deep and regular. Dallin took some satisfaction in that. He wanted to save his own neck, but he wanted to put her through as few hardships as he could in the process.

Despite his best intentions, he dozed off, too, with his back against a tree trunk. Exhaustion dragged him deeper and deeper into sleep until he slumped onto his side without even knowing it and didn't wake up.

That changed abruptly when somebody grabbed him. He bolted up. His hand flailed out in search of the revolver he had placed right beside him. He touched the smooth walnut grips and snatched up the gun. At the same time, he struck out with his other hand and slammed it into something soft and yielding.

Jessie went "Ooof!" as she fell backward.

Dallin realized that he had just hit her. He dropped to his knees beside her. "Dadgummit, dadgummit! Blast it, Jessie, I didn't mean to hurt you. Are you all right? Why'd you grab me that way?"

"I . . . I'm fine. You didn't really hurt me. You just pushed me down. Help me sit up."

He did so and then asked again, "Why'd you grab me?"

"Because I was scared. Didn't you hear that shot?"

"What—" Dallin stopped short. He might not have heard the shot that had spooked Jessie, but he heard the sudden burst of gunfire that shattered the night's stillness.

Somebody was in trouble, and not very far away.

Chapter 22

The flash of a gun going off almost blinded Stonewall, and the roar of the shot half-deafened him.

It had an effect on the man about to kill him, too. The muscular arm that had been pressing against his throat like an iron bar slipped a little.

Stonewall grabbed the bare flesh, hauled down on it as hard as he could, and ducked his head. He sunk his teeth into the man's arm and at the same time drove forward in a dive that sent him and his attacker crashing to the ground. The impact jolted him loose from the man who had grabbed him.

Stonewall struck out blindly with an elbow and felt it crack into something, hopefully the man's jaw. He rolled desperately to one side in an attempt to put some distance between himself and the would-be killer.

The sun wasn't above the horizon yet, but the eastern sky was lighter, giving off enough grayish light for Stonewall to see his enemy as he came up on one knee.

Just as he had suspected, the man was an Apache. He

wore only a breechcloth and high-topped moccasins. A strip of cloth was tied around his head to hold back his thick black hair. He clutched a knife in his right hand and the blade darted forward as he lunged at Stonewall.

Making a grab for the Apache's wrist, Stonewall caught it just in time to twist his arm aside and deflect the knife. He went over backward, pulling the Indian with him. He planted a foot in the man's belly and used his leg to throw him up and over.

Stonewall figured Roy Corbett had fired that shot, but he didn't know where the store clerk was. The Apache might be alone, or he might be part of a group that would fall on the two white men and kill them . . . if they were lucky.

If they were unlucky, the Apaches would capture them and make their dying slow and hideously agonizing. Stonewall fought to bring his fear under control.

As the warrior rolled over and sprang to his feet, Stonewall slapped at his holster, hoping the gun was still there. It was. He drew the revolver. A knife was no match for Colonel Colt's equalizer.

A rifle cracked from the rocks above them. The bullet whined past Stonewall's ear. He threw himself to the side, angled the gun up, and triggered a couple return shots.

The muzzle flashes lit up the little clearing at the base of the bluff where they had camped. Stonewall finally spotted Corbett. His friend was on the other side of the clearing, rolling around and wrestling with another Apache.

The warrior was about to plunge a knife into Corbett's throat.

The wanna-be lawyer finally found the gun he had

dropped when the Apache tackled him, jammed it into the man's side, and pulled the trigger until the cylinder was empty. The booming reports rolled across the rugged landscape.

Stonewall had two threats facing him, the Indian with the knife and the one with the rifle above him in the rocks. Another shot smacked into the ground a couple feet to his right, making him scramble to his left.

That brought him too close to the one with the knife, who lunged at him again. Stonewall felt the blade's fiery bite as it cut across the top of his left shoulder.

As his heart hammered wildly, he swung the Colt, clubbing it across the Apache's face. He felt bone crunch under steel. The warrior fell away from him.

Gravel slid above him. Stonewall looked up and spotted a moving shadow. The third and evidently last Apache was trying to get away. The odds weren't in his favor anymore and so he no longer wanted any part of the fight.

Stonewall fired after the fleeing man, then cursed as the Apache never slowed down. He scrambled over the top of the bluff and vanished in a shower of dirt and gravel. Stonewall knew they would never catch him.

He also knew there was a good chance a larger band was somewhere nearby. More than likely, the three who had attacked were scouts. The one who had gotten away would rush back to his companions and tell them that two white men were camping in the mountains and had killed or wounded two of their people.

That thought reminded Stonewall there was a more immediate threat. He figured the Indian Corbett had shot to pieces was dead, but the other one might not be. The

Apache sprawled on the ground, unmoving, but that could be a trick.

Stonewall looked around until he found the knife lying in the dirt next to the man. He kicked it out of reach, then pointed his gun at the motionless shape and hooked the toe of his boot under the man's shoulder.

When Stonewall rolled him over, the Apache's head lolled limply on his neck. He sure looked dead.

"Roy," Stonewall said with some urgency in his voice as he backed away from the man. "Roy, are you all right?"

Corbett had shoved the man he'd shot aside and crawled out from under him. He was breathing hard. "Yeah, I . . . I think so. How about you?"

Stonewall's shoulder stung where the knife had cut him, but he ignored the pain. "Just a scratch. I'll be fine. We've got to get out of here."

"Why? They're . . . they're both dead, aren't they?"

"Yeah, but the one who was takin' potshots at us from the rocks up there isn't. Chances are he's runnin' back to the rest of his bunch right now, and he'll tell them where to find us."

"You think there are more of them?"

"I'd bet a hat on it," Stonewall said grimly. "That's why we can't stay here. If they're gonna kill us, I want them to at least have to hunt for us first."

Corbett swallowed, and it was audible in the pre-dawn gloom. "You think they're going to kill us?"

"Maybe that's not why they broke off the reservation in the first place, but they sure made a grab for it in a hurry once they got the chance. And since we did for two of them . . ."

He didn't have to say anything else.

Corbett said, "Let's get the horses saddled."

While they were getting ready to break camp, the sky grew brighter still. Stonewall glanced at the man he had clubbed with the gun. There was enough light now for him to see the deep depression in the Apache's temple. The desperate blow had shattered the man's skull.

It wasn't the first man he had killed. He had been part of several running fights with rustlers while the Howell family was bringing their herd from New Mexico Territory to Arizona, and he was pretty sure he had shot a couple wide-loopers out of their saddles.

But he didn't have the lives of many men on his conscience, and this was the first one he had taken close up, where he could see the dead man's face. It wasn't a pretty feeling, even though the Apache had been trying hard to kill him.

He did his best to shove that out of his mind and reached for his Winchester, which was still lying on the ground where he had dropped it when the Indian jumped him.

A sharp voice made him stop short.

"Just leave it layin' right there, Stonewall," the man ordered, "and straighten back up real slow like."

Stonewall's heart thudded. He knew that voice.

The sound of gunfire could travel a long way, especially at night, but as Dallin listened to the shots he could tell they weren't far off. Half a mile, maybe.

The shooting made Jessie clutch at him again. "What is that?"

Dallin had heard a revolver go off—maybe more than one—and the cracking of a rifle, as well. That meant a skirmish of some sort. Nobody fired that many shots if they were just hunting. Besides, it was still too dark for that, although the gray in the eastern sky was a harbinger of dawn.

"Somebody's got a fight on their hands. Could be Indians, I suppose. I ain't heard of any bronco Apaches bein' on the warpath lately, but I been sort of otherwise occupied with my own problems."

"You mean Apaches fighting with each other?"

"Naw, more likely they jumped somebody who was camped hereabouts . . ." Dallin's voice trailed off as the implications of what he was saying soaked into him. It could just as easily been him and Jessie the Apaches jumped, if that was actually what happened. He was putting her life in danger by having her in the rugged mountains.

And not just her life, either, but the unborn one inside her.

In his desperation, he had run risks that seemed completely unacceptable to him. No matter what happened to him, he had to go back to Tombstone and take Jessie with him.

Assuming they survived that long.

"You mean they attacked some whites?" Jessie asked, breaking into his thoughts.

"Yeah, that could be what happened—"

"Then my father and the men who came with him could be in danger."

That idea hadn't occurred to Dallin until she said it, but he knew she was right. It was certainly possible Little Ed and his punchers had been mixed up in that fracas. In fact, that was the most likely explanation.

"Sounds like the shootin's stopped. I'm sure everybody's all right—"

"You can't be sure about that. You can't be sure at all." Her voice rose a little as a note of hysteria edged into it. "My father could be lying out there dead right now for all we know."

"If Little Ed followed us into the mountains, he would've brought a good-sized bunch with him. He's bound to be fine—"

"We have to go see."

"What?" Dallin stared at her in the gray light. "You want us to go traipsin' over to where all that shootin' was on the off chance that your pa was mixed up in it?"

"We have to," Jessie insisted. She drew in a deep breath. "If it's him, I'll do what you want, Dallin. I'll tell him the truth. But I have to make sure he's not hurt."

Dallin narrowed his eyes in thought. What she proposed sounded like a workable bargain, one that might even clear his name. But there were considerable risks, too, not the least of which was that a band of renegade Apaches might be roaming around the area. That could be very bad news indeed.

For that matter, if he came face to face with Little Ed McCabe, the rancher might kill him before Jessie had time to intervene and tell the truth. Or she might double-cross him and stick to her story, although he considered that unlikely.

"You give me your solemn word you'll tell your pa the truth?"

"My solemn word," she said.

He had to take the chance. It might be the best one he'd ever have. "All right, let's go. I'll get the horse saddled up."

A few minutes later, they were riding slowly in the direction of the gunfire. Dallin had the gun in his right hand as he held the reins with his left. Jessie rode in front of him, swaying against him as she rocked back and forth from the motion of the horse.

That wasn't a bad feeling, Dallin thought then immediately tried to put it out of his mind. The girl had accused him of just about the most awful thing she could have, and she had done it knowing that the charge wasn't true.

Not only that, but she also had another man's child growing inside her. A man would have to be plumb loco to start having tender feelings toward a gal in that situation.

It also didn't take into account the fact that they might run smack-dab into a war party of bloodthirsty Apaches at any moment. Or a bunch of angry cowboys bent on stringing him up.

When he thought they had to be getting close to where the shooting had taken place, Dallin reined in and whispered to Jessie, "Slide down. You'll have to hang on to the horse while I go ahead on foot."

"I want to come with you," she whispered back.

"Not until we know what we're dealin' with. Can I trust you to stay here and not try to run off?"

"I'll stay here," she promised. "But be careful, Dallin."

"That's what I'm plannin'." He didn't like leaving her unarmed and defenseless. He looked at her in the growing light. She was scared and exhausted. Her clothes were rumpled from sleeping on the crude pine needle bed, and her hair was a tangled mess.

He thought she sure was pretty.

Again, he had to force his mind back to the problem at hand. He gave her a nod, then started working his way through the rocks that littered the mountainside.

He stopped every few moments to listen, and after he'd done that a couple times he heard voices not far off. Two men were talking.

With every bit of stealth he could muster, Dallin drew closer. He came to the edge of a bluff and looked down. He saw that the two men had camped there, but were saddled up and ready to break camp.

Two dark, motionless shapes on the ground told the grim story of what had happened. A pair of Apaches had jumped the men and died for their trouble.

The two white men were moving their camp in case any more renegades were around.

It came as no surprise to Dallin that he recognized both men, although they weren't who he had expected. One was a fella who worked in the general store in town. Dallin couldn't remember his name, but he had seen the man in the store plenty of times.

The other hombre was his old pard, Deputy Stonewall Jackson Howell . . . and he was about to pick up a rifle lying nearby on the ground.

Dallin had seen indisputable proof that Apaches were roaming around in the Santa Catalinas, and that meant

Jessie was in more danger than ever before. He needed help to get her back to safety, and it was right in front of him . . . if he could convince Stonewall to listen to him.

He didn't really think about what he was doing. As Stonewall reached for the rifle, Dallin pointed the Colt down at the deputy even though he had no intention of using it as anything except a bluff. "Just leave it layin' right there, Stonewall, and straighten back up real slow like."

Chapter 23

Arabella told herself she was being unreasonable; she had no claim on Steve Drake's affections. He was free to indulge his appetites and do whatever he wanted with whomever he wanted.

But a brazen hussy like Copper Farris . . . ?

Arabella had thought better of her old friend and mentor than that.

She prided herself on her ability to put her emotions aside and think clearly and levelheadedly when she sat down at a poker table, and that was exactly what she did that night as the tournament got underway again. At least, it was what she attempted to do.

She wasn't sure she was completely successful. She noticed that she was playing a bit more recklessly and ruthlessly than usual, pushing her raises a little higher, bluffing a little longer, generally putting as much pressure as possible on the other players at her table.

It seemed to be working, too. As the pace of the game accelerated, the size of the pots grew. One by one, the players at Arabella's table were forced into making larger bets than they might have otherwise, and when luck deserted them, they didn't have the reserves to recover. They had to drop out.

Finally, she and the mild-mannered Donald Lockard were the only ones remaining in the game. Jim Snyder and J.D. Burnett stayed at the table to watch after they folded for the last time, while Wade Cunningham had shoved back his chair, bid them all good luck and good night, and headed for the bar.

Arabella had the deal. As she shuffled, she glanced over at the table where Drake was still playing. Copper was no longer in the game, she noticed. She had been concentrating on her own cards so much she was unaware of when the redhead had dropped out of the tournament.

But in all honesty, Arabella had to admit a part of her was glad to see that Copper no longer had a chance of winning. The redhead's lack of success came as no surprise; She had never been that good.

The other tables were down to two or three players, as well. The night had been brutal.

And it had taken most of the night, Arabella realized. She didn't know what time it was, but a glance out the front windows of the Top-Notch revealed the gray light of approaching dawn. They had been playing all night, and she hadn't even noticed the passage of time.

One more night might finish off the tournament, including the final showdown match with Morris Upton.

Win or lose, she was ready for it to be over. The excitement she had felt going into the big game was gone. She was left with a sour taste in her mouth.

"Five card draw," she announced as she began dealing the hand.

Luck didn't smile on her. When she checked her cards she had a four, a five, a nine, a ten, and a jack. Her best possible hand was a straight. The odds of filling it didn't support a big bet. If Lockard opened for very much, she thought, she would fold quickly.

But Lockard's bet was small, so Arabella stayed in. She looked at her cards again. Her best play was to throw away the four and five and try to fill the higher straight.

After Lockard took two cards, a sudden impulse made her do something completely out of character. She threw in the nine, ten, and jack. Her mouth quirked a little as she defied the odds. She could always fold after the draw.

Then she dealt herself a two, a three, and a six.

There was her straight. Only six high, but it would be enough to beat quite a few hands.

Lockard didn't appear to be all that confident in his hand. He made another small bet.

Of course, there was always the chance that he was trying to sucker her. Arabella saw the bet and raised it, but not by much. He returned the favor.

Small bets could add up fairly quickly. As the pot grew, Arabella thought he might fold, but he continued raising stubbornly. She asked herself how confident she was that he was trying to bluff her. She discovered that she wasn't confident at all and considered dropping out herself.

But if she did, she would suffer a significant loss. Not enough to wipe her out; she still had enough money that she would be able to continue. But it would put her in a precarious position where she couldn't afford to lose another hand.

She had never been a reckless player, but something drove her on. Maybe it was the fact that Drake was a dozen feet away from her and she felt his eyes on her from time to time, watching her.

He had taught her to be cautious . . . and look where that had gotten her.

She saw Lockard's bet and raised it.

He thought about it for a long moment. She couldn't read anything in his bland, expressionless face.

"I think I'm all in," he finally said as he pushed the last of his money into the center of the table. "You can cover that, can't you, Lady Arabella?"

"I can. And I call."

He smiled before he laid down his hand, and for a second she thought he had succeeded in tricking her. His cards were good, too. He placed them on the table and said, "Three aces."

Arabella put her cards down one at a time. Her unruffled demeanor and deliberate movements told him all he needed to know by the third card.

He sighed and leaned back in his chair. "It's yours, milady. Well played."

Cheers went up from the spectators as they realized that Arabella had emerged as the first table winner. She smiled and gathered in her winnings.

All she had to do was wait and see who would join her in the bigger game. It wouldn't be Copper Farris, but she might still see Drake across the table from her.

She didn't know whether to dread the possibility . . . or look forward to it.

Oscar Grayson, Jed Muller, and Max Rourke had all been forced out of the tournament, which didn't come as a real surprise to any of the three men despite Muller's bravado and Rourke's arrogant confidence. They all knew they weren't at the same level as many of the other players.

Grayson and Muller were at the bar, watching the games. After Lady Arabella Winthrop won the deciding hand at her table, Grayson nudged his companion in the side and said quietly, "Let's get out of here."

Muller put his empty beer mug on the bar and nodded.

Grayson caught the eye of Rourke, who was alone at a table on the other side of the big room, and angled his head toward the entrance. Rourke's lean, hatchet-like face remained as expressionless as a stone, as usual. Grayson didn't know if the man would take the hint or not.

He hoped that Rourke would. The tournament's first round was on the verge of being over. It might not take many more hands to crown winners at the other three tables. If that turned out to be the case, it was possible the big showdown could occur in less than twenty-four hours.

They needed to be ready to strike as soon as the champion of the tournament was facing Morris Upton across the table with a fortune between them.

As he and Muller left the Top-Notch, Grayson thought about all that money—piles of greenbacks and stacks of double eagles that he would sweep off the table and into a canvas bag while Rourke was dealing with Upton's guards.

What Rourke didn't know was that Grayson wasn't going to wait for him. He was going to be out the back door and gone before Rourke had a chance to catch up. Just to make sure that double cross was successful, Muller would have only two horses waiting in the alley— one for Grayson and one for himself.

Max Rourke would be staying behind to take the blame. Grayson was counting on Upton or one of his men to kill Rourke for his part in the robbery. If Rourke got away, he would come looking for the two men who had betrayed him. Grayson sure as hell didn't want that.

No man with any sense would want a loco killer like Max Rourke on his trail, so it was a big chance to take.

It would be worth the risk if the gamble paid off. And then later, when they were safely south of the border, Muller wouldn't be expecting a bullet in the back of the head . . .

"What're you grinnin' about?" Muller asked, breaking into Grayson's murderous chain of thought.

"Oh, just thinking about what I'm going to do with my share of the money."

That was true enough. Muller didn't have to know that Grayson intended for his share to be . . . all of it.

Rourke came up behind them as they ambled along the boardwalk. Grayson didn't even know the man was there until he said, "All right. What was it you wanted?"

Grayson tried not to jump in surprise. He didn't want the other two to see how much Rourke had spooked him. He turned around. "We need to sit down and figure out the rest of the details. The big finish could come tonight."

"All right," Rourke said. "My room at the hotel."

Neither thought about arguing. You didn't argue with Max Rourke, not if you wanted to stay alive.

It was almost dawn as they walked into the hotel. The lobby was empty, but a few people were in the dining room getting some early morning coffee.

Grayson spotted Sheriff John Slaughter sitting at a table by himself, thumbing through a copy of the *Tombstone Epitaph*. He didn't even glance in their direction, which Grayson thought was a good thing.

The plan was risky enough without attracting the attention of Cochise County's tough-as-nails sheriff.

They went up to Rourke's room and spent the next half hour going over every detail they could think of, from the locations where Muller would place the dynamite to the place where he would be waiting with the horses when Grayson and Rourke fled out the back of the Top-Notch. The more they talked about it, the more Grayson was convinced that it would work.

Muller sat in the room's lone chair and Grayson was leaning against a table. Rourke had taken off his coat and loosened his string tie and collar. He sat on the end of the bed and slipped the silver flask from his pocket and took a nip from it.

Muller frowned and gestured vaguely toward the flask. "Are you sure that's a good idea?"

Rourke's already stony face seemed to grow even harder at the question. "You let me worry about my personal business."

"Yeah, but that stuff ain't like whiskey," Muller persisted, ignoring the warning glare Grayson directed toward him. "It can really muddle your brain."

Rourke capped the flask and put it back in his pocket. "It just so happens this is the only thing that keeps my brain from being muddled all the time from the pain in my head."

"I didn't know about that, Max," Grayson said. "If you've got some sort of condition—"

"Never you mind what I've got," Rourke snapped. "All you have to worry about is getting the money—" He stopped short as his head came up in a listening attitude. He rose quickly to his feet, and Grayson was reminded of a snake uncoiling.

Rourke motioned for his two startled fellow plotters to be quiet, then he stepped over to the door, moving with speed and absolute silence. He grasped the knob and jerked the door open.

Copper Farris practically fell into the room. Rourke wrapped his left arm around her waist and spun her away from the door. At the same time, his right hand clamped over her mouth so she couldn't cry out.

Grayson and Muller both sprang up. Muller said, "Copper!"

Grayson's thoughts whirled in dismay. Clearly, the buxom redhead had been listening at the door while they outlined their entire plan. She might demand to be cut in for a share or she would reveal what she had discovered.

That might be workable, he realized. She might be interested in going to Mexico with him. She had never paid any attention to him other than an occasional sneer, but Grayson was well aware of how much more attractive a man became in a woman's eyes when he had plenty of money.

She struggled in Rourke's grip. Although she was big

enough to overpower some men, she had no chance against Rourke's wiry, cable-like muscles.

"What are we going to do about this?" Grayson asked.

"You two don't have to do anything," Rourke said. "I'll take care of it."

Copper's green eyes widened in terror, and she made muffled sounds against Rourke's palm.

Grayson knew why she was scared. Rourke's method of dealing with problems was direct and final. He and Muller exchanged a glance; the big man obviously knew what Rourke meant, too.

"I'm not sure that's necessary—"

"I wasn't asking you," Rourke said. "I'm telling you. Both of you get out, now. Go down the back stairs and out that way. You were never here."

"Somebody might have seen us come in together."

"It doesn't matter. Not for what I've got in mind."

Grayson wasn't going to ask what that was. He didn't want to know. He looked at Muller again, searching for any hint that Muller thought they should go against Rourke.

Muller looked away and said gruffly, "Come on, Oscar, let's go."

Well, that pretty much settled it, thought Grayson. He couldn't take on Rourke by himself. Hell, there was a good chance the man could kill both of them without breaking much of a sweat, even in the lingering heat.

It was a shame about Copper. A real, damned shame.

"We'll get together again late this afternoon," Grayson said as he started toward the door.

Copper made pleading sounds. Grayson wished he couldn't hear them. He tried to put them out of his mind.

As he and Muller left the room, Muller said, "You know what he's going to—"

"There's no need to talk about it," Grayson cut in. "Just think about the money, Jed."

Muller sighed. "Yeah, I guess you're right. That sure was a bad break for us, though."

And a much worse one for Copper Farris, Grayson thought.

Chapter 24

Despite the weariness that gripped Arabella after beating Donald Lockard to claim the championship of her table, she didn't leave right away. She remained downstairs in the Top-Notch to keep track of the other games, rather than going up to her room to get some sleep.

She sensed that those games would be over soon. The smell of desperation hung in the air. The sooner she knew who she would be facing in the next round, the better.

The table where Drake sat was down to two players. The Virginian was one of them. Arabella wasn't surprised that he was still in the game. Even though she was angry and disappointed in him, she didn't doubt for a second that he was a highly skilled player.

Drake won the hand. His opponent sighed, pulled a silk handkerchief from his breast pocket, and mopped beads of sweat off his face. It was hot in the room, of course; it was still stifling hot everywhere in Tombstone.

But that was the sweat of fear, Arabella thought. The man must have played a good game to reach that point, but he was overmatched and beginning to realize it. Still, the cards took strange turns sometimes. If a man was really a gambler, something inside him compelled him to see how they were going to fall.

"Are you still in?" Steve Drake asked quietly.

"I'm still in." The man shoved his ante to the center of the table.

It didn't take long. A few bets, more money in the pot, then the two men laid down their cards and Steve Drake raked in the last of his opponent's stake.

The man sat back in his chair and shook his head. He seemed resigned to his fate, rather than upset about it. "That was a good game, Mr. Drake. I appreciate being part of it."

"You were a worthy adversary, my friend. You'll allow me to buy you a drink?"

The man let out a small chuckle. "I have no choice in the matter."

Drake smiled and pushed a double eagle back across the table. His vanquished opponent picked up the coin, got to his feet, and headed for the bar.

Drake began stacking his winnings into neat piles.

Arabella wondered if she ought to go over and congratulate him on his victory as she certainly would have done if the incident with Copper hadn't occurred.

She decided not to.

Maybe that was petty of her, she told herself, but she didn't care. Besides, one of the other games looked like it was about to come to a conclusion, too.

Beulah Tillery had her competition on the run. Two men were still at her table, but they were both down to the last of their stakes. When she drew to a royal flush—and filled it—that was the end for them.

One of the men groaned, threw his hands in the air, and said disgustedly, "I feel like I've just lost everything to my grandmother!"

Beulah grinned. "Count yourself lucky that I left you the shirt on your back, friend." She looked around, saw Arabella watching her, and closed one eye in a wink, as if to say that as women, they had to stick together.

Arabella returned the smile. She could understand the sentiment, but when it came time to play cards, she would clean out Beulah Tillery just as fast as she would anybody else.

The game at the fourth and final table might take longer to finish, Arabella realized as she watched it for a few moments. The three men still playing all wore stubborn, determined looks, as if they would stay at it all day if they had to.

Arabella's weariness was catching up to her. She didn't care enough to stay and watch the rest of the game and moved toward the stairs.

Steve Drake wasn't going to take her to breakfast this morning. All she wanted was some sleep.

That didn't mean she was going to get it without being annoyed first. She had almost reached the door of her room when she heard rapid footsteps in the corridor behind her. A glance over her shoulder revealed Morris Upton coming toward her.

"Is that last game still going on downstairs?" she asked him.

"Yeah, it is. Those three may wrestle over it for a good while yet."

"Then shouldn't you be down there making sure everything is done properly?"

That was pretty blunt, she thought, but she didn't really care if she hurt his feelings.

Upton waved a hand as if to dismiss her suggestion. "My men can handle things without any problem. I can't believe how difficult it's been to find the time since you've been here for the two of us to have a visit."

"Well, we've both been busy—"

"I heard about what happened at the American Hotel, you know. Steve Drake's a fool."

Arabella realized that even now, her first impulse was to defend Drake from the buffoon's judgmental words. Then she caught herself. "I really don't wish to discuss the matter, Morris," she said coolly as she reached into her tiny handbag and slipped out the key to her room. "I'm very tired, and I just want to get some rest."

"Of course," Upton said. "Perhaps when you come back down, we can go get something to eat . . ."

That wasn't going to happen, but for now she just gave him a slight, non-committal smile then slid the key into the lock. She turned it, opened the door, and stepped into the room.

The startled cry that she couldn't keep from coming to her lips made Upton stop short as he started to turn away in disappointment. He swung around and took a quick step into the room after her. "Arabella, what—"

The sight of the nude, redheaded corpse sprawled

across the bed on blood-soaked sheets shocked him into stunned silence.

Copper Farris was dead as she could ever be.

Slaughter was having breakfast in the dining room of the American Hotel when Mose Tadrack hurried into the room and went over to his table. "There's trouble, Sheriff."

Slaughter was already setting aside his napkin. "I knew that as soon as I got a look at your face, Mose. What is it now?"

"Another of those gamblers has been killed."

Slaughter was on his feet. "Which one?"

"The woman—"

"Lady Arabella Winthrop?" Slaughter broke in.

"No, sir, one of the others. The redheaded lady. The one they call Copper. But Lady Arabella . . . well, the body was found in her room at the Top-Notch."

Slaughter's eyebrows rose in surprise as he muttered, "Good Lord." His thoughts went back to the day before, when he had come in at the end of what apparently had been a battle royale between the two women. They had appeared to be eager to kill each other then.

Maybe Lady Arabella had finished the job, as difficult as that was for him to believe after having talked to the woman. She just didn't seem the sort to commit murder.

People sometimes did things in the heat of anger, though, that no one would ever dream they would do.

Slaughter put on his hat. "All right, Mose, let's go see about this."

He and Tadrack were on their way out of the room

when a man at one of the other tables stood up and blocked their way. Slaughter frowned in annoyance until he recognized the man as the desk clerk who had been working in the hotel lobby the day before. The clerk had been having breakfast, too, probably before starting his shift at the desk.

"What is it, Alfred?" Slaughter asked.

"I heard what Deputy Tadrack said about that poor woman being killed. I was wondering . . . how was it done?"

"That's a mighty strange thing to be asking," Tadrack said with a frown.

"Please, I have a reason," the clerk said.

Slaughter looked at Tadrack. "How about it, Mose? What happened? Did you see the body?"

Tadrack sighed and nodded. "Yes, sir, I did. I happened to be walking past the Top-Notch when I heard all the yelling. I went inside and settled things down as much as I could. The place sort of emptied out after that. I tried to make folks stay where they were, but there were too many of 'em."

"Yes, yes," Slaughter said as he tried to curb his impatience. "What about the body?"

"The lady's throat was cut, pretty much from one ear to the other. There was more blood than I reckon I've ever seen before."

"Another gambler murdered with a knife," Slaughter mused.

The hotel clerk said, "That's exactly why I asked about it, Sheriff. You see, during that incident yesterday . . .

you know, the one where the ladies had their, ah, altercation . . ."

"Yes, I know. Go on."

The clerk took a deep breath. "Well, when they were falling down the stairs, Lady Winthrop's clothing was in great disarray, and while it certainly wasn't intentional on my part, there was a moment when I saw . . ."

"When you looked up the lady's dress, yes, I understand," Slaughter said. "No one's blaming you for that, son. But if you saw something that might have to do with this killing, you'd better spit it out."

"That's what I was getting at, Sheriff. Lady Winthrop had a knife strapped to one of her lower limbs. I saw it for only a second, of course, but I got a clear look at it. It was in a sheath, you understand, but it appeared to be one of those knives with a very narrow blade. A stiletto, I think they call it."

"You're sure about that?"

"Yes, sir. I'm certain, Sheriff."

That was interesting, thought Slaughter. Angelo Castro had been stabbed with a narrow-bladed knife, and at the time he was ahead in the game at the table where Lady Arabella was playing.

Copper Farris was dead, too, with her throat cut, and she and Lady Arabella had a definite grudge between them. It wasn't proof by any means, but it was enough to make a man think.

"Thanks, Alfred. Later, I may have to call on you to repeat what you just told me."

The man nodded. "Of course, Sheriff. Anything I can do to help."

Slaughter and Tadrack hurried out of the hotel and headed straight to the Top-Notch. They heard the commotion before they got there.

A large crowd had gathered on the boardwalk in front of the saloon. People who had been in the place when the body was found had wanted out, but everybody else in town, it seemed, wanted to know what was going on. Some of them were probably even hoping to catch a glimpse of the dead woman.

Slaughter wasn't going to allow that. He raised his voice and demanded to be let through, and the crowd scattered like a flock of chickens . . . for the moment, anyway.

The two lawmen went inside. Morris Upton stood near the bar with a grim expression on his face. Lady Arabella, looking pale and shaken, sat at a table by herself. Steve Drake stood not far away. He appeared to want to go to her and comfort her, but he held back, probably because of the incident the day before.

A number of the other gamblers were sitting at tables as well, but they weren't playing cards. The low buzz of conversation among them came to an abrupt halt as Slaughter strode into the room.

He walked over to Upton. He didn't waste time with small talk. "Is the body still upstairs?"

"Of course," Upton replied. "I didn't allow anybody to move it or even touch it. In fact, a couple of my men are up there right now guarding the door."

Slaughter was a little surprised that Upton had taken that precaution. He nodded curtly. "That was a good idea. Who found Miss Farris?"

Upton leaned his head toward Lady Arabella. "She went in the room first, but I was right there a step behind her." He made it sound like he had been going into Lady Arabella's room with her.

Somehow, Slaughter doubted that. But he put that aside for the moment. "I'd better go have a look."

"Of course. I'll come with you."

"That's not necessary. You can stay down here. Just don't go anywhere."

"I promise you, Sheriff, I won't," Upton said coldly. "I don't like this any more than you do."

Slaughter could believe that. One brutal murder hadn't been enough to put a stop to Upton's big poker tournament, but two might be.

With Tadrack behind him, Slaughter climbed the stairs. He saw Upton's bouncers standing in front of a door and knew that was where the corpse was. The two men stepped aside to let him in.

Slaughter stopped just inside the door. From where he stood, he could see how Copper Farris was laid out across the bed in the obscene sprawl of death. He saw the hideous grin of the gaping wound in her throat. What looked like all the blood in her body had soaked the bedding around her.

Slaughter's face was bleak as he moved closer. He bent and studied the wound, pointed, and said to Tadrack, "Look how clean that cut is."

"Yeah," the deputy agreed. "Sheriff, I know I gave up the booze . . . but looking at something like this sure makes me feel like I could use a drink."

"Don't think about that, Mose. Concentrate on helping me find out who's responsible for this crime."

"Don't worry. I won't slip. It was too hard getting off the stuff the first time. You reckon somebody used a thin-bladed knife to cut her throat? Like a stiletto?"

Slaughter straightened from the corpse. "I think it's time I had a talk with Lady Arabella."

Chapter 25

When Slaughter and Tadrack got downstairs, the sheriff told his deputy, "You can go and fetch the undertaker now, Mose," then he walked over to Arabella and gave her a polite but rather curt nod. "I'm sure you understand that I have to ask you some questions, Lady Arabella. I'd prefer to do it somewhere privately, though."

"So would I," she said as she got to her feet. "Should we go to your office, Sheriff?"

"That would be fine with me."

She smiled faintly. "Should I consider myself under arrest?"

"Not just yet." But he couldn't rule out what might happen in the future.

Drake stepped forward. "Hold on a minute. Bella, if you'd like for me to come with you—"

"What in the world makes you think I would want that, Steve?"

His lips tightened. "Look, I know you're angry with me, but I just want to help you."

"I'll be fine," she told him. "Shall we go, Sheriff?"

Slaughter held out a hand for her to go first. As they passed Morris Upton, the saloonkeeper said, "If you need a lawyer, Arabella, I have a good one."

"I won't need one," she said as she shook her head. "I haven't done anything wrong."

Slaughter found himself hoping she would be able to prove that.

The crowd parted again to let them through. The hum of excited gossip filled the hot morning air. Lady Arabella ignored it and kept her head high. Slaughter had to admire the way she hung on to her dignity.

Some of the townspeople trailed them the several blocks to the courthouse, gossiping avidly. Slaughter was glad to get inside the sheriff's office and close the door so he wouldn't have to hear them and look at them anymore.

Under some circumstances, he thought, humans had altogether too much in common with vultures.

The outer office was empty at the moment. Jeff Milton, Lorenzo Paco, and several other deputies had set off on the trail of Dallin Williams after Paco located the tracks the day before. It left Slaughter a little short-handed, but he figured he would be able to make do.

He hadn't counted on another murder, especially not such a grisly one.

He escorted Lady Arabella into his private office but left the door open to let in any air that happened to stir a little, knowing it was unlikely.

When they were seated on opposite sides of the desk, he said, "I'm sorry to have to bring you here like this, ma'am, but since you discovered the body I don't have any choice."

"I understand, Sheriff. I want you to find out who killed Copper just as much as you do."

"Is that so?"

"Why wouldn't it be? Just because I had a disagreement with her, that doesn't mean I'm happy that she's dead."

"From what I saw in the hotel, it looked like the two of you were trying to kill each other."

Lady Arabella's eyes narrowed suspiciously. "I was just trying to defend myself from her attack. Do you think I killed her, Sheriff?"

"When somebody turns up dead, a lawman usually starts by looking at whoever they've had trouble with recently."

"Well, you can put that out of your mind. I couldn't have killed Copper Farris. I was downstairs in the Top-Notch the entire time. Copper was still playing when the games started up again last night, so she was still alive then and I didn't go upstairs after that."

"You can prove that?" Slaughter asked.

"You can ask the other players in the game. They'll vouch for my whereabouts. And I'm sure there were dozens of other people who saw me playing after Copper left."

"Did you go upstairs and find her right after the game at your table was over?"

Lady Arabella hesitated before she answered. It wasn't much of a pause, but Slaughter caught it.

"As a matter of fact, I didn't. I stayed for a while to watch the other games."

"Were you with anybody the whole time?"

"Actually, no. I spoke to several people—you know,

the ones who came up to congratulate me on winning the game at my table—but I don't suppose there's anyone who could swear to my whereabouts for the entire time."

Slaughter cocked his head slightly to the side. "It wouldn't have taken long to go upstairs and then come back down again. As crowded as the saloon was, it's possible you could have done that without anybody noticing that you were gone."

Lady Arabella folded her hands in her lap. Her face was still calm and composed, but her eyes revealed the strain she was feeling. "Sheriff, this whole idea is ludicrous. I didn't kill Copper. I had no reason to."

"You could've been holding a grudge because of that fight . . . or because she stole that fella Drake away from you."

Lady Arabella drew in a breath.

She was having to work harder to keep herself under control, Slaughter thought.

"Steve Drake was hardly mine, so she couldn't very well steal him from me. He and I are old friends, that's all."

"Sure," Slaughter said, but it was clear from his voice that he didn't believe it. He changed tacks abruptly. "Do you carry a weapon, Lady Arabella?"

"You mean a gun?"

"Or a knife," Slaughter said.

A couple heartbeats went by then she said, "You may not realize it, Sheriff Slaughter, but sometimes being a gambler is a rather dangerous profession." She pulled back the sleeve of her gown to reveal a derringer in a spring holster. "It's only prudent to be armed. But Copper wasn't shot, was she? I got a good enough look at her body to know that."

"How about a knife?" Slaughter asked quietly. "Do you carry a knife?"

Lady Arabella didn't answer.

After the silence stretched out for a few seconds, Slaughter went on. "I have it on good authority that you carry a stiletto, Lady Arabella. Discretion and decorum prevent me from mentioning where you carry it—"

"Would you like for me to pull up my dress and show you, Sheriff?" she said coldly. "Or would you prefer to search me?"

"I don't reckon that'll be necessary. We both know you've got it. There have been two killings committed with a weapon like that, so you can't blame me for wondering about it."

"Wait just a moment," Lady Arabella said. "Are you accusing me of Angelo Castro's murder, too?"

"He was winning at your table when he was killed."

Lady Arabella shook her head. "The game was very young at that point. I assure you, Sheriff, I wasn't worried about losing to Angelo Castro."

"Can you tell me where you were when he was killed?"

"I don't know exactly when he was killed. And that was several days ago. I can't account for every second of my time." She leaned forward in her chair. "But I didn't kill him. I didn't kill Copper Farris, either. I give you my word. I don't know what else I can do."

"What about Steve Drake? Does he carry a knife?"

"Now you suspect Steve of the murders?" Lady Arabella laughed, but there was no humor in the sound. "Steve had no reason to kill either Angelo or Copper."

"He could have been upset with Miss Farris for causing trouble between you and him."

"It was Steve's own decision to become involved with her. He wouldn't have blamed her for what happened. He's not that sort of man."

"Maybe," Slaughter said. "Castro was robbed—"

"Steve had a good stake. He still does. He had no need to steal from Angelo Castro."

"You're giving me plenty of denials, but no proof of anything."

"I have no proof to give you other than my word. Although . . ." She smiled. "If you'll turn your head for a moment, I can let you see that knife you were so insistent that I have in my possession."

"All right." Slaughter turned and looked at the wall.

The English woman's clothes rustled, and then she said, "Here, have a look."

She had placed the narrow-bladed knife on Slaughter's desk. He picked it up and studied it. The blade was shiny and clean.

"As you can see, there's no blood on it."

"You could've wiped that off," Slaughter said. "No nicks on the blade, either. The cut in Miss Farris's throat was so deep the knife might've scraped on her spine."

Lady Arabella paled slightly. Slaughter told himself that maybe he shouldn't have been quite so blunt.

"There you are," she said. "Another indication that I didn't kill her."

"I said the blade might've scraped on bone. I don't know that it did."

"Sheriff, we've been through everything. Are you going to arrest me?"

Slaughter considered for a moment, then shook his

head. "There's not enough evidence for that. But don't plan on leaving town any time soon."

"I'm not going to. The tournament isn't over, and I'm still in the game. That is, if Mr. Upton continues with it."

Slaughter grunted. "When it comes to making money, Morris Upton isn't going to let a little thing like a murdered woman with a slashed throat stop him."

By the middle of the day, a victor at the fourth and final table had emerged. The tournament was down to four players. Lady Arabella Winthrop, Beulah Tillery, Steve Drake, and Alex Connelly.

Their game would commence at seven o'clock that evening, Morris Upton announced, and as soon as it was over, he would play the winner.

Oscar Grayson's eyes felt gritty from lack of sleep, but he couldn't turn in yet. He had to go over the final details of the plan with Jed Muller and Max Rourke.

They met in Rourke's hotel room as they had before, although Grayson posted Muller inside at the door as a guard to make sure no one tried to eavesdrop on them again.

"She noticed us talking and figured we were up to something. She wanted to find out what it was so she could horn in on our game," Rourke explained when Grayson brought up the subject of Copper Farris. "She told me all about it while she was begging for her life. She spilled her guts and promised me all sorts of things." He smiled thinly. "Not that it did her any good."

Grayson hated the man. Not because he felt particularly sorry for Copper; she had gotten herself into trouble all on her own because of her greedy nature. Rather because Rourke didn't seem to have blood in his veins. Or if he did it flowed coldly, like that of a reptile.

Grayson would be glad when he and Muller took the money and abandoned Rourke to his fate.

"Why'd you decide to kill her in Lady Arabella's room?" Muller asked from the doorway, where he was keeping an eye on the corridor through a narrow gap. "You took a big chance, getting her into the Top-Notch that way."

"I knew those two had had trouble between them," Rourke said. "I wasn't trying to frame Lady Arabella for the killing, just create enough suspicion to muddy the waters and distract that damned sheriff."

Muller grunted. "We don't want Texas John Slaughter on our trail, that's for sure."

"Slaughter will have his hands full when half the town blows up," Grayson said. "You have the dynamite, Jed?"

"Yep. Had to go to three different general stores to get enough, but we don't have to worry about that. I just told the storekeepers I was thinking about doin' some mining once the poker tournament is over."

Grayson nodded. That actually wasn't a very plausible excuse, he thought, but then again, it wouldn't have to fool anybody for very long.

In less than twenty-four hours, the whole thing would be over.

Slaughter had felt the frustration of following a trail to a dead end. He was experiencing that again as he sat in his office late that afternoon. He had questioned everybody he could find who had been in the Top-Notch early that morning, but he hadn't been able to find anyone who could swear that Lady Arabella Winthrop had gone upstairs before she found the body of Copper Farris.

He hadn't found any witnesses who could swear she was downstairs in the saloon the entire time, either.

Morris Upton had been with Lady Arabella when she walked into her room and discovered the gruesome scene. He had told Slaughter he was convinced that her shock and surprise had been genuine.

Slaughter didn't put much stock in anything Upton said, though. Besides, Lady Arabella might be a good actress. What better way to divert suspicion from herself than to pretend to find the body when she knew it was there all along?

But if she was that smart, why would she leave the dead woman in her own room to start with? That didn't make sense, no matter from which angle he tried to look at it.

His instincts told him that Lady Arabella hadn't killed Copper. But a lawman had to go on more than just instinct.

He was pondering the whole thing again when Pete Yardley came into the office. Yardley was a tall, lanky, bespectacled man with a prominent Adam's apple. He owned one of Tombstone's general stores, and Slaughter considered him a friend. Yardley had accompanied him into Mexico during the pursuit of those bandits, and he'd proven to be tougher than he looked.

"Hello, Pete," Slaughter said. "Something I can do for you?"

"Well, if you want to put on an apron and moonlight as a store clerk for a while, one of mine has disappeared and left me high and dry. Roy Corbett walked off, and I don't know where he went."

Corbett's name was vaguely familiar. Slaughter thought maybe the man was one of Stonewall's friends.

"You suspect foul play?" He hoped not; he didn't need another murder to solve when he was having so little luck with the two already on his plate.

"No, no, nothing like that," Yardley replied. "A couple people told me they saw Roy ride out of town. I just can't figure out why he up and quit that way."

"Well, I'm sorry you're short-handed, Pete, but that doesn't really seem like a matter for the sheriff's office."

"No, it's not, and it's not what I came over here to talk to you about, John. I just got sidetracked, that's all. I came about the dynamite."

Slaughter frowned. "What dynamite?"

"I sold every stick of dynamite I had on hand to one of those fellas who came into town for the gambling tournament at the Top-Notch. He said that when the tournament was over he might stick around and do some prospecting."

Slaughter shrugged "One thing's not much more of a gamble than the other."

"Oh, I know that. It struck me as a little odd that the fella would buy all my stock like that, but I didn't really think anything more about it until I happened to talk to Riley Oswalt. He said the same man came into his store and bought all the dynamite he had, too."

Slaughter sat up a little straighter in his chair. "That's pretty odd," he agreed.

"I thought so, too, so I went down to Dobson's Mercantile and asked old Abe Dobson if he'd sold any dynamite lately. Turns out he did. Today."

"To the same man?"

"Yep," Yardley said. "Between the three stores, I reckon he bought enough dynamite to blow up a mountain."

Slaughter scraped back his chair and stood up. "Do you know the man's name?"

"I asked around until I found out. His name's Jed Muller. What are you going to do, Sheriff?"

Slaughter reached for his hat. "I think I'd better go hunt up Mr. Muller and have a talk with him. I want to know what he intends to do with enough dynamite to blow half this town to kingdom come."

Chapter 26

For the second time since he'd been in Tombstone, Oscar Grayson woke up to find Steve Drake in his room in the squalid little hotel. Grayson was ready for trouble. His pistol wasn't on the table beside the bed. It was under his pillow, and as he opened his eyes and saw the bleak look on Drake's face, his hand darted for the gun.

Coming out of sleep the way he was, his reactions weren't quite fast enough. Drake sprang at him, caught his wrist, and twisted. Grayson cried out as bones ground together under his skin.

Drake hauled him out of the rumpled, dirty sheets and dumped him onto the floor next to the bed. He landed hard enough to knock the breath out of him. He lay there in his long underwear, gasping.

"What the hell are you up to, Grayson?" Drake demanded. "What's your connection to Copper Farris?"

Terror shot through Grayson. Drake knew that Rourke had killed Copper!

Grayson forced himself to get control of his galloping fear. The Virginian hadn't said anything about knowing who killed Copper. He just knew there was some sort of connection between the redhead and Grayson.

Sometimes, stubborn denial was the best course of action. Grayson shook his head. "I don't know what you're talking about, Drake. I barely knew the woman." He paused. "You think somebody like her would give the time of day to somebody like me?"

"Well, that's true enough, I suppose." Drake took his gun from under his coat. "I've been asking around. Somebody saw Copper Farris outside the door of Max Rourke's room in the American Hotel not long before she disappeared, only to turn up dead in Lady Arabella's bed later on."

"Then why aren't you talking to Rourke instead of me?" Grayson asked sullenly as he pulled himself to a sitting position with his back against one of the bedposts.

"I'll get around to Rourke. I started with you because you've been seen talking to Rourke and Jed Muller, and you're the biggest weasel of the bunch. Tell me what you're up to and what it's got to do with Copper."

Grayson shook his head again. "You can insult me all you want, Drake, but I still don't know what you're talking about. You're just holding a grudge against me and Jed because of what happened in Wichita."

"If anybody's holding a grudge, it's the two of you." Drake eared back his pistol's hammer. "Now, I'm not going to ask you again. Tell me what's going on, or I'll just shoot you like the little rat you are." He looked and sounded like he meant what he said.

Grayson swallowed hard. He was scared, but didn't want to give up his dream of stealing all that money.

He saw movement behind Drake and realized the

Virginian had left the door into the room open a few inches. It swung wider, and Muller's face peered through the opening.

One of the hinges squealed faintly, warning Drake. He whirled around, but Muller burst through the door, swinging a blackjack he clutched in his hand.

The sap smashed against Drake's head and dropped him like a stone. The gun slipped from his hand and thudded to the floor, unfired.

"Damn, that was a close one," Muller said. "He sure had the drop on you, Oscar." The big man laughed as he tucked his weapon into his jacket pocket. "You were about to spill your guts, weren't you?"

"Hell, no," Grayson insisted as he got to his feet. "I wasn't going to tell him anything."

"What's he doing here, anyway?"

Grayson shook his head "He tumbled to the fact that you and Rourke and I are working together on something. I guess we weren't careful enough about not being seen together. Somebody saw Copper outside Rourke's door while she was spying on us. They told Drake, and he seemed to figure we were responsible for what happened to her."

"Well, that was a pretty good guess, wasn't it?"

"Her death was all Rourke's doing, not ours. I guess Drake was investigating because he wanted to protect Lady Arabella. He didn't want her blamed for the murder." Grayson sighed. "Now we've got a real problem on our hands."

"I don't see how," Muller said. "We'll just kill Drake and hide his body. Chances are nobody will find it until after we're got our hands on that money and rattled our hocks out of Tombstone." He spat on the floor, the kind of crude gesture that nobody would notice in such a place. "I wish I hadn't missed him the first time I made a try for him."

"It was you who tried to shoot him from that alley?"

"Who else? You didn't think I was gonna let him get away with what he did in Wichita, did you? I was willing to forget about settling that score once you came up with your plan, but luck's dumped the chance to get rid of him right back in my lap." Muller picked up Grayson's gun, thumbed back the hammer, and pointed it at Drake's face.

"Wait!" Grayson cried as an idea occurred to him. "A gunshot will draw attention. Use that blackjack of yours and beat him to death with it. You can bust his skull with a few blows. Nobody will hear that."

Muller tossed the gun back on the bed and grinned. "I've always liked the way you think, Oscar." He took the blackjack out of his coat pocket again and stepped closer to his intended victim.

Drake's leg shot up with blinding speed and the heel of his boot crashed into Muller's groin. Muller screamed and doubled over. Drake lunged for the gun he had dropped.

Panic gripped Grayson. Drake could have heard Muller confess everything . . . and the Virginian was going for his gun.

Grayson grabbed his pistol from the bed. The .22 cracked wickedly as flame lanced from its barrel. Drake grunted and rolled over as the bullet dug into his left shoulder. His hand slapped down on his gun and lifted it. He rolled again and brought up the revolver.

The pair of explosions was deafening in the little

room. Grayson felt the double impact as the slugs from Drake's gun pounded into his chest and drove him backward. The back of his knees hit the edge of the bed and made him sit. He perched there, swaying slightly as blood pumped from the wounds. His vision began to blur, but he could still see Muller struggle to his knees, surge upright, and lunge for the door.

Drake twisted on the floor and fired again. The bullet missed and chewed splinters from the jamb as Muller careened into the hallway.

"Not . . . fair." More blood trickled from the corner of Grayson's mouth as he hunched forward against the growing pain. "I just wanted to . . . win for a change."

He toppled forward off the edge of the bed, dead by the time he hit the grimy floor.

Jed Muller wasn't at the Top-Notch or any of the other saloons Slaughter checked. He had a description of the man furnished by Pete Yardley, so he moved on to the hotels. He didn't know where Muller was staying, but there were only so many places in Tombstone he could be.

Slaughter needed to locate that dynamite, too. That much explosive stored in one place represented a danger he didn't want in his town.

Muller wasn't at the American Hotel or any of the better hostelries. Slaughter headed on to the ones that weren't so nice. By the time he reached a rundown, one-story adobe hotel far out on Safford Street, he was running out of patience.

The bald, gangling man who ran the place was dressed in a pair of stained corduroy trousers and a heavily sweated union suit. He acted like a half-wit and didn't seem to know anything, but Slaughter wondered if that was just a clever pose.

"No, I ain't seen nobody like that, mister," the man was saying when shots suddenly erupted from the corridor where the rooms were located. The proprietor dived behind the registration desk, out of the line of fire, while Slaughter swung toward the hall and drew his pearl-handled Colt.

A man staggered out of one of the rooms and started toward him. He seemed to be in pain.

Slaughter felt a shock of recognition go through him as he realized the man matched Jed Muller's description. "Muller! Hold it right there!"

Muller's eyes widened, but he didn't slow down. He lowered his head and crashed into Slaughter, knocking the lawman over backward. The collision jolted the gun out of Slaughter's hand.

Muller tried to scramble past him, but Slaughter twisted and grabbed the bigger man's ankle. Muller spilled onto the ratty rug in the middle of the lobby.

Slaughter went after him and landed with his knees in the middle of Muller's back. He clubbed his hands together and slammed them into the back of Muller's head. The blow pounded Muller's face into the floor.

The gambler went limp. Slaughter had knocked him out cold.

A footstep behind him made Slaughter look around for his gun. As he scooped it up from the floor where he had dropped it, he saw a familiar figure stumbling toward him.

Steve Drake had his right hand pressed to his body

just under his left shoulder. Crimson oozed between his fingers.

"Drake!" Slaughter said. "What are you doing here? What is all this?"

"Madness, Sheriff. But there's a method to it, of sorts." Drake nodded toward the unconscious Muller. "There's the man who shot at me and Bella from that alley. I heard him admit it while I was shamming unconsciousness. But that's not all. He and a man named Grayson and another man named Rourke were mixed up in some sort of robbery scheme. From what I heard, I think they were going after the pot in the final showdown at the Top-Notch tonight."

"Good Lord," Slaughter muttered. "I knew Upton and his loco ideas were going to cause trouble. Where are Grayson and Rourke?"

"Grayson's back there." Drake jerked his head toward the open door of one of the rooms. "He's dead. We shot it out, and he gave me this." Drake nodded at his wounded shoulder. "I put two in his chest."

Slaughter had gotten to his feet. He nodded grimly. "Reckon you didn't have any choice."

"That's not all, Sheriff. Copper Farris was spying on them, trying to find out what they were up to so she could cut herself in on it, and they caught her. Max Rourke killed her."

"Where's Rourke now?"

Drake shook his head. He was starting to look pretty pale from shock and loss of blood. "I have no idea, Sheriff. But I know something about him. When you approach him, be very careful. He's a dangerous man."

"So am I," Slaughter snapped. "We'd better get you to a doctor, Drake."

At that moment, Drake's eyes rolled up in their sockets and his knees folded. He collapsed on the floor.

Probably wasn't the first time somebody had done that.

Arabella asked herself if the awful day would ever end. She had managed to sleep a bit—in a room at the American Hotel, since there was no way she was going to stay at the Top-Notch anymore—but her slumber had been nightmare-haunted and not the least bit restful.

She hadn't eaten anything, either. She hadn't had any appetite since seeing Copper's bloody corpse spread out across her bed.

She wished she had never even come to Tombstone. Even if she won the tournament, she wasn't sure it would be worth the falling out with Steve Drake and being suspected of murder.

Money, after all, wasn't everything.

"Buck up, honey," Beulah Tillery told her. The two women sat together at one of the tables in the saloon. "Connolly's here, and Steve Drake ought to be coming along soon. We'll get started, and once you're holding the cards, you'll forget about everything else."

"You really think so, Beulah?"

"I know so. It's the game. It pushes out everything else. Makes you see that everything in life, hell, it's just a game, too. Play it the best you can, and let the cards fall how they will."

Arabella smiled. "That's good advice."

"It ought to be. I've damn well lived long enough. All those years ought to be good for something."

The blue haze of tobacco smoke that hung in the air began to sting Arabella's lungs. Most of the time, she could tolerate it, but when the air was really still and hot, as it was that evening, the smoke bothered her. "I believe I'll get a breath of fresh air."

"Don't go too far, honey. As soon as Steve shows up, we'll be getting started." The older woman paused. "I hope the two of you can work out the trouble between you. He's a good man. Sure, he makes some mistakes, but shoot, we've got to cut 'em some slack, don't we? After all, they're just men."

"We'll see," Arabella said, coolly reserved. She wasn't sure how she felt about Steve Drake at the moment, and she certainly didn't know how she would feel in the future.

The idea of losing his friendship forever . . . didn't sit well with her, either.

She stepped out of the Top-Notch and moved along the boardwalk. The sun had set not long before, so the western sky was awash with red and gold. The heat was as overpowering as it had been for days. The air didn't stir as shadows gathered.

Something moved behind her, and she stiffened as she felt the prick of a blade against her throat.

"Don't move, Lady Arabella," a man's voice said. "I'd hate to have to open up that pretty neck of yours."

She stood frozen as if the temperature was a hundred degrees colder than it really was.

"That's good. I always knew you had some sense. You're coming with me."

Arabella swallowed. It made the knife dig a little deeper into her skin for a second, but she had to in order to be able to speak. "Who . . . who are you? Why are you doing this?"

"You don't have to know that. Just come along. I'll get us a couple horses—"

"If you don't tell me what this is about, I'm going to scream."

The knife pressed harder against her flesh. "You do and I'll cut your throat."

She didn't doubt it; she thought she heard madness in the man's voice. But even though she knew she was taking a chance by doing it, she said, "You've already cut one woman's throat, haven't you?"

He took hold of her arm with his other hand. The fingers closed cruelly. "How did you know that?"

She didn't answer the question. "You're on the run, aren't you? The sheriff has found you out, and you came here to get a hostage before you flee from Tombstone."

"And you delivered yourself right into my hands, lady. Come on. I won't tell you again."

The brutal grip on her arm steered her toward the edge of the boardwalk and the pair of steps leading down to the street. Several horses were tied at a hitch rail a few feet away.

Arabella knew that if she allowed the man, whoever he was, to take her out of Tombstone, she would never survive the night. She tried to drag her feet, but he forced her on with the knife still at her throat.

As they went through a small patch of light to reach the horses, a powerful voice called from the other side of the street, "Rourke! Stop right there, mister! Let her go!"

Max Rourke . . . ! Arabella knew his reputation, knew she was right about him being mad. She had no idea what was behind it all, but she had no trouble believing that he had killed Copper Farris. There was every chance in the world he had murdered Angelo Castro, too.

"Stay back, Sheriff!" Rourke yelled as Slaughter started across the street toward them.

Arabella saw the glint of the revolver in the lawman's hand.

"Stop or I'll cut her throat! You know I'll do it, Slaughter!"

"Take it easy. You don't want to cause more trouble for yourself, do you, Rourke?"

The man laughed, and it wasn't a pretty sound. "What do you think you're going to do, hang me more than once? I knew when I saw you coming out of that grubby little hotel that Grayson and Muller must've talked. You've got the rats locked up, don't you?"

"Just Muller. Grayson's dead, but he said enough before he died. And Muller won't stop talking. I know everything, Rourke . . . except why you killed Angelo Castro."

"Why the hell not?" Rourke cackled again. "That dirty little Eye-talian had a lot of money on him. That gave me a bigger stake so I could stay in the game longer."

"But you lost anyway," Slaughter said. "In the end Castro died for nothing, just like Copper Farris."

The shouting had drawn people from the Top-Notch and other businesses along the street.

Arabella couldn't turn her head to look, but her eyes darted back and forth and saw the edges of the growing crowd. "Mr. Rourke, you can't possibly get away. Just look around you."

"Nobody's going to stop me as long as I've got you." He forced her another step closer to the horses. "We're going to ride double for now. You'll mount up first. Don't try anything or I'll rip you wide open. Your guts'll spill out all over the street."

She whimpered, "Don't hurt me, please."

"That's more like it," he said with vicious satisfaction in his voice. It was as if he knew she was too terrified to do anything except cooperate with him. He pulled the knife away from her throat. "Now get on that horse."

She reached up with her left hand as if she were going to grasp the saddle horn. At the same time, she twisted her body and brought her right arm around. When she flexed her wrist, the derringer slid smoothly from the spring-loaded holster into her palm.

Rourke might have had time to see the weapon's muzzle about three inches from his right eye before the derringer went off with a little pop, but that was the last thing he saw. The bullet exploded through his eye and into his brain, killing him instantly. He dropped the knife and fell away from her, limp as a rag doll.

Slaughter reached Arabella a couple seconds later and reached out to steady her, but she didn't need his help. She was cool and calm as she said, "I take it you have enough information now, Sheriff, to know that I didn't kill Copper Farris or anyone else."

"Nobody but this fella, you mean. And if anybody ever needed killing, it was him."

"You'll get no argument from me. What was this all about?"

"Somebody else can explain that to you, somebody who wants to see you, anyway. He's over at the hotel, getting patched up by the doctor."

"Steve—" She caught her breath. "Is he all right?"

"He'll be fine," Slaughter told her, "but I've got a hunch he'll be even better once he sees you."

Arabella hesitated. "I'm free to go?"

"We'll talk later, but yes, you are."

"Thank you, Sheriff." Arabella started walking toward the hotel. By the time she had gone a few feet, she was almost running.

Chapter 27

Stonewall recognized Dallin Williams's voice. For a second, he thought about making a grab for the rifle, or spinning around and trying to get his Colt out of its holster, but he discarded the idea. He knew he could never do either of those things in time to keep Dallin from shooting him.

He would have liked to think that the cowboy wouldn't do that . . . but under the circumstances, there was no way he was going to bet his life on that hunch.

On the other side of the camp, Roy Corbett looked like he wanted to make a play, too. Stonewall caught his eye and gave a little shake of his head. He hoped Roy wouldn't do anything to get them both killed.

"You fellas stand next to each other," Dallin ordered. "I want to be able to keep an eye on both of you at the same time."

"Dallin, you're smart enough to know that you can't get away with this," Stonewall said. "The best thing you can do is surrender and let us take you back to Tombstone."

Dallin surprised him by saying, "Well, now, I might

just do that, but we got to take care of some things first. Have you seen Little Ed?"

"No, but he and his men are bound to be around here somewhere. They probably heard those shots, just like you did, and they're gonna be looking for us."

"I hope so. Jessie's got something to tell him."

"She's with you?" Corbett exclaimed.

"That's right." Dallin was in the rocks above the camp. He turned his head and called, "Jessie, come on down here. Bring the horse if you can."

Stonewall heard gravel sliding on the hillside. A few minutes later, several shapes loomed out of the darkness. Two people and a horse, he decided as they came closer.

Dallin's gun was down at his side. "I'm thinkin' that if there are bronco Apaches around here, we need to find us a hidey-hole."

"I thought the same thing," Stonewall agreed. "Someplace we can defend—"

"Roy?" Jessie suddenly exclaimed as she came close enough to recognize him. "Roy Corbett?"

He stepped forward. "Now, listen, Jessie—"

"No!" she screamed. "Get him away from me!"

Before Stonewall or Dallin could do anything, Corbett's gun came out of its holster. He leveled the revolver at them and ordered coldly, "All right, you two, just stand still."

Jessie was breathing hard as she cringed against the horse. The animal was spooked to start with, and it became more skittish.

"Roy," Stonewall said, "what's going on here?"

"It was you!" Dallin said before Corbett had a chance to answer. "By God, you're the one who hurt this girl!"

"I didn't hurt her," Corbett said. "She wanted it. She's been asking for it ever since I rode for Little Ed."

"She was just a kid then!" Stonewall exclaimed. "You said so yourself."

"That doesn't change anything," Corbett said.

Jessie found her voice again. "He . . . he told me he'd kill me if I ever told anybody what he did. I didn't really care about that, but . . . but he said he'd kill my ma and pa, too. He said he'd have to."

"Damn right I'd have to," Corbett said. "I'm not going to let some little ranch slut ruin my career. If I married you like you wanted, I'd have to keep clerking at that store just to make ends meet. I'd never save up enough money to go to school and become a lawyer."

"All that talk about the law and how you wanted to do good," Stonewall said bitterly. "That was just a pile of horse droppin's."

"I do want to be a lawyer," Corbett insisted. "And when I am, I'll marry somebody better than this . . . this . . ."

"Whatever it is, don't you say it," Dallin warned with a tone of menace in his voice. "You've already talked bad enough about this fine little gal."

"Fine little gal?" Corbett laughed. "Her lies nearly got you lynched, you idiot!"

Dallin moved a step forward. "Only reason she lied was because you got her so scared she didn't know what she was doin'. You're the one to blame for all of it, not her."

"Think whatever you want, I don't care." Corbett motioned with the gun in his hand. "Both of you take those pistols out and put them on the ground. Be careful about it, too. I don't have anything to lose by shooting you."

Things had changed so fast Stonewall felt a little dizzy

trying to wrap his brain around the situation. He had considered Roy Corbett a friend, but obviously he had never really known the man at all.

As for Dallin Williams . . . well, Stonewall hadn't forgotten how the cowboy had bent a gun barrel over his head. But he had been desperate, fighting for his life as he saw it. Who was to say that he wasn't right about that? The attempt at lynching him could have turned out very differently.

"I'm not going to tell the two of you again." Corbett's voice shook a little with anger and desperation. "Drop your guns."

Dallin shifted a little, putting himself between Jessie and Corbett.

"I ain't sure we can do that, Roy. Seems to me that since Stonewall and me know the truth now, you can't afford to let us live if you're gonna get what you want."

"He can't let me live, either," Jessie said from behind him. "Because I'm going to tell the truth. I see how wrong I was. I never should have lied about you, Dallin. Can you forgive me?"

Without taking his eyes off Corbett, Dallin smiled. "Why, sure I can. I wouldn't hold a grudge against somebody just 'cause they got scared and didn't know what to do."

"I'm glad to hear that, because I know what to do now." She slapped a hand against the horse's rump and yelled at the animal. The already nervous horse whinnied wildly and leaped forward, straight at Corbett.

He tried to get a shot off, but the horse's shoulder struck his arm just as he jerked the trigger. The gun boomed, but the bullet went high in the air.

The next instant, Dallin crashed into Corbett and drove him backward off his feet.

Stonewall dashed in and kicked the gun out of Corbett's hand, but it didn't really matter. Dallin was smashing his fists into the man's face and Corbett was already knocked senseless.

Stonewall grabbed hold of Dallin and hauled him off. "Settle down! You don't want to kill him."

"The hell I don't! Lemme go, Stonewall. He's got it comin'."

"He'll get what's coming to him, all right," Stonewall argued, "but first we've got to get back to Tombstone, all of us, before the Apaches find us."

Mention of the Apaches seemed to cut through Dallin's anger. He gave his shoulders a shake and nodded. "You can let go of me now. I won't stomp him to death, no matter how much I want to."

Like anybody who had cowboyed for a living, Stonewall carried a rope on his saddle. He got it and tied Roy Corbett hand and foot. They would have to sling him over a saddle and tie him on.

Dallin said to Jessie, "That was a pretty smart move, stampedin' that horse. Corbett might've killed all of us if you hadn't done that."

"I couldn't let that happen. Not now."

Stonewall didn't ask her what she meant. He didn't want to know. But he couldn't forget that Dallin and Jessie had spent quite a bit of time together, and he knew how women just naturally seemed to get around Dallin. . . .

He put that thought out of his head and said, "Let's get out of here while we've got the chance. We'll move back out toward the flats. The Apaches might not chase us out of the hills." He knew that was a slim hope, but it was better than nothing.

They lifted Corbett onto his horse and tied him in place.

The horse Dallin and Jessie had ridden away from the Bar EM had stopped a short distance away and settled down. He led it back over and helped her get mounted before he swung up behind her.

By that time, Stonewall was in the saddle, too. They set off in an easterly direction with him leading Corbett's horse.

It was possible they would run into Little Ed and the rest of the bunch from the McCabe ranch. That would be just fine. As long as there was a chance of being jumped by Apaches, the more men to fight off the attack, the better.

Corbett came to after a while and started cursing through swollen lips. Stonewall got tired of listening to the abuse and stopped long enough to gag him with a bandanna.

The sky began to lighten in the east as morning approached. They continued in that direction and soon neared the edge of the foothills. Another half mile or so and they would be out of the Santa Catalinas.

Dallin and Jessie were in the lead as they went through a little gap between hills. A flicker of movement to his right warned Stonewall and he glanced in that direction just in time to see a knife-wielding Apache in leggings, breechcloth, and a blousy shirt leap from the top of a rock in an attack aimed at Dallin and Jessie.

Stonewall's Colt came up, and he fired faster than he ever had in his life. He knew it was pure luck that guided his shot as the bullet smashed into the leaping Apache and spun the warrior around in mid-air.

Dallin drove his heels into the horse's flanks and sent the mount leaping ahead. The wounded Apache landed right behind the horse.

With savage war cries on their lips, more Apaches swarmed out of the rocks.

As Dallin galloped forward, he told Jessie to lean forward and swung Corbett's Winchester from side to side, blasting shots at the Indians as fast as he could work the Winchester's lever.

Stonewall was right behind him, emptying the Colt at the attackers. "Head for the flats!" he shouted over the pounding hoofbeats. "Maybe we can outrun them!"

It was possible the Apaches didn't even have mounts. They tended to think of horses more in terms of food than transportation, Stonewall knew.

It was a desperate few moments as he and Dallin fought their way through the ambush. Bullets whipped past their heads, and the acrid bite of powdersmoke stung their eyes and noses.

As one of the Apaches leaped at him, Stonewall jerked his foot out of the stirrup and kicked the warrior's bare chest. The man flew backward from the impact with his arms and legs flung out wide. He landed with the sharp edge of a rock slab in the middle of his back. Stonewall would have sworn he heard the Apache's spine break.

Quickly, the riders were past the hills and galloping toward the flats several hundred yards away. The terrain at the edge of the foothills was still rugged. The horses sailed out from more than one ridge top, hooves scrambling for purchase as they landed and continued running.

Shots kept blasting behind them. Stonewall glanced back over his shoulder and saw at least a dozen Apaches mounted on tough little ponies pursuing them. The Indians fired their rifles, but the back of a running horse was a terrible place for accuracy.

Blind luck was always a danger, and that was true as a bullet struck the horse Dallin and Jessie were riding just as they reached the flats. With a sharp cry, it staggered but stayed upright. The horse slowed from the pain of its wound, and Stonewall had to haul back on his reins to keep from running into the animal.

"Take Jessie and get outta here!" Dallin shouted. "I'll fall back and hold 'em off!"

"No!" Jessie cried. "After everything that's happened, I can't let you die for me now!"

"You gotta think about the baby!" Dallin argued as the horse slowed even more.

Stonewall looked back again and saw that the Apaches were gaining on them. "We'll make a stand! That little rise over there!" He waved a hand to indicate the slight irregularity in the ground.

The flats, as usual, weren't completely flat when you got a close look at them.

The rise wouldn't offer them much protection, but it was better than nothing. They angled the horses toward it. Just as they got there, the front legs of the Bar EM horse buckled and the animal collapsed. Dallin slid from the saddle and was able to catch Jessie before she fell.

Stonewall leaped to the ground, dropped to one knee

behind the rise, and fired his Winchester over it. One of the Apaches flew off his pony, but the others kept coming.

Dallin lifted a protesting Jessie onto the saddle of Stonewall's horse and cut the lead rope attached to Corbett's horse. "Go!" he cried. Without giving her a chance to argue, he snatched off his hat and slapped it on the horse's rump. The horse lunged away.

He dropped behind the body of the slain horse and propped his rifle on its corpse. A few feet away, Stonewall stretched out on his belly behind the rise and pointed his Winchester at the charging Apaches, too.

"You know they're gonna overrun us!" Stonewall called.

"Yeah, but maybe Jessie'll have a chance to find her pa!" Dallin replied.

Stonewall glanced over at him. "I'm glad I got a chance to know the truth before it was too late."

Dallin grinned and nodded. "Yeah, me, too," he drawled. "I'd hate to die with you thinkin' I was worse than I really am."

There was no time for anything else. They both opened fire. A couple more Apaches dropped, but there were too many of them and they were too close . . .

Stonewall's Winchester ran dry, and he didn't have time to reload. His Colt was empty, too.

Then he felt a sudden vibration in the ground and heard a sound like thunder. He looked up, but the sky in the east, crimson and gold, was clear. He looked around, not knowing what he was going to see.

Out of the rising sun charged a large group of men on horseback, their guns spurting flame. They swept past Stonewall and Dallin.

Stonewall recognized not only Little Ed McCabe, but also his fellow deputies Jeff Milton and Lorenzo Paco. He knew in that moment what had happened. A posse from Tombstone had run into the McCabe bunch and joined forces with the Bar EM to hunt for the fugitive Dallin Williams.

They had found Dallin, all right, but they had also found a lot more. As bullets flew around the Apaches, the warriors turned to flee, but they had no chance. The men from Tombstone cut them all down in a matter of moments.

Dallin climbed wearily to his feet. "Well, what do you know about that? Never thought I'd be so happy to see ol' Little Ed again." He extended a hand to Stonewall, who gripped it and stood up, too. They watched as several members of the posse dismounted to check the bodies of the fallen Apaches.

McCabe, Milton, and Paco turned their horses and trotted toward Stonewall and Dallin.

"Remember, I'm *your* prisoner," Dallin said under his breath. "I'm countin' on you not to let Little Ed kill me."

"He won't do that," Stonewall promised.

As the riders reined in, Dallin began, "Now, Little Ed, you just listen to what Stonewall here has to say—"

"I don't have to listen to anything," McCabe cut in gruffly. He blew out a breath. "I've already heard plenty from my daughter." He nodded toward the east.

Stonewall and Dallin looked around and saw Jessie riding toward them. Dallin let out an excited whoop.

"You made it!" he told her as she rode up.

McCabe said, "And she, ah, told me the truth about

what happened, Williams. She begged us to come save your sorry butt, along with Deputy Howell here."

"Does this mean you don't want to lynch me no more?" Dallin asked with a grin.

Jessie saved her father the trouble of answering that. She slid off the horse and threw her arms around Dallin's neck.

Jeff Milton said dryly, "I don't think there'll be any lynching in these parts today."

McCabe's eyes narrowed angrily. "I wouldn't be so sure about that. We've still got to round up Corbett. He's got to be around here somewhere. Jessie said he was tied up and had to go wherever the horse went."

"That's right," Stonewall said. "But when we find him, you're not gonna string him up, Mr. McCabe. He's going back to Tombstone to face justice the right way."

McCabe spat and said darkly, "We'll see."

Chapter 28

As it turned out, they were both wrong.

Half an hour later they found the horse with Roy Corbett tied across the saddle. The animal was grazing peacefully on some sparse grass in the shade of a yucca plant. Corbett's head hung down motionless. When Paco took hold of his hair and lifted, they all saw the bullet hole in Corbett's temple.

One of those Apache bullets had found a deserving target and ended forever the threats Corbett had made against Jessie and her parents.

It had ended his hopes of someday having a law career, too, Stonewall thought, but then he corrected himself. Corbett had started that chain of events in motion himself when he decided to be the sort of low-down snake who would do the things he had done.

But they would take him back to Tombstone, anyway, and bury him.

Jessie rode double with Dallin. Little Ed looked like he didn't care much for that arrangement, but he just cleared his throat, shook his head, and rode on without saying anything.

Sometimes, Stonewall thought with a smile, a fella had to just throw his hands in the air and give up.

"You can give up now," Arabella said, "or we can draw this out right to the bitter end."

Morris Upton glared across the table at her. He wasn't interested in flirting with her, not with the large pile of money in front of her and the small one in front of him. "I'm not going to fold," he muttered.

"Very well." She gauged the amount he had left and picked up a sheaf of greenbacks. As she tossed it into the center of the table, she went on. "I'll raise you five thousand."

It would take all he had left to see the bet. He stared at his cards. Silence gripped the saloon, a quiet so profound that Arabella heard a clock ticking somewhere.

She glanced over at Steve Drake, who sat at the next table watching the final showdown. His left arm was in a black silk sling, and the bandages on his wounded shoulder made a slight lump under his suit coat.

Despite his injury, despite the fact that he was no longer in the game, he looked quite pleased.

Beulah Tillery sat with him. She didn't seem to mind that Arabella had beaten her, either. There was always another game in another town, she had said when she was cleaned out.

Alex Connelly had gone somewhere to get drunk after he dropped out of the game. He was still largely a cipher to Arabella. She hadn't exchanged half a dozen words with the man.

The saloon was packed, which didn't help with the heat. Even Sheriff Slaughter was there, leaning an elbow on the bar as he watched.

"Well, Morris," Arabella said softly. "What are you going to do?"

Upton drew in a deep breath and pushed the rest of his stake forward. "I call."

She laid down a full house, kings over jacks.

Upton threw his cards on the table. A flush. A good hand.

But not good enough.

"I believe we're done here," she said when the cheering and applause from the spectators finally died down.

Upton looked like he didn't know whether to curse or cry. He said in a voice that shook a little, "One more hand. The Top-Notch. Everything I own, against whatever you want to stake."

Arabella smiled and shook her head. "I have no desire to own a saloon again, Morris. I've already done that."

"You're sure?"

"Positive."

He nodded. "I suppose I should congratulate you. You played well, especially considering all the distractions."

"Such as nearly being murdered?"

He shrugged. "I'm sorry that happened here. I didn't intend for there to be so much trouble."

Arabella began gathering up her winnings. She looked over at Slaughter. "Sheriff, do you think you could make arrangements for this money to be locked up in your local bank?"

"It's well after hours," Slaughter said with a smile, "but I'll see what I can do."

"I'll leave it with you, then." She stood up, every inch a regal beauty. "Steve, if you could escort me to the hotel . . ."

"It would be my honor, Bella." Drake got to his feet.

As they went out, Arabella heard Beulah Tillery say, "Yeah, she's the big winner, all right," then let out a bawdy laugh.

Once they were on the street, Drake said quietly, "Bella, I hope you can forgive me—"

"There's nothing to forgive, Steve. I never believed you were pining away for me all the years we've gone our separate ways. I was a bit upset, yes, but I shouldn't have been."

"And I shouldn't have been such a damned fool."

"Well," she said as she smiled to herself, "we're all capable of it now and then, aren't we?"

By midnight, Slaughter had seen to having Lady Arabella's fortune locked in the bank's vault. He was making a last turn around the town when he paused in front of the Top-Notch and looked through the window. Morris Upton was sitting alone at one of the tables, looking gloomy even though the saloon was still doing a booming business.

Upton just didn't like being beaten, thought Slaughter, but he would get over it soon enough. He still had the saloon and plenty of money. Slaughter was sure that Upton would remain a thorn in his side for a long time to come.

He walked back to the courthouse. As he came up to the building, he heard hoofbeats in the distance. With a frown, he wondered if more trouble was on the way and shifted the shotgun tucked under his left arm, just in case.

Mose Tadrack, on duty in the sheriff's office, heard the horses, too. He came out of the building and joined Slaughter. "What do you think, Sheriff?"

"I don't know, but we're about to find out."

Slaughter relaxed when the first of the horsemen loomed out of the darkness and he recognized Jeff Milton and Lorenzo Paco. Slaughter's heart leaped a little when he spotted Stonewall riding behind them, apparently unhurt.

Dallin Williams rode alongside Stonewall, and to Slaughter's great surprise, Jessie McCabe was with him, riding double with Williams's left arm around her waist rather possessively. Little Ed McCabe was right behind them, along with some of his ranch hands and the rest of the posse that had gone after the fugitive.

Slaughter stepped out to meet them, knowing that he was about to hear an interesting story. When he spotted the body tied facedown over a saddle, he was even more convinced.

It took half an hour to get everything hashed out.

When Slaughter had the whole story, Dallin Williams asked him, "Are you gonna arrest me for bustin' out of jail, Sheriff?"

Slaughter gave him a stern look. "I don't know yet. I'll have to talk to the judge in the morning. For now, though, I'll release you if you give me your word that you won't try to leave the area."

"No, sir, I sure won't. I give you my word on that."

Dallin looked at Jessie, who smiled at him. "I don't reckon I'll be goin' anywhere any time soon."

"Miss McCabe," Slaughter went on, "you'd better stay here in town, too. You'll have to talk to the judge and persuade him not to file charges against you for making a false accusation."

Little Ed McCabe looked angry.

Slaughter held up a hand to forestall any protest from the rancher. "Don't cloud up and rain, Little Ed. If you'll just be a little patient—I know that's not easy for you— I think everything's going to turn out all right."

"I ain't so sure about that," McCabe said as he gave Dallin a dubious look. "But I reckon we can wait and see."

Well after midnight, Tombstone was finally settled down. Roy Corbett's body was at the undertaker's. Dallin and Jessie had rooms in the hotel. Little Ed and his men had gone back to the Bar EM.

Slaughter stood outside the jail with his shotgun, wondering if he ought to take one more turn around the town.

Stonewall came out of the building behind him and yawned. "I don't know about you, John, but I'm ready to turn in. These last few days have been a mite tiring."

Slaughter chuckled. "You could say that. Make some rounds with me first, Deputy."

"Sure, Sheriff."

As they walked side by side along Toughnut Street. Stonewall said, "I never did hear how that poker tournament turned out. Is it over?"

Slaughter told him the story, bringing a low whistle of astonishment from Stonewall's lips. "Did you ever find all that dynamite?"

"Muller told us where he'd cached it," Slaughter said. "It's back in the stores where it ought to be."

Stonewall shook his head. "I can't believe I missed all that excitement."

"You had plenty of excitement of your own," Slaughter pointed out to his young brother-in-law. "What about Williams? Did I detect something going on between him and the McCabe girl?"

"Dallin says there is. He claims he's gonna give up his womanizing ways and try to settle down. He even said he might start courting Jessie."

"It would be good for her to have a husband before that baby's born. I'll believe Williams can settle down when I see it, though."

"You never know. Stranger things have happened, I reckon." Stonewall lifted his face and added, "Like that. Unless I'm imaginin' things, that's a cool breeze I feel. I think the heat wave's broken, John."

"I do believe you're right," Slaughter said, and they walked on into the night.

Keep reading for special preview of . . .

**The First Mountain Man
PREACHER'S KILL**

*A fur trapper by trade, Preacher can smell a bad deal
from any direction, no matter how well it's disguised.
It wasn't always that way—he's got the scars to prove it.
Now he's ready to pass on his deadly survival skills
to a boy named Hawk, who just might be his son . . .*

Preacher and Hawk ride out of the Rockies
and into St. Louis loaded with furs. It's Hawk's first
trip to civilization, and the moment he lays eyes on
young Chessie Dayton he's lost in more ways than one.
When Chessie unwisely signs on for a gold-hungry
expedition into the lawless mountains,
Hawk convinces Preacher to trail the outfit, because
they're all headed straight to the sacred Indian grounds
known as the Black Hills—a land of no return.
To come out of it alive, a lot of people will have to die.
And Preacher's going to need a heap of bullets
for this journey into hell . . .

Available now wherever Pinnacle Books are sold!

Chapter 1

A rifle ball hummed past Preacher's head, missing him by a foot. At the same time he heard the boom of the shot from the top of a wooded hill fifty yards away. He kicked his feet free of the stirrups and dived out of the saddle.

Even before he hit the ground, he yelled to Hawk, "Get down!"

His half-Absaroka son had the same sort of hair-trigger, lightning-fast reflexes Preacher did. He leaped from his pony and landed beside the trail just a split second after the mountain man did. A second shot from the hilltop kicked up dust at Hawk's side as he rolled.

Preacher had already come up on one knee. His long-barreled flintlock rifle was in his hand when he launched off the rangy gray stallion's back. Now, as he spotted a spurt of powder smoke at the top of the hill where the ambushers lurked, he brought the rifle to his shoulder in one smooth motion, earing back the hammer as he did so.

The weapon kicked hard against his shoulder as he fired.

Instinctively, he had aimed just above the gush of dark gray smoke. Without waiting to see the result of his shot, he powered to his feet and raced toward a shallow gully ten yards away. It wouldn't offer much protection, but it was better than nothing.

As he ran, he felt as much as heard another rifle ball pass close to his ear, disturbing the air. Those fellas up there on the hill weren't bad shots.

But anybody who had in mind ambushing him had ought to be a damned *good* shot, because trying to kill Preacher but leaving him alive was a hell of a bad mistake.

Before this ruckus was over, he intended to show those varmints just how bad a mistake it was.

From the corner of his eye, he saw Hawk sprinting into a clump of scrubby trees. That was the closest cover to the youngster. Hawk had his rifle, too, and as Preacher dived into the gully, he wasn't surprised to hear the long gun roar.

He rolled onto his side so he could get to his shot pouch and powder horn. Reloading wasn't easy without exposing himself to more gunfire from the hilltop, but this wasn't the first tight spot Preacher had been in.

When he had the flintlock loaded, primed, and ready to go, he wriggled like a snake to his left. The gully ran for twenty yards in that direction before it petered out. Preacher didn't want to stick his head up in the same place where he had gone to ground. He wanted the ambushers to have to watch for him.

That way, maybe they'd be looking somewhere else when he made his next move.

No more shots rang out while Preacher was crawling along the shallow depression in the earth. He didn't believe for a second that the men on the hill had given up, though. They were just waiting for him to show himself.

Over in the trees, Hawk fired again. A rifle blast answered him immediately. Preacher took that as a good time to make his play. He lifted himself onto his knees and spotted a flicker of movement in the trees atop the hill. More than likely, somebody up there was trying to reload.

Preacher put a stop to that by drilling the son of a buck. A rifle flew in the air and a man rolled out of the trees, thrashing and kicking. That commotion lasted only a couple of seconds before he went still . . . the stillness of death.

That luckless fella wasn't the only one. Preacher saw a motionless leg sticking out from some brush. That was the area where he had placed his first shot, he recalled. From the looks of that leg, he had scored with that one, too.

Were there any more would-be killers up there? No one shot at Preacher as he ducked down again. The mountain man reloaded once more, then called to Hawk, "You see any more of 'em movin' around up there, boy?"

"No," Hawk replied. Preacher recalled too late that he didn't much cotton to being called "boy." But he was near twenty years younger than Preacher and his son, to boot, so that was what he was going to be called from time to time.

"Well, lay low for a spell longer just in case they're playin' possum."

Now that Preacher had a chance to look around, he

saw that his horse, the latest in a series of similar animals he called only Horse, had trotted off down the trail with Hawk's mount and the pack mule they had loaded down with beaver pelts. The big wolflike cur known as Dog was with them, standing guard, although that wasn't really necessary. If anybody other than Preacher or Hawk tried to corral him, Horse would kick them to pieces. But Horse and Dog were fast friends, and Dog wouldn't desert his trail partner unless ordered to do so.

That was what Preacher did now, whistling to get Dog's attention and then motioning for the cur to hunt. Dog took off like a gray streak, circling to get around behind the hill. He knew as well as Preacher did where the threat lay.

Preacher and Hawk stayed under cover for several minutes. Then Dog emerged from the trees on the hilltop and sat down with his pink tongue lolling out of his mouth. Preacher knew that meant no more danger lurked up there. He had bet his life on Dog's abilities too many times in the past to doubt them now.

"It's all right," he called to Hawk. "Let's go take a look at those skunks."

"Why?" Hawk asked as he stepped out of the trees. "They will not be anyone I know. I have never been in . . . what would you say? These parts? I have never been in these parts before."

"Well, they might be somebody *I* know," Preacher said. "I've made a few enemies in my time, you know."

Hawk snorted as if to say that was quite an understatement.

"What about the horses?" he asked.

"Horse ain't goin' anywhere without me and Dog, and that pony of yours will stay with him. So will the mule."

Taking his usual long-legged strides, Preacher started toward the hill.

As he walked, he looked around for any other signs of impending trouble. The grassy landscape was wide open and apparently empty. Two hundred yards to the south, the Missouri River flowed eastward, flanked by plains and stretches of low, rolling hills. Preacher didn't see any birds or small animals moving around. The earlier gunfire had spooked them, and it would be a few more minutes before they resumed their normal routine. The animals were more wary than Preacher, probably because they didn't carry guns and couldn't fight back like the mountain man could.

"Since you ain't gonna recognize either of those carcasses, as you pointed out your own self, you keep an eye out while I check 'em."

Hawk responded with a curt nod. Preacher left him gazing around narrow-eyed and strode up the hill.

The man who had fallen down the slope and wound up in the open lay on his back. His left arm was flung straight out. His right was at his side, and the fingers of that hand were still dug into the dirt from the spasms that had shaken him as he died. He wore buckskin trousers, a rough homespun shirt, and high-topped moccasins. His hair was long and greasy, his lean cheeks and jaw covered with dark stubble. There were thousands of men on the frontier who didn't look significantly different.

What set him apart was the big, bloody hole in his right side. Preacher could tell from the location of the wound that the ball had bored on into the man's lungs and torn them apart, so he had spent a few agonizing moments drowning in his own blood. Not as bad as being gut-shot, but still a rough way to go.

Remembering how close a couple of those shots had come to his head, and how the ambushers had almost killed his son, too, Preacher wasn't inclined to feel much sympathy for the dead man. As far as he could recall, he had never seen the fellow before.

The one lying in the brush under the trees at the top of the hill was stockier and had a short, rust-colored beard. Preacher's swiftly fired shot had caught him just below that beard, shattering his breastbone and probably severing his spine, too. He was dead as could be, like his partner.

But unlike the other man, Preacher had a feeling he had seen this one before. He couldn't say where or when, nor could he put a name to the round face, but maybe it would come to him later. St. Louis was a big town, one of the biggest Preacher had ever seen, and he had been there plenty of times over the years. Chances were he had run into Redbeard there.

Now that he had confirmed the two men were dead and no longer a threat, he looked around to see if they'd had any companions. His keen eyes picked up footprints left by both men, but no others. Preacher crossed the hilltop and found two horses tied to saplings on the opposite slope. He pulled the reins loose and led the animals back over the crest. Hawk stood at the bottom of the hill, peering around alertly.

Preacher took a good look at his son as he approached the young man. Hawk That Soars. That was what his mother had named him. She was called Bird in a Tree, a beautiful young Absaroka woman Preacher had spent a winter with, two decades earlier. Hawk was the result of the time Preacher and Birdie had shared, and even though Preacher had been unaware of the boy's existence until recently, he felt a surge of pride when he regarded his offspring.

With Preacher's own dark coloring, he hadn't passed along much to Hawk to signify that he was half-white. Most folks would take the young man for pure-blood Absaroka. He was a little taller than most warriors from that tribe, a little more leanly built. His long hair was the same raven black as his mother's had been.

One thing he *had* inherited from Preacher was fighting ability. They made a formidable pair. Months earlier, to avenge a massacre that had left Hawk and the old man called White Buffalo the only survivors from their band, father and son had gone to war against the Blackfeet— and the killing hadn't stopped until nearly all the warriors in that particular bunch were dead.

Since then, they had been trapping beaver with White Buffalo and a pair of novice frontiersmen, Charlie Todd and Aaron Buckley, they had met during the clash with the Blackfeet. During that time, Todd and Buckley had acquired the seasoning they needed to be able to survive on their own, and they had decided to stay in the mountains instead of returning to St. Louis with the load of pelts. Preacher, Hawk, and White Buffalo would take the furs back to sell. Todd and Buckley had shares coming from that sale, and Preacher would see to it that they got them when he and Hawk made it back to the Rocky Mountains.

White Buffalo had surprised them by choosing to

remain with a band of Crow they had befriended while they were trapping. Cousins to the Absaroka, the Crow had always gotten along well with Preacher and most white men. They had welcomed Preacher, Hawk, and White Buffalo to their village . . . and White Buffalo had felt so welcome he had married a young widow.

Preacher had warned the old-timer that the difference in age between him and his wife might cause trouble in the sleeping robes, but White Buffalo had informed him haughtily, "If she dies from exhaustion, I will find another widow to marry."

You couldn't argue with a fella like that. Preacher and Hawk had agreed to pick him up on their way back to the mountains, if he was still alive and kicking, and if he wanted to go.

That left just the two of them to transport the pelts downriver to St. Louis. Preacher figured they were now within two days' travel of that city on the big river, and so far they hadn't had any trouble.

Until today.

Hawk heard Preacher coming and turned to watch him descend the rest of the way.

"Two men," Hawk said as he looked at the horses Preacher led. "Both dead."

"Yep."

"Old enemies of yours?"

Preacher shook his head.

"Nope. One of them sort of looked familiar, like maybe I'd seen him in a tavern in the past year or two, but the other fella I didn't know from Adam."

"Then why did they try to kill us?"

Preacher pointed at the heavily laden pack mule

standing with Horse and Hawk's pony and said, "Those pelts will fetch a nice price. Some men ask themselves why should they go all that way to the mountains, endure the hardships, and risk life and limb when they can wait around here and jump the fellas on their way back to St. Louis. I can't get my brain to come around to that way of thinkin'—if you want something, it's best just to go ahead and work for it, I say—but there are plenty of folks who feel different."

Hawk grunted. "Thieves. Lower than carrion."

"Well, that's all they're good for now."

Hawk nodded toward the horses and asked, "What are you going to do with them?"

"Take them with us, I reckon. We can sell them in St. Louis."

"If those men have friends, they may recognize the animals and guess that we killed the men who rode them."

Preacher blew out a contemptuous breath.

"Anybody who'd be friends with the likes of those ambushers don't worry me overmuch."

"And what about the dead men themselves?"

"Buzzards got to eat, too," Preacher said, "and so do the worms."

Chapter 2

Preacher's estimate was correct. Two more days on the trail found them approaching St. Louis. Above the point where the Missouri River flowed into the Mississippi, he and Hawk crossed the Big Muddy on a ferry run by a Frenchman named Louinet, a descendant of one of the trappers who had first come down the Father of Waters from Canada to this region a hundred years earlier.

Preacher saw the wiry, balding man eyeing the two extra horses and said, "Found these animals runnin' loose a couple days ago, back upstream. You have any idea who they might belong to?"

Louinet shook his head. "*Non.* Since you found them, I assume they are now yours."

"Reckon so. I just figured I'd get 'em back to whoever rightfully owned 'em, if I could."

"If those animals were running loose with saddles on them, then the men who rode them almost certainly have no further need for them."

"You're probably right about that," Preacher said with a grim smile.

He wasn't worried about who the two ambushers had been, but if Louinet had been able to give him some names, it might have helped him watch out for any friends or relatives of the dead men. But if they came after him and Hawk, so be it. They had only defended themselves and hadn't done anything wrong. Preacher was the sort who dealt with problems when they arose and didn't waste a second of time fretting about the future. It had a habit of taking care of itself.

That attitude was entirely different from being careless, though. Nobody could accuse Preacher of that, either.

Once they were on the other side of the river, Preacher and Hawk rode on, with Hawk leading the string that consisted of the pack mule and the extra mounts. They didn't reach St. Louis until dusk, and as they spotted the lights of the town, Hawk exclaimed softly in surprise and said, "They must have many campfires in this village called St. Louis."

"Those ain't campfires," Preacher said. "They're lights shinin' through windows. Lamps and lanterns and candles. You'll see when we get there."

"Windows, like in the trading posts where we stopped from time to time?"

"Sort of, but a lot of these have glass in 'em." Hawk just shook his head in bafflement, so Preacher went on, "You'll see soon enough, when we get there."

More than likely, window glass wouldn't be the only thing Preacher would have to explain to his son before this visit was over. This was Hawk's first taste of so-called civilization, which held a lot of mysteries for someone accustomed to a simpler, more elemental life.

As they rode into the settlement sprawled along the

west bank of the Mississippi, Hawk gazed in wonder at the buildings looming in the gathering shadows. He wrinkled his nose and said, "Ugh. It stinks."

"You're smellin' the docks and the area along the river," Preacher said. "It's a mite aromatic, all right. There are a lot of warehouses along there full of pelts, and not everybody's as careful about cleanin' and dryin' 'em as we are. They start to rot. Then you've got spoiled food and spilled beer and lots of folks who ain't exactly as fresh as daisies. It all mixes together until you get the smell you're experiencin' now."

Hawk shook his head. "The high country is better."

"You won't get any argument from me about that, boy . . . but this is where the money is."

"This thing you call money is worthless."

"Oh, it has its uses, as long as you don't get too attached to it. Your people trade with each other, and it's sort of the same thing."

"We trade things people can *use*," Hawk said. "It is not the same thing at all."

"Just keep your eyes open," Preacher said. "You'll learn."

And the youngster probably would learn some things he'd just as soon he hadn't, the mountain man thought.

The pelts were the most important thing to deal with, so Preacher headed first for the local office of the American Fur Company. Founded by John Jacob Astor in the early part of the century, the enterprise had grown into a virtual monopoly controlling all the fur trade in the United States. In recent years, the company had declined in its influence and control, a trend not helped by Astor's departure from the company he had started. But it was still operating, led now by a man named Ramsay Crooks, and Preacher knew he wouldn't get a better price for the furs anywhere else.

Despite the fact that night was falling and some businesses were closing for the day, the office of the American Fur Company, located in a sturdy building with a sprawling warehouse behind it, was still brightly lit. Preacher reined Horse to a stop in front of it and swung down from the saddle.

"Tie up these animals and keep an eye on 'em," Preacher told Hawk. "I'll go inside and talk to Vernon Pritchard. He runs this office, unless somethin's happened to him since the last time I was here." He added, "Dog, you stay out here, too."

Preacher wasn't sure it was a good idea to leave Hawk alone on the streets of St. Louis, but the youngster had to start getting used to the place sooner or later. Besides, Dog wouldn't let anything happen to him or any of the horses. Preacher took the steps leading up to the porch on the front of the building in a couple of bounds, then glanced back at Hawk, who was peering around wide-eyed, one more time before going into the building.

A man in a dusty black coat sat on a high stool behind a desk, scratching away with a quill pen as he entered figures in a ledger book. He had a tuft of taffy-colored hair on the top of his head and matching tufts above each ear, otherwise he was bald. A pair of pince-nez clung precariously to the end of his long nose. He looked over the spectacles at Preacher and grinned as he tried to straighten up. A back permanently hunched from bending over a desk made that difficult.

"Preacher!" he said. "I didn't know if we'd see you this season."

"You didn't think anything would've happened to me, did you, Henry?"

"Well, of course not," the clerk said. "You're indestructible, Preacher. I fully expect that forty or fifty years from now, you'll still be running around those mountains out there, getting into all sorts of trouble."

Preacher laughed. "I'm gonna do my best to prove you right." He jerked a thumb over his shoulder. "Right now, though, I've got a load of pelts out there. Vernon around to make me an offer on 'em?"

Henry's smile disappeared and was replaced by a look of concern. "You just left them out there?"

"Dog's guardin' 'em. And I told my boy to keep an eye on 'em, too."

"You have a partner now?"

"My son," Preacher said.

That news made the clerk look startled again. He hemmed and hawed for a moment and then evidently decided he didn't want to press Preacher for the details. Instead he said, "Mr. Pritchard is in the warehouse. You can go on around."

"Thanks." Preacher paused. "Henry, why'd you say that about me leavin' the pelts outside, like it wasn't a good idea?"

"St. Louis has gotten worse in the past year, Preacher. There are thieves and cutthroats everywhere. I hate to walk back to my house at night." Henry reached down to a shelf under the desk and picked up an ancient pistol with a barrel that flared out at the muzzle. He displayed the weapon to Preacher and went on, "That's why I carry this."

"Put that sawed-off blunderbuss away," Preacher said. "You're makin' me nervous."

"Preacher being nervous." Henry shook his head. "I'll never live to see the day."

Preacher lifted a hand in farewell and went back outside. Just as he stepped onto the porch, he heard a harsh voice say, "Damn it, Nix, Jenks, look at that. That's a redskin sittin' there with a nice big load o' pelts. Hey, Injun, where'd you steal them furs?"

Preacher paused and eased sideways, out of the light that spilled through the door. He drifted into a shadow thick and dark enough to keep him from being noticed easily. He wanted to see what was going to happen.

Hawk had dismounted long enough to tie the animals' reins to the hitch rail in front of the office, then swung back up onto his pony, which he rode with a saddle now rather than bareback or with only a blanket, the way he had when he was younger. He stared impassively at the three men who swaggered toward him, but didn't say anything.

They were big and roughly dressed. Preacher could tell that much in the gloom. He didn't need to see the details to know what sort of men they were. The clerk had warned him about the ruffians now making St. Louis a dangerous place, and Preacher knew he was looking at three examples of that.

"I'm talkin' to you, redskin," continued the man who had spoken earlier. "I want to know where you stole them furs. I know good an' well a lazy, good-for-nothin' Injun like you didn't work to trap 'em."

Hawk said something in the Absaroka tongue. The three men clearly didn't understand a word of it, but Preacher did. Hawk's words were a warning: "You should go away now, before I kill you."

One of the men laughed and said, "I guess he told you, Brice—although I ain't sure just what he told you."

Brice, the one who had spoken first, stepped forward enough so that the light from the doorway revealed the scowl on his face. He said, "Don't you jabber at me, boy." He waved an arm. "Go on, get outta here! You don't need them furs. Leave them here for white men, and those horses, too." He sneered. "You can keep that damn Injun pony. It probably ain't fit to carry a real man."

After spending months with Preacher, Charlie Todd, and Aaron Buckley, Hawk spoke English quite well. Only occasionally did he stumble over a word or have to search for the right one. So Preacher knew Hawk understood everything Brice said.

He also knew that Hawk had a short temper and probably wasn't going to put up with much more of this.

Brice came closer. "Are you not listenin' to me, boy? I said git! We're takin' those pelts."

"They are . . . my furs," Hawk said in English, slowly and awkwardly as if he wasn't sure what he was saying. "Please . . . do not . . . steal them."

In the shadows on the porch, Preacher grinned. Other than that, he was motionless. Hawk was baiting those would-be thieves, and Preacher had a pretty good idea what the outcome was going to be. He wouldn't step in unless it was necessary.

"Don't you mouth off to me, redskin," Brice blustered.

"Get outta here, or you're gonna get the beatin' of your life."

"Please," Hawk said. "Do not hurt me."

Brice grunted in contempt and reached up.

"You had your chance," he said. "Now I'm gonna teach you a lesson, you red ni—"

He closed his hands on Hawk's buckskin shirt to drag him off the pony.

Then, a split second later, he realized he might as well have grabbed hold of a mountain lion.

Hawk's leg shot out. The moccasin-shod heel cracked into Brice's head and jolted his head back. As Brice staggered a couple of steps away, Hawk swung his other leg over the pony's back and dived at the other two men.

They both let out startled yells when Hawk kicked their friend, and one of them clawed at a pistol stuck behind his belt. Before he could pull the weapon free, Hawk crashed into them and drove them both off their feet.

He hit the ground rolling and came upright as Brice recovered his balance from the kick and charged at Hawk with a shout of rage. The young man darted aside nimbly as Brice tried to catch him in a bear hug that would have crushed his ribs.

Hawk twisted, clubbed his hands together, and slammed them into the small of Brice's back as the man's momentum carried him past. Brice cried out in pain and arched his back, then stumbled and went down hard, face-first, plowing into the hard-packed dirt of the street.

Hawk whirled to face the other two men, who were struggling to get up. One of them he met with a straight, hard punch that landed squarely on the man's nose. Even from where Preacher stood on the porch, he heard bone and cartilage crunch. The man went back down a lot faster than he had gotten up and stayed down this time.

The third man had a chance to spring toward Hawk and managed to get his right arm around the youngster's neck from behind. He clamped down with the grip and used his heavier weight to force Hawk forward and down. His left hand grasped his right wrist to tighten the choke hold. He brought up his right knee and planted it in Hawk's back. That move proved the man was an experienced brawler, because now with one good heave, he could snap Hawk's neck.

Chapter 3

Preacher wasn't going to stand by and do nothing while his son was killed. He had two flintlock pistols shoved behind the broad leather belt around his waist. He reached for the guns, then realized that if he blew a hole in the man about to break Hawk's neck, there was a good chance the heavy lead balls would pass on through his body and into the youngster. Preacher couldn't risk that.

Instead he grabbed the tomahawk that was also stuck behind his belt. A perfect throw would lodge the sharp flint head in the back of the man's skull without endangering Hawk.

As it turned out, the mountain man didn't need any of his weapons. Hawk writhed like a snake, and his opponent couldn't hold him. Hawk worked his way out of the grip seemingly by magic and dropped to a crouch. His elbow drove back sharply into the man's groin, causing a startled, high-pitched yelp of pain. As the man began to double over, Hawk turned and lifted an uppercut with all the deceptive strength in his slim body. His fist crashed into the man's jaw and made his feet come off the ground as he flipped over backward, out cold.

A voice said, "That was as fine a display of pugilism as I've seen in a long time, lad!" A man with a thatch of gray hair and bushy side whiskers came toward Hawk. He must have been watching the fight from the corner of the building. "Who are you, my friend? Do you speak English?"

"I speak the white man's tongue," Hawk said. He pointed toward the porch. "And I travel with him."

Preacher chuckled and moved forward to the top of the steps. "You knew I was up here watchin' the whole time, didn't you, Hawk?"

"Of course. I am not blind as so many of your people seem to be."

The newcomer looked up at the porch and said, "Is that you, Preacher?"

"Howdy, Vernon," Preacher said by way of answer. "Good to see you again. The sprout over there"—he nodded toward Hawk—"is Hawk That Soars." Preacher paused. "My son."

"Is that so?" Vernon Pritchard said. He thrust out his hand toward the youngster. "I'm pleased to make your acquaintance, Hawk That Soars."

Hawk hesitated, still not entirely comfortable with the customs of the white men, but he gripped Pritchard's hand and shook it.

"I didn't know you had any children, Preacher," the trader went on.

Preacher scratched his jaw and said, "You and me both. But I've never been good at keepin' up with that sort of thing."

"I take it those are your pelts on that pack mule?"

"Mine and Hawk's and a couple of other fellas. You want to make us an offer on 'em?"

Pritchard went over to the mule, opened one of the packs enough to check the furs bundled inside it, then said, "All of them the same quality?"

"Yep."

With the keen eye of an experienced trader, Pritchard estimated the load's weight, then stated a figure.

"You can do a mite better than that," Preacher said.

Pritchard laughed. "You drive a hard bargain, my friend. I'll raise my offer by . . . ten percent."

"Twenty-five."

"Fifteen," Pritchard countered.

"Done," Preacher said.

"I'll have my men unload. What about the mule?"

Preacher pointed along the street and said, "We're gonna take the horses down to Fullerton's. If one of your boys can bring the mule along when you're done, I'll tell Fullerton to be lookin' for him."

"I can do that."

Preacher nodded toward the three men lying sprawled in the street. They were starting to come around, stirring a little and letting out an occasional moan. The bubbling noises coming from the one whose nose Hawk had broken sounded miserable.

"You know these varmints?" the mountain man asked.

"Not to speak of. There are dozens of crooked brutes just like them around now. Do you want me to send for the constable so you can have them arrested?"

"No, I reckon Hawk already dealt 'em out enough punishment for bein' stupid."

"I considered killing them," Hawk said, "but I thought the other white men might be upset and cause trouble for you, Preacher."

"Don't ever hold back on killin' somebody who needs it on account of me," Preacher advised. "If I worried overmuch about what other folks think, I never would've taken off for the tall and uncut when I was still just a younker."

With the deal for the furs settled, Preacher and Hawk walked toward the stable, leading the four horses. Dog padded alongside the mountain man.

After a minute or so, Hawk said, "I am pleased you did not try to help me back there. I can fight my own battles."

"Never doubted it," Preacher replied. He didn't say anything about how he'd been preparing to take action when Hawk got loose from the third man. His help hadn't been needed . . . but he had been ready if it was.

Full night had fallen by the time they reached Fullerton's Livery Stable. The proprietor, Ambrose Fullerton, was a short, round man with a white beard and a genius's touch with animals. Preacher wouldn't trust Horse to anybody else in St. Louis, and he knew Fullerton wouldn't mind if Dog stayed here, too.

Fullerton came out of the office as Preacher and Hawk led the four horses into the barn's broad center aisle. He shook hands with Preacher and patted Horse on the shoulder and Dog on the head. They wouldn't accept such familiarity from many people.

"And who's this?" Fullerton said as he smiled at Hawk.

"My son, Hawk," Preacher explained. "We've been doin' some trappin' together."

"It's good to meet you, Hawk. You'll find that your pa has a lot of friends here in Sant Looey."

Hawk nodded solemnly and said, "I am beginning to understand this. He likes to talk about how many enemies he has made, but I think he has made more friends."

"Not necessarily," Fullerton said. "Most of Preacher's enemies are dead."

Preacher ignored that and jerked a thumb toward the two extra horses. "Seen these mounts before?"

Fullerton looked the horses over, studying them for a couple of minutes before he said, "As a matter of fact, I think I have. I believe they were stabled here for a few nights, a week or so ago."

"Remember what their owners looked like?"

"One was a tall, dark-haired fella. Had a lean and hungry look about him, as Audie might say when he's spouting old Bill Shakespeare. The other one was shorter. Had a red beard, as I recall."

Preacher nodded. "That's them, all right."

Fullerton regarded Preacher intently for a second, then said, "I don't suppose they'll be needing those horses anymore."

"Nope, they sure won't."

"In that case, I can take them off your hands if you want. Give you a fair price."

Preacher didn't bother haggling this time. He took what Fullerton offered him, then said, "You don't happen to know the names of those two fellas, do you? Or if they had any family around here? If they did, the money for the horses should rightfully go to them."

Fullerton shook his head. "They didn't offer their names, and I didn't ask. They didn't act like they were from around here, though. Fact is, they rode into town with some other fellas. All of them were new to these parts, seems like."

"How many other men are we talkin' about?" Preacher asked.

"Fourteen or fifteen, I'd say. Some kept their horses here, some didn't. But they're all gone now. I didn't get names for any of them, either." Fullerton rubbed his chin. "I can tell you about one of them, though. Hard to forget him. He was even bigger than you, Preacher. Didn't have a beard, but he was sporting one of those long mustaches that curl up on the ends. Funny-lookin' thing. The way the others acted, he was sort of the leader of the bunch."

"But they're not around anymore, you say?"

Fullerton shook his head and said, "I haven't seen any of 'em for a few days. I reckon they took off for greener pastures, wherever that might be."

Greener pastures, thought Preacher. Like lurking around west of the settlement to rob and kill trappers on their way to St. Louis with a load of pelts. Well, two members of the gang wouldn't be doing that anymore.

As they left the stable, Hawk asked, "Where will we stay tonight? We should make camp before it gets much later."

"We won't have to sleep on the ground tonight," Preacher said. "A friend of mine has a place here in town. It's mostly a tavern, but he rents rooms, too, and we can get something to eat there. That's where we're headed now."

"Sleep . . . in one of these buildings?"

"You've slept in tepees your whole life."

"Those are different."

Preacher laughed. "We're gonna have this same conversation about everything when it comes to civilization, ain't we?"

"Sleeping in a building." Hawk shook his head. "It seems wrong."

"Well, you'll just have to see if you like it. The place we're headed is called Red Mike's."

Preacher led the way to the tavern not far from the waterfront. He stopped here every time he visited St. Louis and considered the burly Irishman who ran the place to be a friend. More than once, Preacher had gotten into fights either inside Red Mike's or near the place, but that didn't stop him from returning.

The streets were busy, and now that night had fallen, it was likely there weren't too many innocents out and about. Preacher and Hawk passed a number of hard-looking men, but those fellows gave them a wide berth. Preacher supposed some of them recognized him and figured it wouldn't be a good idea to tangle with him. Others just instinctively gave him room.

He knew he had something of a lean and hungry look himself. He recognized the quote because he'd heard it often enough from his friend Audie, who had been a college professor many years ago, before giving up that life to come west and take up trapping.

There were also women in the windows of some of the buildings they passed, calling down coarse invitations to the men in the street and sometimes displaying their charms by lantern light. Preacher could tell Hawk was trying not to stare at them but only partially succeeding.

"There are too many people here," Hawk said with a scowl as they walked along.

"I hear tell there are even bigger, more crowded settlements back East, and I've even spent some time in one called New Orleans, down near the mouth of the Mississippi."

Hawk shook his head. "It cannot be. That many people would breathe up all the air."

"Sometimes I feel that way myself," Preacher agreed.

They came to an unimpressive-looking building which had no sign on it because everybody knew where Red Mike's was. Preacher opened the door and went inside. Hawk followed him but stopped short, making a face at the thick clouds of grayish-blue smoke that filled the air. At least half of the men in the tavern were puffing on pipes. Some of the serving wenches were, too. Adding to the miasma in the air were odors of spilled beer and whiskey, vomit, and human waste.

"How do you stand it?" Hawk asked when Preacher looked back to see what was keeping him.

"I'd say you get used to it, but I ain't sure if that's true or not, because I've never been here long enough for that. I spend a night or two now and then, but after that I'm on my way back to the mountains."

"That sounds like a good plan. Let us go now."

Preacher laughed and clapped a hand on his son's shoulder. "Come on. It ain't that bad. I'll introduce you to Mike."

Hawk allowed himself to be led reluctantly toward the bar at the side of the low-ceilinged room. On the other side of the tavern, stairs led up to the second floor, where those rooms for rent Preacher had mentioned were located.

The bar was crowded, but when Mike spotted Preacher, he bellowed, "Step aside there, step aside! Make room!"

"What the hell, Mike!" one of the drinkers protested. "We got as much right here as anybody else." The man glanced around to see who was going to displace them, then added with a frown, "More right than a damn Injun!"

"That's my son you're talkin' about, mister," Preacher said in a flat, hard voice.

"Then he's a dirty half-breed, and he shouldn't even be in here!"

Preacher stiffened. He was proud of his boy, and he wasn't going to let anybody insult Hawk that way. It was an insult to Bird in a Tree, too, and that was even more intolerable. He was about to throw a punch, despite the look he got from Mike that implored him not to start anything, when a voice like beautiful music from a bell cut through the hubbub in the room.

"Gentlemen, wouldn't you rather drink than fight?"

A bare arm, complete with smooth, creamy female flesh, was thrust in front of him, and the hand at the end of that arm held a foaming, brimming tankard of beer. He lifted his gaze to the prettiest pair of blue eyes he had seen in a long time, and behind him he heard Hawk exclaim softly in what sounded like awe.

Connect with Us

Visit us online at
KensingtonBooks.com
to read more from your favorite authors, see books
by series, view reading group guides, and more.

Join us on social media

for sneak peeks, chances to win books and prize packs,
and to share your thoughts with other readers.

facebook.com/kensingtonpublishing
twitter.com/kensingtonbooks

Tell us what you think!

To share your thoughts, submit a review,
or sign up for our eNewsletters, please visit:
KensingtonBooks.com/TellUs.